— PRAISE FOR —
Flame & Crystal Thorns

"Flame and Crystal thorns is a beautifully written faerie fantasy that I was instantly hooked on! The epic romance and magically detailed world building will reel you in, and absolutely leave you wanting more!" –Ashley Nicholas

"This book is everything I had hoped it would be. Romance, fantasy, bravery, and cleverness all rolled up into a fantastic story. The ending will make you want for more! Kay L. Moody truly never disappoints." –Cheyenne Mcdonald

"An enchanting adventure through Faerie. This book is perfect for fans of fantasy and romance! You won't want to put it down!" –Laura Fincher

"I thought I loved Elora, but Chloe is perfection! Filled with rapid speed twists and turns, unexpected consequences, smart-mouth humans and fae, and all the trickery we have come to expect in Faerie, Chloe, who has always put others before herself, must decide what matters most, who she can save, and if she will survive any of it. It's a thrilling adventure!" –Sara Lawson, editor

"I am thrilled that the book-reading, everyone-healing younger sister of the previous series' main character gets her own story! Can't wait for the second book!" –Zara Gennert

Flame of Crystal Thorn is a thrilling read for all fae lovers. Holly Black and Elise Kova fans would be delighted! Transport yourself into the pages of this book and you will devour it as I did! You will not regret it. 5 magnificent stars." –Gladys, Nerd Girl Official

ALSO BY KAY L. MOODY

Fae and Crystal Thorns
Flame & Crystal Thorns
Shadow & Crystal Thorns
Blade & Crystal Thorns
Curse & Crystal Thorns
Wrath & Crystal Thorns
Standalone: Nutcracker of Crystalfall

The Fae of Bitter Thorn
Heir of Bitter Thorn
Court of Bitter Thorn
Castle of Bitter Thorn
Crown of Bitter Thorn
Queen of Bitter Thorn

The Elements of Kamdaria
The Elements of the Crown
The Elements of the Gate
The Elements of the Storm

Truth Seer Trilogy
Truth Seer
Healer
Truth Changer

Visit **kaylmoody.com/bitter** to download a prequel novella, *Heir of Bitter Thorn*, for free.

KAY L. MOODY

FLAME &
CRYSTAL THORNS

FAE AND CRYSTAL THORNS 1

Flame & Crystal Thorns
Fae and Crystal Thorns, #1
By Kay L. Moody

Published by Marten Press
3731 W 10400 S Ste 102, #205
South Jordan, UT 84009

www.MartenPress.com

Cover by Angel Leya
Edited by Deborah Spencer and Justin Greer
Under the dust jacket illustration by ArtByArtemis

ISBN: 978-1-954335-09-7

Dedication

If you have ever forgotten to take care of yoursef,
this book is for you.

1

FOR SOMEONE WHO HAD ONCE visited Faerie, Chloe found strange comfort in the simplicity of the mortal realm.

A crackling fire in one corner warmed her small sitting room. She sat in a plush chair with a leatherbound notebook perched open on her lap. The feather quill she used to take notes often left smudges of ink on her fingers. Today's smudges were especially dark.

Across from her, a neighbor woman whose dark hair had turned mostly gray sniffled. She kept dabbing her eyes, but a few tears still escaped her embroidered handkerchief.

Chloe tapped her quill against a notebook page as she felt her mouth screw into a knot. "And did you say your husband developed a fever along with his rash?"

"Yes, but…" The woman's lip quivered, slow at first until it shook as fast as a lone leaf clinging to a tree amidst an icy winter wind. She squeezed her handkerchief as if it might save her from pain. "It's not a normal fever. I know it is not. Everyone says it's winter sickness and that the rash will soon be gone, but I am certain it is something much worse."

Before the woman could soak her handkerchief with a puddle of tears, Chloe reached across the space between them until her hand dropped over the woman's. "Mrs. Nash, I agree with you. This does not sound like winter sickness."

The lightest flicker of hope sparked in the woman's red rimmed eyes.

With a nod, Chloe sat deeper into her plush velvet chair. No weaver in the mortal realm could craft such fine material as the rich maroon velvet of Chloe's sitting room furniture. Luckily, everyone in town spent too much time whispering about the strange stories Chloe's nieces and nephews told or about the inhuman color of her brother's eyes to worry about her too-fine furniture.

Her gaze swept across her notebook, scanning the notes she had taken. "I'll need to do a bit of research, but I am certain I can find a remedy for your husband."

"Truly?" Mrs. Nash sat forward in her seat with eyes as wide as clocks.

Chloe snapped the notebook closed before standing up. "There is a reason I've gained the reputation as best apothecary in town. I am certain I can help."

The woman clutched her handkerchief tight as she brought her hand over her heart. Tears welled in her eyes.

Reaching out a hand to help the woman up, Chloe donned a light smile. "You can return to your home now. I'll do my research, then I'll fix something up and bring it to your home later tonight."

Tears slid down Mrs. Nash's splotchy red cheeks as she got to her feet. "Thank you."

She took a few steps but then turned back. Shadows from the fire danced across her face as she inhaled deeply. "I know you only moved here because your parents died and your older brother was the only family you had left, but—" She shook her head. "It's awful about your parents, truly awful, but…"

Her chin trembled as she attempted to steady her breathing. "I don't know what would happen to my husband without you. I'm so glad you're here and not wherever you used to live."

At least the woman had refrained from asking exactly *where* Chloe used to live. Chloe and her younger sister always evaded those questions as skillfully as possible. How else could they explain that they used to live not just in a different town but also in a different time?

Having a fae brother who masqueraded as a mortal certainly made life difficult to explain. By mortal standards, he wasn't even her brother. They did share blood, though, which still made him family. And since Faerie had no time, he was able to bring Chloe and her sister back to the mortal realm to live with him after their parents' deaths.

Even more important, her brother's wife and their children knew about his true fae nature. Maybe her nieces and nephews' stories sounded strange and outlandish to outsiders, but those in her house knew how true they really were.

A tight smile stretched across Chloe's face as she waved goodbye to Mrs. Nash. The woman had been too deep in her grief to notice Chloe's tension at the mention of her parents and her previous town. Chloe gripped her notebook a little too tight as she made her way down the hall leading to her workroom.

This entire wing of the house had been added when Chloe and her younger sister, Grace, moved in. Her fae brother had done it all in one night, which took almost no work at all since he could conjure clothing, gold, and even buildings with his fae magic.

What *did* take work was trying to convince the people in town that the extra wing had been there all along. People had whispered about it for months. In the end, they all collectively agreed their memories had to be faulty, since it was clearly impossible for one man to build an entire wing in one night. Impossible for a mortal, maybe, but not for a fae.

A wave of earthy scents rushed into Chloe's nose when she opened the door to her workroom. Dried lavender, rosemary, and a few other herbs hung from thin strings tied to the ceiling. Notebooks, loose papers, heavy books, and empty pots of ink littered a worktable at one end of the room. On the other worktable, herbs and crystals sat next to a stone mortar and pestle.

Ignoring both tables, she knelt down and unlatched the trunk in one corner. No matter how many times she opened the trunk, she still held her breath while lifting the lid. The air ignited with an unseen energy. Tingles spread over her skin as she reached into its depths. The tingles only multiplied when her fingers met the book sitting at the bottom.

She pulled the suede and leather book cover tight to her chest as she breathed in its mossy scent. She had stolen it from Faerie, which she didn't feel guilty about in the least. Magic pulsed between the pages, but no matter how many times she tried, she could never capture or absorb any of that magic for herself. For good measure, she tugged it even closer and took one last deep breath. Still nothing.

Sighing, she stood and set the book onto her worktable. After getting comfortably situated, she thumbed through the pages. The book held information on Faerie, including the creatures there, the flora and fauna, a little history, and more. She had skimmed every page multiple times, but with her current occupation, she now usually just referred to the sections on illnesses, injuries, and remedies.

Mr. Nash's sickness seemed eerily similar to scurpus. The sickness probably had a different name in the mortal realm, but the book from Faerie called it by its fae name.

While fae had healing abilities that could heal almost any sickness without help, they also had a host of remedies that sped up the healing process. Luckily, their remedies worked on mortals too.

Her finger tapped on the book once she found the page for scurpus. She set her notebook right next to it and compared the symptoms. A fever, rash, and excessive weakness were followed by a tinge of gray along the hairline and at the tips of the fingers. Mrs. Nash hadn't mentioned anything about the gray tinge, but it probably wouldn't be long before her husband exhibited that symptom too. A simple poultice could heal him, as long as Chloe administered it before the gray tinge in the fingertips spread far enough to reach the palm of his hand.

Wiping her hands on the homespun apron protecting her silk dress, Chloe began gathering herbs. After reading the first ingredient off the list, she found it and set it neatly next to the book. Then she moved onto the next ingredient, placing it right next to the first. A wisp of blonde hair fell into her face while she worked, but she just tucked it back into her messy bun. Soon she had nearly all the ingredients gathered.

Her finger trailed down the page until she found the last ingredient. The sight of it sent a wrench through her heart.

Salt from the Faerie Court of Swiftsea.

Chloe gulped. Swiftsea salt had magical properties that not even the other Faerie courts possessed. Her fingers instinctively reached for the hidden pouch under her homespun apron. Tight knots wound in her chest as she touched the drawstring opening. A tiny wave of nausea churned in her belly.

But just before she opened the pouch, the knots in her chest loosened. Shaking away her worry, she held her page with one finger and then flipped to the back of the book.

She had encountered this problem a few times before. Thanks to an intelligent mortal who was long since dead, an appendix had been added to the book, which gave mortal ingredient substitutions for all the ingredients specific to Faerie.

A breath of relief fell from her lips when she found that Swiftsea salt did indeed have substitute ingredients that existed in the mortal realm. Her relief only lasted a moment. She needed juniper, goldenrod, and fennel. She had a few bundles of juniper and a handful of goldenrod—but not the other herb.

She hadn't bothered to collect and dry any fennel during the summer since she had never used it before. Without all three of the herbs, she couldn't make a proper substitution for Swiftsea salt.

Her mouth went dry as she stared at the page. A part of her hoped staring would change the words in front of her. The book *was* magic, wasn't it? It came from a magical realm at least.

The hope was fruitless. Of course the words never changed. If she wanted to save Mr. Nash, she knew what she had to do. Biting her lip, she reached under her apron and opened the small pouch. That same wave of nausea turned her stomach again, even stronger this time.

Only a handful of items sat at the bottom of the pouch. It contained a seashell that could make any liquid taste like honey, but even more important, the shell could also cleanse liquids of impurities or even poison. A light purple ribbon cut from a skirt that once belonged to her mother sat next to the shell. There were a few other trinkets, including a loose harp string she probably should have gotten rid of long ago. Last of all, there sat a small bag of Swiftsea salt.

Most of the Faerie items had come from Chloe's older sister, Elora. A lump formed in her throat as she stared at the open pouch. Her sister lived in Faerie now. She occasionally came to the mortal realm to visit, but Chloe still missed her terribly.

Seeing the items did the same thing it always did. It made her miss *Faerie* too. She let out a wistful sigh as she plopped onto the nearest chair. Chloe hadn't spent long in Faerie, but her time had been filled with adventure. Even three years later, she still pined for it sometimes.

But Faerie was dangerous. It had all sorts of rules and consequences, many of which could be deadly for a mortal. She had never been the type who loved adventure anyway. Reading epic poems provided as much adventure as she ever wanted from life.

Still, the land had been enchanting. Beautiful. It had a whole host of magical books just begging to be read.

Her eyes slammed shut as she folded her arms over her chest. Not this again. She had already decided. She would never return to Faerie. She was mortal. She belonged in the mortal realm.

Letting out a heavy breath, she ran through all the reasons the mortal realm was better for her. Here she'd be able to find someone to fall in love with, someone to grow old with.

Not a fae.

If she had stayed in Faerie and fallen in love with a fae, there would be no growing old together. She knew this more intimately than anyone. Her immortal fae brother had been married for years without trouble, but now his mortal wife was starting to age…and he was not.

Trouble brewed whether they wanted to admit it or not. Pretty soon, her fae brother would have to start wearing a glamour that made him appear older to match his wife's age. If anyone caught sight of his true face, he might have to leave the mortal realm. Then his wife would be forced to grow old all alone.

Gritting her teeth, Chloe snatched the bag of Swiftsea salt from her pouch. She *would* use it for Mr. Nash's poultice, every last bit of it. Yes, it had valuable properties that would keep fae from enchanting her food, but what did that matter when she never intended to return to Faerie anyway?

Despite her surety, it still hurt to see the last sprinkles of her Swiftsea salt drop into the small wooden bowl she used for mixing. One of her last reminders of Faerie would be gone forever.

Her eyes stung as she crushed and cut the other herbs and dropped them into the bowl. The wisp of hair fell into her face again, but she was too busy wiping away a tear to bother with it.

The moment of weakness still ached in her throat, but she did her best to focus on her mixing bowl. It didn't take long to finish after that.

With the dry ingredients for the poultice secured in a cloth binding inside a small basket, Chloe grabbed her fur-lined cloak and pulled it over her shoulders. Getting to the Nashes' house would be easy since they lived just down the lane.

Chloe hardly noticed the ice crunching under her boots. Memories of Faerie flitted in her mind, no matter how she tried to shake them away. The moon shone bright in the sky, lighting the path ahead. When she arrived at the house next to the large ash tree at the end of the lane, she knocked hard on the front door.

Mrs. Nash answered it, her eyes now puffy and swollen. The woman ushered Chloe into a dark room lit only by the fire in the fireplace. "Here he is." She whispered the words, as if speaking out loud might upset her ill husband.

The man's eyes snapped open. His gaze darted around the room while fear seized his features. But once he caught sight of his wife, the tightness of his muscles vanished with a relieved exhale. "Mirielle."

His fingers shook as he attempted to lift his hand from the bed he rested on. The weakness plaguing him prevented him from bringing his hand more than a palm's length above the blankets. Just as Chloe had suspected, the lightest tinge of gray dappled his fingertips. After another moment, his hand dropped heavily back onto the bed.

Mrs. Nash rushed to his bedside and took his hand in both of hers. She squeezed it and then brushed the hair off his forehead. A tinge of gray stretched along his hairline. Her whisper came out even gentler than before. "Don't you worry. Miss Chloe Rosenbel is here to make you feel better, just like I promised."

She continued to speak soothing words to her husband while Chloe opened the poultice and added water to make a thick paste. Once ready, she spread the paste over the man's chest.

With each movement, Mrs. Nash spoke gently to her husband and offered comfort.

Warmth spread in Chloe's heart at the sight of it. Growing old with someone wouldn't always be perfect. Maybe it would mean sickness and heartache and wrinkly skin, but moments like this would make it worth it.

Once finished, she offered a short nod to the Nashes and promised to return the next evening to check on Mr. Nash's progress. By the time Chloe returned to the wintery air outside, her full heart warmed her against the chill.

It lasted three full steps before a tall figure just ahead forced her to jerk to a stop. She gulped as she glanced up, but then her entire body went rigid. She gasped.

The man before her stood taller than the average mortal, but that wasn't too out of place. His pointed fae ears, on the other hand, would make anyone stare. Not to mention, he had gloriously perfect features that made him impossibly attractive, especially for a mortal.

"Quintus." She spoke his name like a warning. If he weren't so beautiful, she would have glared. He never should have entered the mortal realm without masking himself with a glamour that made him appear more like an imperfect mortal.

His eyes locked onto hers with a fervor she hadn't known since leaving Faerie. His expression commanded the utmost attention. Surely, his voice would too.

"You have to return to Faerie."

2

A CLATTER SOUNDED FROM A nearby house, bringing Chloe to her senses. Her head shook as she gripped her basket tight. Just like the Faerie book, Quintus's mere presence seemed to ignite the air with energy. Only after clenching her stomach tight could she counteract the effect his presence had on her.

Stepping to the side, she marched right past him. "I told you I would never return to Faerie."

He fell into step beside her but did not immediately offer a rebuttal. It surprised her enough to glance his way.

He stared at her.

She hated it because her insides tumbled at the sight of his rich brown eyes. Her stomach flipped and burst with a frightening delight.

As town apothecary, Chloe had healed her fair share of handsome young men. The surrounding farms all employed strapping young men with work-hardened muscles and sun-tanned faces. She secretly loved it when one of them suffered a minor injury and required her services.

Maybe her hands always lingered a little longer than necessary on their arms or hands while working, but their gazes always lingered longer than necessary on her figure, so in her mind, they were even.

Still, after more than a year of blushing and batting her eyelashes at every handsome young man she healed, no one had ever affected her the way Quintus did—the way he was doing right now. Her cheeks flushed with heat, but they also tingled with an icy cold. The sensation snaked down her arms, giving her the strong desire to smack him upside the head just for daring to show his face again. She huffed loud enough for him to hear.

He only narrowed his eyes and stared a little harder. "Your hair is different than last time I saw you."

It was a good thing the moon lit their path because the sun would have betrayed the even deeper surge of heat rising in her cheeks. She had to clear her throat before she could respond. "Yes, I'm older now. I just turned eighteen."

The tiniest spark lit in his eyes. Was that a hint of a smile on his lips?

Her stomach devolved into flutters.

To hide her involuntary blush, she tipped her nose into the air. "I'm sure my hair—and my face even—look terrible compared to you fae with your perfect features and ageless skin."

Whatever distraction her changed appearance had provided, it vanished now. His face grew serious once again. "Can you come now? Do you need to bring anything?"

Her basket nearly slipped from her hands. "Come now?" She scoffed. "I'm not coming at all. I have a life here." She stood a little taller as she turned away from him. "People depend on me."

Even with her face deliberately turned away from him, she could still see how his eyebrow raised. "I can bring you back to this exact moment when we return."

She huffed again. "Yes, I remember how Faerie time works. Or rather, I remember how you don't have time at all. *Time* is not the issue."

They had reached her home now. Any mortal would have known to stop at the door and offer a farewell as she stepped inside. Apparently, Quintus had no desire to follow mortal customs. He walked in right behind her and followed like he had been invited. "You must come."

After burning him with a glare, she stomped into her workroom. The mess she had left behind still had to be cleaned, after all.

At least the room kept him quiet for a few moments. He looked around with almost as much awe as she felt when she had been in Faerie. One of his hands reached toward the dried herbs hanging from the ceiling, but he did not touch them.

He scanned the room again. This time, the sight of something caused him to smirk. Pointing to the open book on her worktable, he raised one eyebrow. "Did you take that from Faerie?"

Snapping the book closed, she shoved it into the trunk in the corner of the room. "If Brannick wants it back, he can come get it himself."

The slightest chuckle escaped Quintus's lips. He mouthed the name *Brannick*, though no sound came out.

With the trunk securely fastened, Chloe stood and shoved her hands onto her hips. "He is not royalty here in the mortal realm. There's no reason I have to use his full title, nor Elora's. I can call him just plain Brannick if I want to."

"What is this?" He had stopped listening to her mid-sentence, which reminded her of one of the many things she found infuriating about him. Now, he trailed a finger along a pile of herbs atop a white cloth square at the edge of the table.

A frown tugged her lips down. "It's a poultice." She flopped onto the nearest chair. "My neighbor is ill. I used half of it on him earlier, and I hoped it would be enough." She shook her head, which sent a few blonde strands into her face. "But he is worse than I thought. If he needs more than the rest of that poultice, I do not have the ingredients I need to make another."

Taking the chair from the other worktable, Quintus sat across from her. His eyebrows danced upward as he reached into his pocket. "I saw the recipe. You need Swiftsea salt?"

She clenched her jaw. "The poultice can be made with mortal ingredients as well."

He didn't respond. Pulling his hand from his pocket, he revealed a woven ball of glowing blue energy. She didn't even notice herself leaning forward or widening her eyes.

He caught her eye just long enough to raise an eyebrow. Then the glowing ball expanded until it hovered above his palm as large as a round loaf of bread. The energy inside it sizzled with crackling sparks.

Her mouth hung open as she leaned even closer than before. "What is that?"

"It is magic. Why worry about mortal illnesses when you can experience magic in Faerie?" He whispered the words, throwing the same energy into his tone that filled the air around him.

One hand lifted from her lap, mostly involuntarily. She went to touch the glowing magic, but before she could reach it, the door to her workroom burst open.

Two children with ruddy cheeks and fiery red hair stumbled into the room.

"Aunt Chloe, Mother wants everyone in the sitting room to hear a poem before bed." Even though he was only ten, as the oldest of his parents' children, Gideon always took it upon himself to relay all announcements.

His eight-year-old sister, Eliza, pouted. "I wanted to tell her." Now she stuck out her tongue at him.

He just poked her in the shoulder, preparing to stick out his own tongue. At that precise moment, both he and his sister caught sight of the glowing ball of energy above Quintus's palm.

"Magic," they said in unison.

Quintus sat up straight with a sharp exhale. The glowing ball shrunk to the size of a thumbnail before he shoved it back into his pocket. He jerked his head toward Chloe, his eyes shimmering with a strange expression. Guilt, maybe?

"You two run along," Chloe said, ushering the children out of the room. "I'll be right there."

They obeyed her, though Gideon looked over one shoulder as he darted down the hallway. "Bring the fae too. Father will want to talk to him."

By the time Chloe turned back toward the room, Quintus had stood from his chair. He now towered over her, angling himself just enough to see into the hall. When he caught her staring, he raised an eyebrow. "Do those younglings know about magic already?"

Chloe laughed out loud as she cleared a few broken herb stems off her worktable and into the little garbage where she collected them. The dilemma with the poultice would have to wait until tomorrow. Hopefully Mr. Nash would be better by then and it wouldn't even matter that she had no more Swiftsea salt.

"They're Vesper's children, of course they know about magic. Their mother, Cosette, tries to teach them how to keep quiet about fae and magic around others, but you know how Vesper is. Everything is a great adventure to him, including the possibility of mortals discovering his true fae nature. He keeps as quiet about Faerie as a baby does when he's starving."

Quintus tilted his head. "What do mortal babies do when they are starving? Do they just sit there?"

She rolled her eyes and unclasped her cloak, hanging it on the peg near the door. "They cry. Loudly. Just forget it."

"Hello, Grace."

Chloe's younger sister stopped at the sound of Quintus's voice. She had been walking nonchalantly down the hall, but now she turned toward the pair of them. Her red hair didn't have as much vibrance as Cosette's or any of the children, but it still had the same hue.

Her eyebrows tipped upward as she took in the fae. Her gaze immediately flicked over to Chloe's. Several expressions danced across Grace's face at once, most of which triggered a tingling sensation through Chloe's suddenly sweaty palms.

With a smirk, Grace glanced pointedly at Chloe, then continued down the hall.

Quintus didn't seem to notice how she failed to answer. Like before, he stood deep in thought, as if these mortal interactions barely deserved his attention.

"You recognized Grace?"

Now he turned toward Chloe with a question in his eyes. "Yes." His eyes narrowed. "She looks the same as when I saw her before."

"The same?" Chloe shook her head. "She's fifteen now. She was twelve last time you saw her."

He shrugged.

Chloe touched a hand to her forehead. "Grace went from looking like a child to looking like a young woman, but somehow, she still looks the same to you? But me, who looks virtually the same as I did at fifteen, I look different?"

"I do not think I will go into the sitting room after all." Apparently, he had no interest in answering her questions. He took a step toward the nearest chair. "I will stay here until you return."

Grabbing him by the elbow, she shoved him into the hallway. "Oh yes, you're coming. If you have the nerve to show up here after I specifically told you I never wanted to see you again, then you absolutely have to deal with my fae brother. I warn you, Vesper probably won't be so friendly with you now that he's had three years of me complaining about how you're the worst male that has ever entered my life."

The words scorched her mouth, which gave her the fuel to shove Quintus even harder down the hall. He probably didn't even try to stop her, but it still felt good to be forcing him to go somewhere he didn't want to go. For once.

When they reached the sitting room, the three children inside it raced to get to him first.

"What's it like to have pointy ears?" the third child, Danielle, asked. Her eyes sparkled with the fascination only a five-year-old could have.

Eliza stepped in front of her sister. "Do the points of your ear improve your hearing? Father hears much better than us mortals. He says that even though we have a fae father and a mortal mother, children are always born fully fae or fully mortal, so we don't know anything about being fae since we're all mortal."

"Except we know what Father has told us," mumbled Danielle from behind her sister.

"True." Eliza nodded solemnly before glancing up at Quintus again.

But now Gideon stepped in front of her. Eliza tried to push him away, but he just caught her by the wrist and yanked it down. He did all this while maintaining perfect eye contact with the fae in front of him. "Does our mortal food taste terrible to you? Or is it like mortal music, and it's actually even better than fae food? Father says our food is delicious, but I think he's lying."

Jabbing her foot into the back of her brother's knee, Eliza finally managed to step out from behind him. "Fae can't lie, Gideon. Not even Father."

His hand danced across the air as he tried to catch his sister's wrist again. "I know, but he only ever says the food here tastes delicious. He won't say it tastes *better*, so I think it's just his way of avoiding the true answer."

"Children."

The sound of their father's voice acted like an enchantment on them. Gideon, Eliza, and Danielle froze in place for a split second. Then they immediately dropped their hands and slinked over to the sofa where they usually sat.

Vesper and Cosette stepped into the room with matching stern expressions, though neither of them directed the look toward their children. A boy with chubby cheeks and a mop of brown hair held tight to Cosette's hand. At three years old, Tucker never strayed far from his mother. Grace stood a step behind them, looking like she had just spilled a juicy secret.

Folding his arms over his chest, Vesper glared at Quintus. "You better have a good reason for being here."

Quintus met the glare with one of his own. "A group of mortals is trying to take over Faerie."

Over his blue and gray eyes, Vesper's eyebrows raised. "What?"

Cosette pinched her mouth in a knot, clearly trying to smother a chuckle.

Only Chloe chose to say the words they were all thinking. "But they're mortals. What can mortals do against fae?"

Whipping his head toward her, Quintus clenched his jaw. "They have iron."

She kept her expression even. "How much iron?"

He stepped closer to her, moving straight into her personal space. If anyone else in town had seen, they'd probably assume he was moving in for a kiss. But he didn't. He just clenched his jaw tighter. "Too much. They figured out how to weaponize the iron. They have trapped fae inside confined spaces. They're trying to take over Crystal Thorn Castle."

That declaration forced a gasp from the edge of the room. Grace clapped a hand over her mouth while the weight of those words settled.

Chloe's older sister, Elora, lived in Crystal Thorn Castle. And Elora was now fae. She had once ended up on her own unwilling quest to restore Faerie, and it had changed her forever. If the mortals had learned how to weaponize iron, then she was in trouble.

Quintus's expression softened once he saw that his words had sank in. He still didn't move away though. "Only a mortal can save us now, a mortal who already knows about Faerie and who cares about someone living there."

The words came out as dark and rich as Faerie velvet. He leaned down capturing Chloe's gaze with an intense stare of his own. "We need *you*."

Her mouth went dry. It heated and thickened her throat at the thought of her sister, but no one, *especially* not Quintus, would manipulate her into doing anything she didn't want to do. "This town needs me. I'm not going anywhere until Mr. Nash feels better."

3

EARLY THE NEXT MORNING, CHLOE donned her cloak again. If she didn't have any more Swiftsea salt, then she'd have to check the town market for some fennel. Maybe one of the market stalls would have it, though not many would be open if it had snowed overnight.

The outside of her cloak had a dark blue fabric with a weave tight enough to block almost all rain and snow from soaking through. White fur formed the underside of the cloak, providing incredible warmth. Since the fabric and the fur both came from Faerie, she knew the other townspeople didn't have such effective winter protection.

She snatched up her basket anyway, hoping at least a few people would be brave enough to open their market stalls. Inside the basket, she stuffed the second half of the poultice she had made the day before. On a whim, she also threw in the magical book from Faerie. A red and gold fabric square went on top, hiding the contents from any curious eyes. If snow had fallen through the night, she'd just head straight to the Nashes' house.

Luckily, when she stepped outside, only a light dusting of frost covered the cobblestone road. Her boots made a noise with each new footprint she pressed into the icy frost. Her thick petticoats behind her nearly erased them.

Swathes of red and orange blazed above as the sun climbed into the sky. Drops of golden sunlight dappled her cloak, though it did little to warm her on such a cold morning. Luckily, the fur in her cloak still kept the temperature bearable.

By the time she reached the market, the sun had risen completely over the horizon. Now the swathes of red and orange had turned to feathery wisps.

The brisk walk should have given her plenty of time to think about Faerie and the supposed danger it was in, but her mind kept spinning back to the Nashes instead. She only had half a poultice left. If Mr. Nash had improved since the night before, the second half would heal him completely after she administered it that morning.

But what if his illness hadn't been scurpus? Or what if she had made some error while preparing the poultice? She had never made an error before, but that didn't stop her from fearing this might be her very first time.

Her fingers tapped the handle of her basket as she scanned the different market stalls. One man did have a bit of goldenrod. Since she was low on that too, it might be worth a look.

The moment she stepped toward his stall, his gaze immediately fell to the bundle of herbs in his hands. When she leaned over his table, he muttered under his breath. "A *woman* apothecary. I've never heard such a thing."

"I can hear you." She pinned him with a stare that would hopefully crumble his insides.

He responded with a deeper scowl than before, which meant her stare had not done its job.

No matter. She didn't need any goldenrod at the moment anyway, just fennel, of which he had none. Tipping her nose into the air, she continued down the frozen cobblestone path. The man usually only sold to the male cooks in town. She should have known better than to approach him.

As she scanned another row of stalls, her gaze fixed on a young man purchasing a brown cloak from a nearby stall. Her lips curved upward at the sight of him. Dunstan Bennett. Dunstan's father owned the largest farm in the town.

Usually that would mean he'd grow up stuffy and being served to his whole life, but his father wisely forced all his sons into manual labor with the rest of the servants. Now he had the same work-hardened muscles as the other young men in town, but he also had money.

He must have felt her gaze because he looked up just then. Biting her bottom lip, she offered a tiny wave. She decided to forgo the batting eyelashes this time.

His light-colored eyes gleamed at the sight of her. Dunstan turned to the man in the stall in front of him and reached into his pouch, probably to end the deal as quickly as possible so he could have a word with Chloe. Or maybe she just hoped those were his intentions.

"Miss Chloe."

Turning on her heel, Chloe faced the child who had just called her name. Little Maisie from the Fletcher family stood before her. Her brown hair had been braided into two tight plaits that hung over her shoulders. Yellow ribbons tied each one off. "Could you come check on my grandfather? He isn't feeling well."

"Of course." Chloe reached into her pocket and fished out a wooden top. "I have to check on Mr. Nash first, but you can play with this while you're waiting for me. I'll pick it back up later today when I come to check on your grandfather."

Maisie did a little jump at the sight of the toy. If she heard any words Chloe spoke after revealing it, her face did nothing to show it. Now her thick-mittened hands reached for the top. She darted away without another word.

Chloe stood up straight again, intending to inconspicuously trail closer to Dunstan, but a solid figure stood directly in her path. A sigh puffed out of her lips strong enough to ruffle the loose strands of hair that had escaped her messy bun. "Hello again, Quintus."

At least he wore a glamour this time. His fae magic now made his pointed fae ears look like round, mortal ones. He still appeared a little too handsome and a little too tall for a mortal, but he had clearly tried.

"Faerie needs you."

She waved a flippant hand through the air. "Yes, I know, but my town needs me too. I told you I'm not going anywhere until Mr. Nash is doing better."

He opened his mouth, which sent fire into her belly strong enough to make it tingle. She clenched her jaw and gestured toward the man at the stall who had been so rude to her earlier. "Go see if that man has any fennel."

Instead of complaining, Quintus merely tilted his head. "What is fennel?"

"Does it matter?" She shoved him away. "Just ask him if he has any. The man knows what it is."

She found it highly unlikely that the man would have an herb hidden somewhere, instead of on his table for buyers to see. But at least this way, she could get rid of Quintus for a few minutes.

He stalked off just in time for her to reach the edge of the cobblestone path. As she hoped, Dunstan stepped toward her without question.

"Miss Chloe Rosenbel." He pulled a brown cap off his head and bunched it up in his hands. Despite the cap, his light brown hair was combed with precision over his head. He cleared his throat. "I wondered if I might stop by your home this evening."

"Are you feeling unwell?" She paired the question with her most charming smile.

Of course she knew full well what he meant to imply with his question, but hearing him say it out loud would be five times as good as the question itself.

A gentle smile graced his lips. "You always forget yourself completely when someone is in need." The smile stretched wider. "You have such selflessness, which is the most admirable quality a woman can have."

The words twisted in Chloe's gut. She did like helping people, but knowing it was the *only* thing that made her worthy of attention never sat well with her either. Luckily, Dunstan didn't seem to notice the slight wrinkle of her nose.

His gaze dropped to the cap in his hands while a bright pink colored the tops of his ears. "But no, I am not unwell. I thought perhaps—"

"Who is this?" Judging by how fast Quintus had appeared, he had most likely used fae speed to get there. A vein in his jaw pulsed when he clenched it tighter. Even worse, he stared at her and not Dunstan. Etiquette in their town clearly dictated that a man should always be addressed before a woman.

After letting out a huff that flared her nostrils, she relaxed her face and turned forward again. "I'm so sorry, Mr. Bennett. You must excuse my…"

The words trailed off incomplete. What should she call Quintus? A relation? That felt wrong. Friend? He definitely *wasn't* a friend.

The vein in Quintus's jaw pulsed again. He turned even farther away from the young man and even closer to Chloe. Now she could nudge him with her shoulder without even having to move her feet. Not that she would. She had no desire at all to touch him, though that didn't explain why her clothes suddenly felt itchy.

Quintus tilted his head toward the road leading to the Nash's house. "We have more important things to do than bother with *him*." His lip curled as he finished the sentence.

He reached for her arm, but she jerked it away just in time. "*We?*" Now she narrowed her eyes, staring directly into his. "You have no claim on my time. And on that note, you're standing too close to me. It's inappropriate for a young man to stand so close to a young woman unless they are betrothed."

When that didn't garner the reaction she expected—from either of the men—she tacked on an even deeper explanation. "Or *married.*"

Wearing the same scowl as before, Quintus continued to tilt his head toward the path. He continued to stare at her though, and she could practically feel him wanting to roll his eyes.

Dunstan Bennett, on the other hand, suddenly blinked several times. He seemed to realize it might be his duty, by rules of etiquette, to defend Chloe's honor in this situation.

He puffed his chest out, curling his hands into fists. "Is he bothering you, Miss Chloe? I could…"

His gaze strayed from her just long enough to glance toward Quintus. He looked up first, probably just now realizing Quintus stood a few inches taller than any other man in town. Then his gaze strayed to Quintus's arms. Even though Dunstan had spent years laboring on a farm, the fae still had larger muscles. Dunstan's puffed out chest immediately caved in. He swallowed, and didn't step back, but he did lean away a bit. "You better leave her alone."

Rolling his eyes, Quintus turned away from the young man completely. Again, he addressed only Chloe. "Are you not anxious to see if your neighbor needs another poultice or not?"

Her insides leapt at the question. Mr. Nash. She *was* anxious to see how he was doing. "Fine."

She got a few steps down the frosty cobblestone path before she remembered Dunstan. That couldn't be a good sign. Swallowing, she turned back to him with an attempt at a charming smile. "I'm so sorry, Mr. Bennett. I think tomorrow might be better."

He nodded, but he took a step back as he did it.

She didn't have time to worry about how Quintus's inopportune presence might have ruined her prospects with the most eligible young man in town. Now she could only worry about Mr. Nash.

But by the time she got to their house, she found she should have been worried about something else entirely. Mrs. Nash answered the door with her back hunched over. A bright red rash covered her hands and face. Sweat beaded at her hairline, indicating a fever.

Even if Mr. Nash was doing better, his wife clearly had gotten worse.

4

TWO PEOPLE IN TOWN HAD the same illness, and Chloe didn't have the ingredients to heal it. Her heart stuttered as she stepped into the Nashes' home. At least she had half a poultice. That is, *if* the poultice had even helped.

Mrs. Nash didn't seem to notice when Quintus slipped into the house behind Chloe. In fact, she hardly even seemed to notice Chloe. Her feet moved, but that almost looked like a reflex more than anything.

When Chloe ushered the woman into her bed, she moved without argument.

"I told her I would get the door." Mr. Nash sat up in the bed right next to his wife. He shook his head. "I still have trouble getting to my feet, but I'm not as weak as yesterday. I'm slow, but I would have done it if she had let me."

His rash remained in small splotches on his cheeks, but it did look much lighter and smaller than last evening. Pulling his damp gray hair off his forehead, Chloe found his hairline no longer had any gray tinge at all.

The poultice *had* helped.

"Mirielle." Mr. Nash turned to his wife now. He attempted to help her into a more comfortable position on the bed, but his arms shook with the effort of it.

In the end, Mrs. Nash just slumped down where she was, despite how her arm jutted out awkwardly to one side. The sweat across her forehead beaded thick enough to now slide down into the sheets. The gray tinge at her hairline spread down to the middle of her forehead, proving she was in even worse condition than her husband had been the night before.

Chloe dropped her basket onto the nearest table and threw the red and gold fabric square off it. Her fingers wrapped around the cloth holding the other half of the poultice. If she used it on Mr. Nash now, he would likely heal completely in another day or so.

But what would happen if she used it on Mrs. Nash instead? Would they both heal completely? Or would they both get worse since neither of them got a full dose?

Her fingers trembled as she attempted to untie the string securing the poultice. Being an apothecary meant she had ample opportunities to research and solve difficult problems. It also meant she could help others in their greatest time of need. Both of those things made her job more than rewarding. They did nothing for situations like this though.

Heat surged in her eyelids as tears welled. She stared at the poultice, blinking the tears back before any of them could fall. This was no time for crying. She could be sad, or delighted, *later*—when she knew whether her decision had been the right one. For now, she had to decide.

"Mirielle, please." Mr. Nash's voice broke over the words. The sound of that ache tugged at Chloe's heart even more than seeing him despondent the day before had. "Won't you try to drink a little water?"

His question was followed by an unintelligible grunt from Mrs. Nash.

The tiniest whimper escaped his mouth.

Taking the open fabric square into her hands, Chloe made her decision. The poultice would go to Mrs. Nash. Chloe knew other methods, mortal methods, for caring for the sick. She'd just have to hope those would work well enough when paired with the poultice.

Rubbing the heel of his hand into his chest, Mr. Nash caught Chloe's eye. He cleared his throat, but it didn't take any of the ache from his voice. "You can help her, can't you?"

Truthfully, she didn't know if she could. If she didn't get more Swiftsea salt or at least some fennel, she didn't have the ingredients for another poultice. But Mr. Nash didn't need to share the same worry as her. He and his wife needed someone who could be steady and sure even in times of uncertainty.

"I will do my best." Chloe said it in her most confident voice possible. Though her fingers still trembled, she didn't allow any of the shakiness into her voice. Now she gestured toward Mrs. Nash. "Will you lower her blouse please? I need to apply a poultice to her chest."

Mr. Nash didn't bother nodding or speaking. He just reached for the top edge of his wife's blouse and pulled it down as much as possible while still maintaining some level of modesty.

After adding water to make a paste, Chloe began spreading the poultice across Mrs. Nash's chest. She worked methodically, keeping the poultice thick while still spreading it out as much as possible.

Throughout the process, Mrs. Nash's skin only seemed to grow warmer, especially her shoulders and arms. If the poultice had any chance of helping, Chloe needed to bring that fever down.

Once the poultice had been applied, she threw the blanket off the bed and lifted Mrs. Nash's underdress up high enough to remove her socks. A little of the poultice still remained on Chloe's fingers. Normally, she would have wiped it away, but putting a little extra poultice on the ankles and lower legs of the woman couldn't hurt.

Chloe's hands worked in larger motions now, rubbing Mrs. Nash's ankle and then her leg up to the knee. Chloe kept the same methodical rhythm as before. Tiny bits of the poultice settled deeper into the woman's skin with each massage.

The fire in the corner of the room had died down to embers, making it only a little warmer inside than outside. Still, Mrs. Nash's skin gave off heat like a loaf of bread just pulled from a fire. After only a few minutes, Chloe had to take a break just to let her own hands cool after touching such heated skin.

Only now did her eyes stray over to another corner of the room. Quintus stood in the shadows staring at her as intensely as he had when she first saw him the night before. He didn't move. He didn't speak. He just watched with those dark brown eyes that held as much magic as Faerie itself.

Her mouth screwed into a knot as she shot him a rueful glare. "Are you going to stand there and do nothing the whole time? You could help me, you know."

He raised an eyebrow. "Why bother? They will not survive."

A sharp inhale stung in her nose. She did her best to turn the glare on her face to a murderous one. "Hush."

She probably should have known better than to speak to him. Her head jerked over to Mr. Nash. Luckily, he was too busy dabbing a rag across his wife's damp forehead to have noticed the interaction between Chloe and Quintus.

Considering how neither of the Nashes even acknowledged Quintus's presence, it was possible Quintus had done some fae magic or other to keep himself hidden from them. Or maybe the Nashes were just too sick to care.

After taking a deep breath, Chloe crossed the room and reached for Mrs. Nash's ankles again. They gave off even more heat than before. If it had been summer, Chloe's options would have been limited, but with a thin layer of frost still covering most of the ground outside, she had a few ideas.

Dashing out the front door, she gathered little bits of frost into her hands. When she pressed into the skin of Mrs. Nash's legs, the woman moaned. Luckily, her illness stole away her ability to resist.

It took Chloe until midday to get the woman's fever down to an acceptable level, except then, Mr. Nash's fever had returned. The once-faded rash on his cheeks had turned to angry red splotches that filled his whole face.

At least the gray tinge across his forehead and at the tip of his fingers hadn't returned. Her eyes narrowed as she lifted his hand closer to her eyes. On second thought, his fingertips did look a bit dull. Shaking her head, she dropped his hand back onto the bed again.

No. The poultice had helped him, and it would help Mrs. Nash. She just had to give it time.

Undoing the clasp of her cloak, she draped it over the nearest chair. In the corner of the room, even the small embers of the fire had died down completely. Despite the chill, her bustling around to bring down the fevers kept Chloe more than warm enough. She probably wouldn't need her cloak again until she finally had a chance to sit down and rest.

With a clunk, she dropped the magical book from Faerie onto a table. Thumbing through the pages, her gaze darted over the words to find the page on scurpus. Just when she thought she found it, she instead found a page on areas of Faerie where magic could keep feet planted in place.

Letting out a frustrated huff, she skipped forward until the paragraphs on scurpus finally sat in front of her. Before, she had only focused on the poultice and its recipe. Now, she skimmed through the causes and the other information about scurpus.

She read a short paragraph on the cause at least three times before she realized it wouldn't sink in. The room and the Nashes distracted her mind too completely. She tried to read it one last time.

Apparently, iron poisoning caused scurpus in Faerie, but that obviously wasn't the cause here in the mortal realm. Iron didn't harm mortals the way it did for fae. Shaking her head, she flipped to the next page. Maybe that one would have something helpful.

When Mrs. Nash began coughing, Chloe scurried to offer her a cup of water. The woman brought the cup to her lips, but when she tried to swallow, the water just drizzled out of her mouth instead. With a whimper, she pushed the cup away and dove deeper into her bed.

"Quintus." Chloe whirled around. She had nothing to offer, but maybe the desperation in her eyes would be enough. "Go get me some Swif—" Her mouth snapped closed as she remembered to check herself. "I need more of *the* salt. I can't save them without it."

Standing in nearly the exact position he'd been in all day, Quintus just stared. But then a light glinted in his eye. He leaned ever so slightly forward. "I propose a bargain."

"What, now?" Pursing her lips, she gestured toward the Nashes. "In front of…"

"They are unlikely to survive." He shrugged. "And even if they do, they are too unwell to remember this conversation later."

She flashed her teeth at him. "Stop saying they won't survive. They will if you bring me the salt."

He narrowed his eyes skeptically and then repeated the same words from earlier. "I propose a bargain."

"No." Chloe stomped her foot. "I'm not making a bargain with you. I know better. Just go get the salt."

Keeping his stare steady, he leaned into the wall behind him. That alone was answer enough. He wouldn't help without a bargain.

But she knew about the fae. She knew how they tricked mortals and twisted words. No matter how carefully she tried to phrase the bargain, it would always end up benefiting Quintus more than her.

Even if it had been a life and death situation with her *own* life on the line, she still wouldn't make a bargain.

She just had to find another way to save the Nashes.

Throwing open her magical book again, she tried to get more creative. Now she searched the remedies for common fevers and common rashes. When she dashed across town to return to her apothecary workroom, Quintus followed close behind.

He said nothing when she gathered tinctures and tonics. He watched her crush herbs and pour liquids into small vials. She dropped the new items into her basket and hurried back over to the Nashes' even faster than she had left them.

Once inside, Quintus went right back to his corner, and Chloe went right back to administering any and every remedy she could think of.

But each new herb and tonic did nothing. Neither did the tinctures.

The gray tinges had returned.

Mr. Nash only had a bit of gray along his hairline and at his fingertips, but it didn't bode well that it had returned. Even worse, Mrs. Nash's entire forehead had turned a deep ashy gray. The gray tinge spread up past her fingers and onto her palms.

Throwing an empty glass vial across the room, Chloe let out a scream. "It's not working." She huffed at the sight of the broken glass that was strewn across the floor.

Neither of the Nashes reacted to her outburst. They just lay in bed blinking and moaning. Sweat beaded across their skin everywhere, not just the forehead.

Whirling around, Chloe jabbed her pointer finger toward Quintus. "I'm blaming you if they die."

"It was too late to save them anyway." Quintus didn't even look at her as he spoke. He had produced a sketchbook and pencil, probably from his pocket, and now focused on whatever he drew on its pages.

A lump lodged deep in Chloe's throat. "It's not too late." She swallowed. "It can't be."

That managed to lift Quintus's eyes from his sketchbook. "It may be too late for them, but it is not too late for Faerie. We need you, Chloe. You must come with me."

"How dare you?" She marched forward just enough to snatch the sketchbook away from him and throw it to the ground. "Your kind is not more important than mine. Just watch me." She lifted her chin. "I *will* save them."

But she didn't.

Only an hour later, just as the first tendrils of night crept in through the windows, Mr. Nash's life slipped away. His wife had died only a few minutes earlier.

Chloe knelt on the ground with her arms draped over the side of the bed. She sobbed into her arms. Her thoughts writhed, but they kept going back to the one moment she tried to forget.

What if she had given the second half of the poultice to Mr. Nash instead of to his wife? If she had given him the full poultice, would he have recovered at least? It had been too late for his wife, but could she have saved him if she had made a different choice?

Her sobs shook the sleeves of her underdress. Tears soaked the entire upper sleeve of her right arm. After so much crying, the cold in the air finally started to chill her. It wrapped around her arms and back even tighter than her cloak. But her heart was too icy to warm anyway.

An apothecary was supposed to take care of people. To heal them.

And she had failed.

"Perhaps we should return to your home."

As much as the sound of Quintus's voice gave her the desire to strangle him, she knew deep down that he was right. She'd stop by the undertaker's home and let him know Mr. and Mrs. Nash had died. He would make all the arrangements after that.

Now, she just had to get out of that house.

She gathered her things and donned her cloak once again. Tears still slid down her cheeks, but they dropped slower than before. By the time she arranged the red and gold cloth square over the items in her basket, she had finally stopped her tears completely.

Using the bottom edge of her wide sleeve that fell nearly to the ground, she wiped away the remaining tears on her face. Now she stepped out onto the cobblestone path. The sun had melted away the last of the frost throughout the day, but more would start forming soon now that the sun had dipped below the horizon.

Her nose was puffy as her boots hit the cobblestone. After only a few steps, a child dashed out into the road. It was little Maisie Fletcher with yellow ribbons still in her hair.

"Are you ready to check on my grandfather now, Miss Chloe?"

The lump in Chloe's throat grew to the size of a fist. She had forgotten all about Maisie's grandfather. She'd much rather throw herself into a bed and sob herself to sleep, but she had a duty as an apothecary. She couldn't give up when someone else needed her. "Of course, Maisie. I can come now. Tell me, what kind of sickness does your grandfather have?"

The child lifted one shoulder until it reached her ear. "Mother says it's just winter sickness. Grandfather's skin is hot, and his arms are all red and splotchy." The little girl wrinkled her nose. "But he also has this strange gray shade on his fingertips. Father says it's unnatural."

Just like that, the ice in Chloe's heart spread out until it filled her entire chest. She tried to breathe but couldn't. The truth gripped her too tight.

Someone else had scurpus.

5

NO FEWER THAN THREE PEOPLE in the Fletcher household had scurpus. Chloe confirmed it, then sent them all to bed with cool rags on their foreheads. She had administered tinctures and uncovered their feet to keep their fevers from getting worse, but without Swiftsea salt or some fennel, there wasn't much else she could do.

Once home, Grace suggested that Chloe get some sleep before she tried to do anything else. Naturally, Chloe ignored the idea and stayed up all night looking for a solution to this horrible problem. By morning, Chloe's bun, which had once been only *slightly* messy, now had strands poking out at every angle. She kept tucking the little pieces back into the bun, but they'd fall away after a minute or two.

At the earliest possible hour, a knock sounded on the door to her workroom. If the knock had been slightly less forceful, she would have assumed Grace had come to call on her. But it wasn't Grace.

Quintus stood in front of her wearing a deep scowl. "I do not understand why Vesper forced me into another room for the night.

You clearly didn't sleep anyway, so what was so bad about us being in the same room?"

Her fingers dug into her hair, attempting to push a particularly annoying strand of hair deep into her bun. "What do you want?" She spat the words out, delivering as much ice with them as she still had coiled around her heart. Then she marched across the room and slumped back into the chair she'd been sitting in a moment earlier.

His scowl deepened. "You must return with me to Faerie. We need you."

"Go get me some Swiftsea salt then." Her eyelids drooped as she turned another page in a book she had only started a few minutes ago. So far, it had no information that the other five books she'd skimmed didn't have. Keeping her eyes open got harder with each second that passed.

Quintus stepped into the room until he stood right at her side. Too close. He always stood too close. "I will not bring you Swiftsea salt unless you make a bargain promising to help save Faerie from the mortals who are destroying it."

She stood up from her chair so fast that it clattered to the ground. Holding out one arm, she showed him the red ribbon that decorated her sleeve just above the elbow. The red ribbon acted as a fae ward. The ward made it impossible for a fae to enchant her.

She gestured toward her neck now. "I have ward necklaces too, one from Vesper and one from Brannick. They're invisible, so you might not remember when I got them, but they still protect me. And do you see the dress I'm wearing?"

Her arms gestured down at herself. She wore a cream linen underdress with a full skirt. Its sleeves were fitted around her upper arms, but at the elbow, the sleeves went wide and fluttered down nearly the same length as her skirts. On top of that underdress, she wore a dark red overdress that opened in the front to show off the underdress beneath it. The overdress had corset lacing around her middle, tied with a golden cord.

"Do you see it?"

His gaze raked over her, lingering a little too long and too appreciatively at her figure.

She smacked him in the chest, forcing his eyes back up to hers. "It's red. I know that red can attract fae, but it also provides protection to the wearer. I've worn red nearly every day since I left Faerie because I know its dangers better than almost any mortal."

Though he continued to look at her, his rich brown eyes—that nearly sparkled—still gave off the supremely annoying impression that he was bored.

With a huff, she slammed her hands onto her hips. "I know better than to make a bargain with a fae. Once that bargain is made, it will be physically impossible to break the bargain. I'd never do something so rash."

He lifted his perfect eyes just enough to glare. "Then you will never get more Swiftsea salt."

Her own glare clenched her jaw. She stepped closer, getting into *his* personal space for once. "Go get me some Swiftsea salt and then maybe I'll *think* about returning to Faerie."

His eyes changed then. The moment she stepped just a little too close to him, his breath stopped, and his throat bobbed with a swallow. His expression stayed as hardened as before, but a spark lit in his eyes. Or maybe a shadow crossed over them, making the light in them more prominent afterward.

He gave no other indication to his thoughts or feelings other than that flicker in his eyes, but something about his voice seemed softer than before. "After you help us, I can return you to this exact same moment in the mortal realm. You can save your own people when you return."

Without warning, her lip trembled. She scratched her nose to hide the movement, but he had probably seen it anyway. "What if I can't save Faerie? What if I die? If I save the people in this town first, at least I know I did one thing right."

Her lip trembled even more. Even if Quintus couldn't see it, he wouldn't miss how her posture stooped.

She swallowed. "Get me the salt. It's the only way I'll think about returning to Faerie."

His eyes did that same strange flicker again. This time, his eyebrows even pinched together. For the briefest moment, she got the bizarre impression that he wanted to reach for her. To comfort her? But no, a fae would never do something like that. Not Quintus.

"Fine." Quintus's voice came out deeper than usual, and possibly even a bit strained. "I will get you some Swiftsea salt, but I expect you to come back with me after that."

When he disappeared down the hall, her heart ached at seeing him leave. But why? She tried to shake away the feeling as she sat back down.

The moment she slumped into her chair a knock sounded at the door.

This time, little Eliza stood on the other side of it. She stood tall with her shoulders rolled back as she announced that someone in the Carpenter household was sick. Her eyes gleamed with pride for finally delivering a message of her own, but Chloe could only nod.

Another person in town had an illness. Maybe it was winter sickness or an infection from a wound, but her gut told her it had to be scurpus. More scurpus.

She didn't have time to wait for the Swiftsea salt.

And then it hit her.

She knew where fennel grew, didn't she? Winter was far from an ideal time to harvest the herb, of course. If any of it had survived autumn, it would be shriveled and probably under a layer of frost. But a small clump of it might still be there. Shriveled and frozen fennel had to be better than no fennel at all.

Nodding to herself, she reached for her cloak. Exhaustion tugged at her eyelids as she forced her feet forward.

She didn't need Faerie, and Faerie didn't need her.

Her older sister had always been better at fighting than Chloe anyway. Elora was the one who convinced their father to teach her sword fighting. And her beloved, Brannick, was the most powerful fae in Faerie. Only Elora came close to matching his skill. If anyone was going to save Faerie, it was them, *not* Chloe.

She was better suited to caring for people, for researching. When entertainment was needed, Chloe could recite an epic poem with all the heart of the greatest bard. But she couldn't save Faerie, not even from mortals.

Now that she had something to do, her hands moved quickly. She gathered her magical book and a few other items to take with her. They could go into the basket, but it would get heavy after such a long walk. A bag might be better, though she didn't have anything in her workroom large enough for everything she wanted to bring.

"Where is Quintus?" Vesper stepped inside. His gray and blue eyes flashed at each corner of the room as he examined it.

Chloe waved off his concern. "I sent Quintus away to get me more Swiftsea salt. It will help with the sickness that is going around."

Vesper raised an eyebrow "You *sent* him?" He stepped closer, which ruffled the brown hair on his head. His arms folded in front of his chest. "Did you make a bargain with him?"

"No." She scoffed, lifting her basket again. Definitely too heavy for that long of a walk. "I'm not stupid. I don't think I need the salt anyway. I might be able to…"

Now her head whipped around. She narrowed her eyes at her brother. Her *fae* brother, who had magic. Her eyes flew open wide. "Can you conjure fennel?"

"Fennel?" He tilted his head to the side. "I do not know what that is."

Her lips curved upward. Why hadn't she thought of this earlier? Now she bent over her worktable to sketch the herb on a spare piece of paper. "It's an herb. It looks like—"

"No, you do not understand." His chin dropped to his chest. "If I do not know what it is, if I have never seen it before, I cannot conjure it."

The little spark that had lit in her chest faded to an ember. "And you cannot conjure Swiftsea salt either, right?"

"No. I am from the Court of Noble Rose. Only fae from Swiftsea can conjure Swiftsea salt."

The little ember in her chest got swallowed by ice once again. "That's what I thought." She let out a sigh, mostly to keep herself from tearing up again. "Can you conjure me a bag then? Something with a strap that will hang on one shoulder and across my body. The bag should be big enough to fit this book, but I need it to have a few extra pockets for herbs, vials, bandages, and such."

With only a wave of his hand, he conjured the perfect bag. It was made of dark brown leather but had soft suede pockets inside.

She grabbed it from him, daring to wear the tiniest smile. "Perfect."

He dropped a hand onto her shoulder as soon as she took the bag from him. "Be careful, Chloe." He leaned closer. "With Quintus, I mean."

Her gaze stayed fixed on the bag in her hand. "I know."

Vesper squeezed her shoulder gently. "He was kind to you before, but he also forced you into a battle you had no reason to join."

"Yes, and then I fainted in front of everyone. I remember."

Now Vesper tilted his head downward until she finally met his eye. He frowned. "Fae are selfish by nature. Just because your sister's beloved and I have both learned to love, it does not mean Quintus is capable of learning the same thing."

"I know."

And she did. She truly did. Maybe Quintus was devastatingly handsome, incredibly strong, and ridiculously tall, but he would be trouble of the worst kind. Nothing could convince her to give him a second chance. Not even a bag of Swiftsea salt.

6

FENNEL GREW ON THE OUTSKIRTS of town in a little meadow near a river. With her new leather bag slung over one shoulder, Chloe donned her dark blue cloak. It hugged her shoulders, bringing warmth along with it right away.

The moment she stepped outside, a blast of icy wind slapped her cheeks. It wasn't until Quintus failed to appear that she realized she expected him to be back with the Swiftsea salt already. He did promise he could return to that exact moment.

Did his absence mean something had happened to him?

That thought couldn't linger because Grace stepped out from around a corner. The chilly wind had turned her cheeks red. She wore her dark red hair up in a bun that was much neater than Chloe's. It was mostly hidden under her green cloak, though. She took a step closer to her sister with a set jaw. "I'm coming with you."

Digging into her pockets for woolen mittens that covered her arms up to the elbow, Chloe chuckled. "Do you even know where I'm going?"

"Yes," Grace said defiantly. "I heard you talking to Vesper. You're going to get fennel, right?"

She followed after Chloe, but on her first step, she tripped over a dip in the cobblestone. Her cloak flew out behind her as she took several steps to catch her balance.

In the end, Chloe had to grasp her little sister by the arm before she stopped stumbling. Chloe chuckled again. "You're lucky you're better with a harp than you are with those feet."

Grace's cheeks turned an even brighter pink, but she let out a giggle. "I know. If Mother were here, she'd probably regret naming me Grace now. I'm the least graceful of us three sisters by far."

Joy danced between them at the thought and then dimmed as the mention of their dead mother sank in. Chloe brushed a wrinkle from her sister's skirts. "Mother would be proud of you if she were here. Only you can play the harp as beautifully as she did."

Hooking her arm around her sister's, Grace squinted at the path ahead. "Where does fennel grow?"

Their mittened arms rested against each other as they started down the path. With her other hand, Chloe gestured toward the river. "Some of it grows in a meadow out there. It needs lots of sun, so it doesn't grow as well in places with shade and trees."

"Do you think we'll even find any? It is winter, after all." Grace's eyes always looked too big for her face when she asked questions. It also made the blue in them brighter than ever.

Even at fifteen, her eyes still had the childlike wonder of a toddler.

"I don't know if we'll find any." Chloe decided to not dwell on that fear. She also decided to not dwell on the reason Quintus hadn't returned yet. He promised he could return to the exact same moment in the mortal realm when he had left. So where was he?

"Don't you usually have bundles and bundles of every herb imaginable?" Grace continued to stare like Chloe's answer might cure an entire civilization, not just a few people in their small town.

A smile pricked on Chloe's lips. She stood a little taller as they walked. Their boots trailed past the frosty cobblestone of their main town road and onto the frozen dirt of an outer path. "I have bundles of all the important herbs, but I've never needed fennel before."

Grace nodded solemnly. "And what's the best spot to get fennel?"

Chloe frowned, though the smile underneath it was probably still obvious. "You always stare at me like my answers are the most important thing in the world. Do you even care about what I'm saying or are you just trying to make me feel important?"

Grace giggled again, her blue eyes brightening when she did. She glanced over her shoulder, as if judging the distance they had walked from town. When she turned back, she gestured toward the river. "Look at the ice. Do you think it's thick enough to try walking on it?"

Throwing her sister a sideways glance, Chloe pursed her lips. "Not going to answer my question?"

"You are important. To me you are." After flashing a wide smile, Grace gestured toward the river again. "What do you think about the ice?"

Chloe chuckled. "No, the ice isn't thick enough to walk on. It hardly ever gets cold enough for that, especially because the water in the river flows so fast. Stepping on that ice is a sure way to die an icy, drowning death."

After staying awake the entire night, exhaustion still weighted down Chloe's limbs, but the cool air and the walking helped to keep it at bay.

"Excuse me, Miss Chloe!" A young man just a few months older than Grace called out to them from a nearby house. He sprinted toward them so fast he had run out of breath by the time he got to them.

"My uncle." He sucked in a breath. "He's sick. And my cousin." Two huge puffs of air escaped his mouth. "They both have a fever with an ugly rash. And my uncle's head—he's bald, you know—looks strange. It's almost gray."

The childlike wonder of Grace's sweet questions had warmed Chloe's insides just enough to forget about the scurpus, but now two more people in town had it. Her teeth clenched together tight before she could relax enough to speak to the young man.

"Yes, I know the sickness." She attempted to unwind her tight expression so the young man wouldn't worry, but that didn't go as well as she hoped. "I have to gather an herb to create the remedy, but I will visit them as soon as I can."

With a hurried nod, the young man sprinted back toward town again.

All the innocence had left Grace's eyes now, but they still opened wide. She gulped. "How many people have it now?"

Chloe shook her head, stomping down the path with more determination than before. "Five." But then she remembered the message Eliza had delivered before she left the house. She winced. "No, sorry, it's six. Six people have it that I know of." She sighed. "We should probably hurry."

Grace marched forward. And promptly tripped on a frozen bush.

Since they still walked arm in arm, it was easy for Chloe to steady her sister before she fell. Grace had stopped being the baby of the family once they moved in with Vesper's family. He had four children younger than her, after all, and little Tucker had been only a few months old when Chloe and Grace arrived. But even with four younger children, and even now that she was fifteen, Chloe couldn't help thinking of Grace as her baby sister.

They walked in silence the rest of the way. Grace looked over her shoulder at least two more times, though she didn't say why.

Once they reached the meadow, she dropped her hands to her sides and opened her mouth. Perhaps now that they were far enough away from town, Grace finally felt it safe to say what had clearly been on her mind the whole time. "Do you really think Elora is in danger?"

As soon as the question left her mouth, she reached up and pinched her lip with her mittened hand.

"Our oldest sister? In danger?" Chloe let out a playful chuckle. "That's impossible. She saved all of Faerie once, didn't she? I'm sure she can do it again."

Grace pushed her eyebrows together until a crease formed between them. "But Elora is fae now, and the mortals have iron." The crease between her eyebrows faded away when Grace bit her bottom lip. "Iron can hurt Elora. We saw it."

Dropping her knees onto the frozen dirt, Chloe used her mittened hand to brush a pile of frost off a plant. It was mullein, not fennel. "Would you go to Faerie to save her then? Would you leave your harp and all your music students, knowing you might never return?"

Grace's skill with the harp had been the talk of the town nearly from the day they arrived. People in town would beg her for concerts. People even came from surrounding towns just to hear her play.

Many of the townspeople assumed the money she made from her harp playing sustained their entire family. It was the only explanation they could devise for why their family was so rich. Grace did make a fair bit of money from harp playing, but of course, the fact that Vesper could conjure gold coins from thin air helped their finances more than anything.

She brushed the ground with her mitten, clearing away frost just like Chloe had. They worked in silence for several minutes.

In that time, Chloe only found one fennel plant. Just as she feared, it was shriveled and frozen. She'd have to warm it by a fire before attempting to use it. And even then, it wouldn't have the same level of medicinal value as if she had collected it in the summer and dried it. She didn't have much choice, though. It would have to do.

"I don't want to go." Grace stopped clearing away frost and dropped her hands into her lap. She stared downward for several breaths, then finally looked up at her sister. "I don't want you to go either, but I also don't want anything to happen to Elora."

Chloe nodded. She didn't say anything because what was there to say? The situation wasn't good for anyone. Instead, she focused on the fennel. Minutes passed. Then several more minutes passed.

She had only found three small fennel plants, and Grace had only found one. Her gaze drifted across the river, which did look frozen over. The larger meadow across the river always had more fennel than this one.

She shook her head at the thought. The river almost never froze over completely, no matter how it looked on the top. No one could cross it during the winter. It always had too much ice to take a boat but not thick enough ice to walk across.

"I found another one." Grace's eyes sparkled with delight as she yanked a sad fennel plant from the ground. Half of it crumbled in her hands, but she still held it out to her sister like she had unearthed a jewel.

"I'll add it to the rest." Chloe tried to borrow some of the hope her sister seemed to have in abundance. But after watching Mr. and Mrs. Nash die, she didn't have much hope left, not even fake hope.

She stuffed the plant into her bag and scanned the area for what was probably the hundredth time. They had scoured the entire meadow now. Those five little plants were all they would get.

Her lips tugged lower as she moved toward the path. "We should head back. I don't think we'll find any more, and I need to hurry and prepare the remedy."

The cold wind and careful work had kept Chloe awake, but standing there now, her eyelids scratched against her eyes. Staying up all night to research had seemed perfectly logical the night before, but she regretted it now.

Maybe she'd ask Grace to stay in the workroom with her while she prepared the poultices, just to be certain she didn't make any mistakes.

Rising to her feet again, Grace stepped toward the path. She leaned forward slightly, as if anxious to say something. But then she leaned back. Her mittened fingers reached for the edges of her dark green cloak, pulling it tighter.

Just as Chloe went to step forward, Grace finally spoke.

"I'll do it."

A fog of sleeplessness clouded Chloe's mind, but she felt certain that comment had come from nowhere. Her eyes narrowed as she turned toward her sister. "What?"

Grace took a deep breath and stepped closer. "I'll go to Faerie in your place if needed."

Pressing a hand to her forehead, Chloe let out a deep sigh. "Grace." She rubbed her forehead until the knots in her chest finally loosened. When she looked up again, she did it with determination. "I know I'm not very brave. I know I fainted the last time I was in a battle. But I would never, *ever* allow you to go to Faerie in my place."

Chloe reached for her younger sister's cheek, stroking it with sisterly affection. "You have a good life here. You have more respect that I have, certainly more than Vesper has. I would never do anything to jeopardize that."

"But you don't want to go to Faerie."

Dropping her hand, Chloe rested it on her hip instead. "I refuse to put your life into danger, which would happen the moment you stepped into Faerie."

"So, *you'll* go then?" Grace's eyes looked both relieved and frightened at the same time.

"Maybe." Chloe checked the contents of her bag once more before finally starting down the path. "I have to deal with this spreading illness first. And anyway, I think Quintus might be exaggerating this whole situation with the mortals and the iron. I need to ask him more questions and wait until he gives direct answers."

Grace nodded. "It's uncanny how fae can be so devious even when they have no ability to lie."

"Exactly." Chloe brushed the frost off her mittens, grateful that their fae-made fabric had prevented any frost or ice from soaking through to her fingers.

Deep in her gut, part of her wondered if Quintus had made up this whole situation just so he could see Chloe again. He had said mortals were trying to take over Faerie, and since he couldn't lie, that had to be true. But just because the mortals were trying to take over Faerie didn't mean they had come even close to succeeding. And maybe their iron weapons weren't as bad as he made them sound.

If he had exaggerated everything just to see her again, she refused to be flattered by it. She wouldn't mistake his obsession for love.

Her lips pursed tight as she focused on the town ahead. "I just need to cure this illness from our town and then I can figure out how problematic this situation with the mortals actually is."

7

THE FROZEN FENNEL CHLOE AND her sister gathered only made enough for three poultices. After rubbing her tired eyes, she examined them. They were lined up neatly, each pile of dry ingredients on its own cloth square. Three poultices and at least six people with scurpus.

She dug into the bottom of her new leather bag for the eighth time. Not a single shriveled stem remained of the fennel she had gathered, but her hand still swiped across the bottom of the bag hopefully. It returned nothing.

Heat prickled at her nose as she let out a huff. Collapsing into the nearest chair, her gaze fixed on the three small piles. Her shoulders slumped forward with exhaustion. She did her best to ignore it.

If she split the poultices in half to have one for each person, no one would survive. Thanks to the Nashes, she knew that a little too well. Each person needed a full dose.

Three poultices. Six sick.

Her lips pinched as she glared at the ingredients. She had already asked Vesper to conjure more fennel. She hoped that with fennel to see and hold he would then be able to conjure it. But his sad conjurings only produced fennel so shriveled and dead that it wouldn't have any medicinal properties at all.

Her head dropped into her hands, half from fatigue and half from desperation. She allowed herself an entire minute to bemoan the situation. After that, she forced herself to her feet and began tying off the little square cloths into neat pouches.

Only three people could be healed. That much she knew for sure. Should she administer the poultices to those who had summoned her first? Or should she give them to those most likely to survive?

Maisie Fletcher's grandfather had very little chance of surviving at such an advanced age. But could Chloe deliver poultices to some of the sick members of that household without delivering it to all of them?

Usually, her apothecary work gave her strength on difficult days. Usually, she helped. And even when she had to sit at the edge of someone's deathbed, she could always find a way to help ease their passing. It gave relief to their family members to know their last moments had not been spent in pain.

But now six were sick, and she could only heal three.

Heat rose up the back of her neck, leaving behind a tingle that spread along her hairline. If she didn't check herself, she'd be in tears again soon. But she couldn't cry when she had work to do.

Icy air stung her ears as soon as she stepped out into the cold. The sun dipped below the horizon just as she pulled the hood of her cloak over her messy bun. Cold already bit into her fingertips.

Pulling her mittens on, she stepped around a corner…and ran right into a man with light brown skin and brilliant brown eyes. Quintus glanced down at her, then pulled from his pocket a small pouch woven from dried seaweed. He held it up with his eyebrows raised.

Ignoring it, Chloe shoved one hand against his upper arm. "There you are." She meant to pull her hand back right away, but it lingered against the soft suede of his dark green coat. Tan leather strings hung from the seam of the sleeve to just below his bicep. The suede and leather were nice but feeling the lean muscle under her fingertips was even nicer.

She stepped back, shaking her head to clear it. "What took you so long?"

Quintus held the bag out to her, but his gaze lingered on the part of his arm she had just been touching. "What do you mean?" He turned to face her now. "It is still dark."

"Still dark?" She rolled her eyes and grabbed the pouch from him. "It is evening now. It was morning when you left. You insisted you could return to the exact same moment when you left, but the entire day has passed."

Her focus stayed so intently on opening the seaweed pouch, she nearly missed how his eyebrows bounced upward.

"It is evening?" Now a true look of concern flashed in his eyes. "Things are getting worse. We need to hurry."

The look might have worried her more, except she had just gotten the pouch open. It only contained enough salt to fit in the palm of her hand. "This is *all* you brought? I need more than this."

His normally even expression turned wild. He flashed his teeth. "We are at war in Faerie. You are lucky I managed to get this much."

"At war?" She eyed him carefully, pretending not to notice how his muscles had bulged under his coat sleeves. "Is that what you call it when a few mortals awkwardly throw some pesky iron objects at you?"

He took a step closer until his breath skimmed her hairline. "Pesky? Queen Lyren herself helped me obtain this salt from her court." He leaned in closer until she could feel heat from his forehead. "You do not seem to realize just how dangerous these mortals are."

Her breath filled the space between them, which had grown even smaller since he first started speaking. Quintus huffed loudly, sending his own breath to mix with hers.

She stared into his eyes, if only to distract herself from the space their breath shared. Fae had multi-colored eyes, usually just two colors but sometimes more. Quintus's eyes had always been the exception. They were a beautiful, rich brown, but just brown, nonetheless.

Up this close though, she realized they did have a second color after all. Golden yellow rings like the light of the moon shimmered on the outside edges of his irises. Star-like sparks of the same golden yellow flecked inside his irises too, giving the brown its brilliant and rich color she had always admired.

Her stomach flopped over on itself. When had she started holding her breath? Ripping her gaze away from him, she took a step back.

He immediately grabbed her by the wrist.

When she went to yank her hand out of his grip, she realized he had stopped her from inadvertently dropping the bag of the precious Swiftsea salt. She blinked at it, unable to breathe like normal.

Stepping just as close as before, he closed the seaweed pouch once again. "Do you really think I would have come here if not desperate?"

She yanked her arm away from him once the pouch was secure and stuffed it into her brown leather bag. "I think you've probably dreamed of returning. How many times did you beg me to stay in Faerie with you instead of returning to the mortal realm?"

He flashed his teeth again. His hand still hung in the space between them, frozen in the same spot where he had grabbed her wrist.

Since he said nothing, she lifted her chin. "I know you wanted to see me again. I can see it in your eyes."

She could see no such thing in his eyes, but maybe she could trick him into admitting it still.

He leaned closer, angling his arm so that it hovered just next to her waist. "Ask yourself this, then." One eyebrow arched up high. "If Crystal Thorn Castle is under attack—which it is—then why did *I* come to get you instead of your sister?"

The very breath between them froze as she blinked at him. Her hand snaked up to her mouth until she covered it completely. "Elora," she whispered. And then she swallowed.

Quintus had just said plainly that Crystal Thorn Castle was under attack. While under attack didn't mean all hope was lost, it did mean the mortals had some power after all. Maybe Quintus *hadn't* been exaggerating. Maybe she only hoped he had been.

Her fingers curled into fists as she reached her arms over her stomach. "Is Elora dead?"

The question probably could have used less serious questions preceding it, but Chloe had no patience for that now. She had to know before she learned anything else:

Shaking his head, Quintus took a tiny step back. "She is alive, but the mortals have control of Crystal Thorn Castle now. They seized it just before I left Faerie. Your sister and every other fae inside the castle are captured and at the mercy of the mortals."

Chloe's throat ached as she tried to swallow again. If she wanted to know exactly what was going on in Faerie, she needed to ask direct questions and get direct answers. She had to make sure Quintus couldn't deceive her with answers that were technically true but still deceptive.

Taking a deep breath, she grabbed him by the hand and led him toward the Fletchers' home. "Do you believe my sister is in true danger?"

He nodded. "Your sister is strong. I never thought anyone capable of defeating her until the mortals attacked the castle with their iron weapons." His head dipped. "If you do not help us, I am certain all of Faerie will be destroyed."

She whirled around to face him. "Destroyed? But even if the mortals hurt the fae, surely Faerie itself would not be destroyed."

A deep breath filled his chest as a solemn look spread into his eyes. "Iron poisons fae, but it poisons Faerie too. And since our two realms are connected, a poisoned Faerie will lead to problems in the mortal realm as well."

Bringing a finger to her lips, she stopped him from continuing. They had reached the Fletchers'. Their conversation could continue after she had administered the poultices and they returned to her workroom to make more poultices with the Swiftsea salt.

When she knocked on the door, no one answered. Her second round of knocks pounded even louder than the first. When that still didn't produce an answer, she called out for someone, anyone. Silence met her plea. In a panic, she burst into the home.

Maisie sat in the hallway, crawling on her hands and knees toward the door Chloe had just burst through.

With a gasp, Chloe fell to her knees at Maisie's side. She helped the child onto her back, and quickly prepared a poultice to spread across the girl's chest.

"Grandfather is dead." Maisie's voice came out in a rasp. "Everyone is sick now, but Father is the worst."

"Hush, little one." Chloe tried to use a soothing voice, but her words came out stilted. She swallowed. "I will take care of everyone. You hold still."

She used the entire poultice instead of using half now and half later. Maybe it would be a mistake since she only had two poultices left and not nearly enough Swiftsea salt to make the two dozen she wanted to have on hand. But it would have to do.

After finishing Maisie's poultice, she carried the girl into the main room and laid her down on a sofa. No one stopped her when she wandered through the rest of the house to find the other family members. Maisie's father got the second poultice. Maisie's oldest brother got the third.

Chloe's heart ached as she spread the poultices on. Why? Why had she been forced to make such an awful decision? If she had enough ingredients, she could have healed all of them. Instead, she had to choose who to save.

Maisie's father was the highest priority since he provided for the family. Without him, the rest of the family would be left with nothing. Maisie's oldest brother brought in money for them too, so he needed a poultice as well.

But what about Maisie's mother who cooked all their meals, mended their clothes, and kept the household running? The woman had given so much of herself through the years, she barely had any of her own self left, and now she was just supposed to die? To sacrifice herself yet another time so that her husband and son could survive?

And what about Maisie's older sister, who pressed flowers between book pages and sang cheerful songs the whole town enjoyed? The women's lives had just as much value, even if town etiquette didn't allow them to provide for their families.

Chloe should have saved the women instead of the men, just to spite the stupid rules about who was allowed to do what in their town. But if she did so, the women truly would lose everything. Chloe's family members were already considered eccentric since they lived with Vesper, who not only treated his wife like an equal but also allowed his sisters to do whatever they wanted.

Even still, Chloe only became an apothecary because the last town apothecary died unexpectedly without an apprentice to take his place. As soon as any man in town decided he wanted to be the next apothecary, she would lose all her credibility and all business overnight.

In her heart, she was secretly grateful she had already given Maisie the first poultice. In terms of value, the child didn't help the family much at all. But how could Chloe ever choose to let a child die?

The moment she finished administering the last poultice on Maisie's brother, she dashed out the door in a flash. Quintus followed her without question. Maybe he had no interest in hearing her plans, but right now, she didn't care. She needed to work through everything to keep herself from losing her mind.

"Now that I have the Swiftsea salt, I can make more poultices. If you help me crush some of the herbs—which you will, this isn't a request, it's a demand—then I can get the other poultices done more quickly. I'll bring them straight to the Fletchers' house first for Maisie's mother and sister. After that, I'll visit the other two homes."

It was a good plan, except it had one glaring flaw.

The Swiftsea salt only provided for nine more poultices. She dragged Quintus along as she administered each one. After the Fletchers, she visited the other two households of people who had gotten sick.

As expected, others in the same household had contracted scurpus too. She had just enough poultices for everyone, but now, on her way back home, they were gone.

Her heart skittered at the thought. It had to be enough. The Nashes had still died after getting a poultice, but she had only given them half of one each. These others she had given an entire poultice all at once. It would be enough.

Chloe refused to consider anything else. Everything would be fine. She could save everyone.

As long as no one else got sick.

She shoved open the door to her house with Quintus still trailing behind her. Her body creaked and groaned with every step, ready to collapse into a pile to force her to sleep. But she ignored it just like she'd been ignoring it all day.

First, she'd go to her workroom to clean up the mess she had made in her rush to get all those poultices finished. But before she could reach the room, Grace stopped her in the hallway.

Her red hair limped over her shoulders with a dull quality it didn't usually have. She stared ahead with bloodshot eyes. Her chin quivered as her lips curved into a twisted almost-smile. This was her brave face.

But why?

Forcing the smile again, Grace lifted her hand. A light gray tinge dappled her fingertips.

Chloe's entire heart dropped to the bottom of her toes.

Grace had scurpus.

8

CHLOE TOOK A DEEP BREATH, steeling herself for the reality before her. "It's going to be fine, Grace. I'll fix it." The declaration probably would have held more weight if Chloe hadn't started yawning right at the end of it.

Why had she been so foolish to stay up the entire night before? Now she could barely keep her eyes open.

Grace put on her same brave smile and dropped her hand to her side. "I know you ran out of ingredients again."

"No, it's fine." Chloe pinched her own arm, hoping it might wake her up more. "I'll get more fennel. Or maybe Quintus can go get more Swiftsea salt from—"

"I cannot do that." His nostrils flared as he whirled around to face her. "I told you it was difficult enough just to get the amount I already brought."

Her jaw clenched tight as she sucked in a deep breath. With a polite, but definitely fake, smile, Chloe turned to her sister.

"Excuse us." An edge cut across the polite tone she had attempted to use, but Grace wouldn't care. Pressing the palms of her hands against Quintus's chest, Chloe shoved him into the workroom. Glancing over her shoulder at her sister, Chloe pressed her lips together. "Everything is going to be fine. I promise."

She didn't wait for her sister to respond. She pulled the door closed tight and turned on Quintus.

His eyes flashed, making the golden yellow in them glow. "Just come with me to Faerie and help us defeat the mortals. I can get you more Swiftsea salt after that. Then you can return to this same moment and heal your sister."

She raised an eyebrow. "You were supposed to return to the exact same moment this morning, but you didn't return until evening. How am I supposed to believe you actually have the ability to return to this exact same moment?"

His nose twitched as he ran a hand through the black strands of his hair. "That was a tiny mistake. And her scurpus hasn't progressed far. Your sister will not die if a day passes without your return."

Heat surged into her cheeks. Her jaw clenched tight as she jabbed a finger at him. "If Elora's life is in danger, then my life will be in danger too. You know I might never come back. We are going to save my baby sister first and then we can go to Faerie."

"You will come?" He spoke so much softer than he had a moment ago. His body leaned toward her, but then he jerked himself back. "But you have no more Swiftsea salt. How are you supposed to save her?"

Turning away from him, she began sweeping broken stems and stray herb crumbs into her hand. "We aren't getting Swiftsea salt. We're getting more fennel."

He stepped closer until his breath ruffled the top of her messy bun. He spoke in a lethal tone. "You have fennel, and you still made me get Swiftsea salt? You have no idea the sacrifices made to obtain that for you."

Her fingers shook as she swept away the last of the debris on her table. Heat still burned in her cheeks, but a needling prickle joined it too. She swallowed. "The fennel is across a half-frozen river. I cannot get across it by myself, but I don't need to now. You are going to use your magic to get me across."

Another yawn interrupted what should have been a poignant moment. His nose twitched at the sight of it. "You should have gone to sleep last night."

He had turned away, so he didn't see when she rolled her eyes. Of course she should have slept. She knew that now, though she also couldn't do anything about it. She'd just have to get through the next hour, then sleep extra as soon as she had the chance.

Lifting the strap of her new leather bag over her head, she rested it on her shoulder. She tucked her magical book inside as well as a short book of her favorite epic poems. The ingredients to make a poultice for scurpus went in next, just in case she didn't have time to return to her workroom before she needed the poultice.

She even removed the pouch that usually hid under her apron. The pouch tucked neatly in an interior pocket of her new bag. With everything inside, she clasped her cloak and headed down to the river.

Freezing wind accosted her the moment she stepped outside. It whipped under her hood, loosening the strands of her hair that only barely stayed in place in her bun. The whole thing would fall out soon.

Despite the cold, she still had to rub her eyes a few times, just to stay awake. Each time, Quintus would throw her a sidelong glance that was entirely judgmental.

But it didn't matter that she was so tired. She just needed a bit more fennel. With Quintus's help, she could get across the river in no time at all.

Once they arrived in the meadow she and Grace had visited earlier, Chloe gestured to the even bigger meadow across the river. "We need to get over there."

He narrowed one eye at her. "You want me to open a door?"

She nodded and flashed a big smile to hide the yawn that tugged at her lips.

After a quick shrug, he waved his hand in a small circle in front of his body. At once, a swirling tunnel appeared before them. The edges of it looked like a blurry forest scene. Lush trees and moss-covered rocks seemed to swirl around, forming the walls of the tunnel. Smudges of black wove through the forest scene, each one lit by small golden lights that glowed.

The door even had its own unique scent. It smelled of moss, fresh wood shavings, and a bit of parchment. Though she had walked through one of his Faerie doors before, something about it seemed more exquisite than she remembered.

It took all her self-control to keep from breathing in deeply as she stepped into the swirling tunnel. Quintus definitely didn't need to know how much she enjoyed the smell of his door. She couldn't help admire the golden lights twinkling all around her.

When she stepped inside, Quintus followed.

But the moment her foot touched the bottom of the swirling tunnel, her body jerked to one side. It felt as though someone had tied a rope around her middle and now yanked it every which way.

A split second later, she landed with a thud onto the same frozen ground she had stood on only a moment ago. Pain shot through her shoulder as she pushed herself off the ground. The hood of her cloak fell to her shoulders. Most of her bun did too.

Quintus landed on all fours, hitting the ground even harder than she did. He huffed as he slammed a fist against the ground. "Stupid iron poisoning."

Forcing herself to her feet again, Chloe removed the ribbon holding only a third of her hair in its bun. The remaining blonde hair fell in stringy strands down her back. Her shoulder winced when she tucked the ribbon into her bag. "Why didn't you take us across the river?"

"I tried." Quintus brushed icy dirt off his dark green pants, but some of it still stuck to the tan cross stitching along the seam. Now he stared at his hands. "Something is wrong."

She rubbed her shoulder as her stomach coiled in on itself. "The iron poisoning in Faerie is affecting your ability to open a door?"

He glared at his hands once more before dropping them to his sides. "I am not sure, but I do not usually struggle with this sort of magic. *Something* is happening."

With a deep breath, Chloe eyed the river next to them. She bit her lip, eager to discover some other solution.

None came.

Although... Her head tilted to the side. It had been unseasonably cold the past two days. She stepped forward, eyeing the ice over the river more carefully. Her heart clenched at the sight of it, but she didn't have much of a choice now.

Curling her mittened fingers into fists, she took a step onto the ice.

From behind, Quintus immediately went to follow her.

"No." The word came out breathless. She inhaled slowly, afraid to move her body any more than necessary. "The ice is not thick enough to support two people."

His eyes widened as a flash of understanding lit inside them. "Is the ice thick enough to support you?"

She didn't answer.

"*Chloe.*"

But she ignored him. Her boot slid across the ice at a glacial pace. She pushed her weight down slightly before resting her full weight on the next foot. Then she began the painstaking process of moving her other boot forward.

Step after step, she moved forward as slow as possible. Halfway across, the ice showed no sign of breaking.

From behind, she heard Quintus's footsteps pace across the meadow. Then the whisper of an open Faerie door fluttered through the air. A heavy thud followed immediately after. Quintus had probably tried, and failed, to open a door that led to the other side of the river again. It only proved she had no choice but to continue.

Just when she thought she'd get across with no trouble, the distinct sound of cracking ice cut into the air. She lifted her foot, which immediately stopped the cracking noise.

Cold tingles spread into her fingertips. She took the time to inhale and exhale before she moved again. But with a half-frozen river so close by, everyone in town knew what to do in a situation like this.

Slowly and carefully, she bent at the waist and moved downward until her stomach met the ice. With her weight spread out across such a large distance, the ice would be able to support her better.

Once in position, she inched herself forward.

"Should you not come back? Is the ice cracking?"

The strain in Quintus's voice was as sharp as a knife.

"Hush." Her answer came out just louder than a whisper.

She inched herself forward again. The cracking had stopped, but tiny pops sounded every few seconds still. She tried to ignore them. Only a few more pushes and she'd reach the riverbank.

If she just moved slowly enough, she'd surely make it.

Her fingers stretched out. The end of her woolen mitten brushed across the icy grass at the riverbank.

Just a little farther.

But then the ice snapped.

She sank under water before she could even take a breath. The ice-cold temperature forced her to gasp, which immediately filled her lungs with water.

She held her breath now, but how much good could it do when she'd already sucked in a mouthful of liquid? Her lips pressed together while her chest heaved with the desire to cough.

But if she coughed, she'd just draw in more water.

Her hand flailed outward, desperate to find the riverbank. The fae magic in her mittens kept her hands from getting wet, but her dress had already soaked through.

She found the riverbank with her hand, and immediately brought the other to it. But cold locked up her fingers. She couldn't bend them enough to grab onto anything.

Her arms flailed again, trying to reach farther up the riverbank to find something easier to grab. But whatever strength she had a moment ago had already withered. She could barely kick her legs.

Light from the moon shone above her, but it grew smaller as she sank lower.

Water waved all around her, faster than the usual flow of the river. A shadowy figure swam toward her, but black spots appeared in her vision now. She couldn't see the figure clearly.

The figure swam closer. His arm reached for her shoulder, but he caught a fistful of her hair instead.

Quintus had finally moved close enough for her to see his grimace. He let go of her hair to reach for her shoulder, but immediately grabbed onto her hair again when she started sinking lower. His other hand reached and reached, stretching his fingers toward her arm, her cloak, anything to grasp besides her hair.

At the coldest, darkest edge of her mind, it occurred to her that it might be helpful if she stretched her hand toward him. Then he could grab her hand instead of her hair.

She opened her mouth to yawn, and that same dark edge of her mind screamed at her to slam her mouth shut and reach out for Quintus. But maybe she'd just close her eyes and go to sleep instead.

She was so tired.

So tired.

9

A FIRE CRACKLED NEARBY. CHLOE could hear it, which meant she wasn't dead. At least, she didn't think they had fires in the afterlife. Not ones that crackled delightfully and gave off a pleasant warmth, anyway.

Damp fabric clung to parts of her legs and arms, proving she had definitely been soaking wet at some point. So the river excursion hadn't been a nightmare. Her dress had mostly dried now though. The fire had probably taken care of that.

Daring to take a peek through her eyelids, she found a lush forest surrounding her with a bright blue sky up above. The scents of moss and fresh rain drifted all around.

She turned herself, attempting to lay on her side instead of her back. The moment she tried to move, her chest screamed in protest. She pressed a hand against her sternum and closed her eyes. Though they were clear now, her lungs still remembered the feel of icy water inside them.

Steeling herself, she threw twice as much effort into it and managed to turn over on her side. The fire crackled a little more than an arm's length away from her. Quintus sat on the other side of it, staring at her. He looked angry, but that seemed to be his favorite expression anyway.

Pushing herself up onto her elbow, she spoke to him. "We're in Faerie."

A vein in his jaw pulsed. "I will not take you back to the mortal realm until you help us."

Rolling her eyes, she managed to sit up. "Typical." At least her chest didn't hurt so much now. Moving hurt it tremendously, but it also seemed to help the aches in her body feel better afterward.

To her surprise, Quintus broke eye contact to stare at the sketchbook in his lap. He worried at the corner of the page, which had curled from all his fiddling. "I fear my door will not bring you back to the moment it should. It would be safer if we wait until your older sister or someone else can bring you back."

Her throat thickened at his admission. After he had failed to open a door to take them across the river, she believed he might be telling the complete truth with no intention to deceive. He had also returned later than expected when he came back from getting the Swiftsea salt. Maybe his door had brought him back to Faerie with no trouble, but he clearly had some problem when opening doors to and inside the mortal realm.

She kneaded her sternum again, which pressed away the last of the most painful knots inside it. Now she dug into the bag that had been set neatly at her side. The brown leather clearly had more magical properties than she had first realized because her magical book sitting inside it didn't have a single drop of liquid, or remnants of liquid, on it. Everything else in the bag had been protected from the cold river water as well.

Pulling the book out, she set it gingerly onto her lap.

Quintus shifted his legs until they were crisscrossed underneath him. "You wake up from near death, and the first thing you want to do is read?"

"Never underestimate the value of reading." She shot the words at him but then followed them with a huff. "If you must know, I'm not reading for pleasure anyway. I had a thought while drowning, and now I want to confirm it."

She thumbed through the pages, trying to tie together the loose thoughts in her mind. "What did you say about the connection between our realms?"

He shrugged. "Just that they are connected." But then his head tilted to the side. "If Faerie is poisoned with iron, the mortal realm will be affected too. Is that what you meant?"

"Exactly." She found the pages on scurpus just as he finished speaking. While at the Nashes' house, she vaguely remembered reading something about how scurpus was caused by iron poisoning. At the time, she'd been too distraught for the words to stick.

They did now though. Every piece came together as her fingers trailed across a handwritten sentence in the margin of her book. The previous mortal owner of the book must have added it, just like he had added the appendix.

Scurpus always originates in Faerie, but it has been known to trickle into the mortal realm when the iron poisoning in any place in Faerie has reached toxic levels.

Her fingers rubbed her chest again as the words settled in. The scurpus in her town hadn't been a mortal illness with a different name at all. It was scurpus, the real scurpus, and only saving Faerie would cure it completely.

At least she was here now. She could save Faerie and return back to the same moment she left. By then, maybe Grace wouldn't even need Swiftsea salt or a poultice at all. Maybe the scurpus would already be gone.

She just had to save Faerie first.

Quintus had nothing to say on the subject when she told him. He just nodded like he had already guessed as much anyway. Before she could tuck the book back into her bag, a large flying creature made entirely of black thorns swooped from the sky down toward them.

She shrieked and threw her bag over her head, as if that might provide enough protection against a magical creature made of thorns.

"The demorogs are not dangerous anymore." Quintus pinched the bridge of his nose as he let out a sigh. "Do you not remember how your sister freed them from their curse?"

Lowering the bag back onto the ground, Chloe glanced at the flying creature. The demorog's thorns looked shinier than she remembered. The creature nearly sparkled in the light around it.

Quintus shook his head as he closed his sketchbook and slipped it into his inner coat pocket. "They never come all the way to the caves anyway."

Her ears perked up at those words. She stood and moved closer to the fire under the guise that she needed to dry off the damp spots in her dress, but really, she wanted a better look at those caves Quintus had mentioned.

Before she could get a good look, he eyed her dress, probably noting how the back side of it was wetter than the front. Her chest ached again, but she didn't rub it. Part of her wanted to ask how he got the water out of her lungs, but another part—a stronger part—decided she'd rather not know.

After eyeing her, Quintus gestured toward a ghastly dress made of stiff cotton that had been laid across a mossy rock. It had a hideous frilly collar and a garish yellow pattern on top of a brown background.

"I was going to change you into dry clothes, but then I thought you might try to murder me if you found out I had removed your clothes while you were unconscious, so I decided against it."

Her chest squeezed, but for an entirely different reason than pain. Heat pinched the tops of her ears and up the sides of her neck. She tried to hide the reaction by lifting her chin. "Good choice."

Her focus turned more fully to the fire now. Its flames heated the damp parts of her dress, which then warmed her as well. Now she began using her fingers to comb through her tangled hair. The tangles won that battle almost immediately. Her hair didn't have much hope without a brush.

After grabbing her bag again, she dug inside it, searching for the ribbon that had secured her bun earlier. She checked each pocket of the bag, and even looked inside the little pouch of her Faerie things that she used to keep hidden in her dress.

While working, the harp string inside her pouch slipped out and fell to the ground.

Quintus stood up right away. "Is that a harp string?"

He crossed the empty space between them before she could blink. His fingers curled around the harp string as he brought it closer to his face.

"It's not." She grabbed onto the end of the harp string, but he wouldn't release his hold on it.

"You are lying." His words came out steady, not angry but certain.

With one end of the harp string still between her fingers, her gaze lifted to his. The moment she caught his eye, the golden rims around his dark brown eyes flashed with brilliance. Her hand moved of its own accord until it hovered only a hair's breadth away from his. She could feel heat coming off his hand.

He held her gaze the entire time. He didn't move toward her, but each time he inhaled, his chest would expand, and it *felt* like he moved closer. It would take only one step, and she'd be close enough to drop her head against his shoulder.

The gaze between them intensified as his lips parted. Tingling spread across her fingertips. They itched to reach for him. To touch his hands, his shoulders, his face. Anything.

Instead, she yanked the harp string out of his grip and took several steps away. She buried the string at the very bottom of her special pouch and then buried that in a deep pocket at the very bottom of her bag.

Undeterred, Quintus stepped toward her. "That is the harp string I used to tie off your braid the last time you were here in Faerie."

She kept her gaze fixed on the inside of her leather bag until she *finally* found her red silk ribbon. Turning away from him, she began to pull her hair into its usual messy bun. "It's a good thing I never wear my hair in a braid then. That harp string is useless to me now."

He had moved close again, and now he smirked at her. "Then why do you still have it?"

Warmth spread into her cheeks, certainly enough to turn them pink. She spun on her heel, determined to get a better look at her surroundings.

The lush forest she saw when she first opened her eyes didn't actually surround them completely. Spongy moss and sturdy trees with vibrant green leaves filled the space only on one side of them.

On the other side, black soil with pearl-like pebbles covered the ground. The soil circled the black caves she had only barely glanced at earlier. A trickling stream with a black-soiled bottom flowed into one of the caves. But its opening was too dark to see inside.

She looked back over her shoulder at the lush forest that smelled like rain. Then she glanced back at the black caves with the pretty pebbles. Her eyebrows lowered.

"Where are we?"

Quintus had gone back to sitting crisscross near the fire. "In the Court of Crystal Thorn." He glanced back at the caves. "Sort of."

She eyed the soil in the spot where it went from light brown to a dark black. "This must be the border where one court leads into another."

"It certainly looks that way, does it not?"

Her eyes narrowed as she walked over to the black soil and nudged it with her boot. "I thought Dustdune was the only court to border yours. And isn't Dustdune orange and dry and full of sand dunes?"

"It is, yes." He reached into his coat to retrieve his sketchbook once again.

She raised an eyebrow. "I know Swiftsea is near Crystal Thorn as well, but a sea separates the two courts. And this," she gestured toward the caves, "doesn't look like Swiftsea at all. Those caves had soft white sand everywhere and seashells in the stone."

"True." His pencil scribbled across a fresh page of his sketchbook. "We are not near Swiftsea."

Her boot stomped on the black soil as she folded her arms over her chest. "Then what is this place? Why won't you just tell me?"

His pencil froze mid-scribble. He closed his eyes for an extra-long second and then he let out a sigh. "I do not know." He shook his head, then opened his eyes and began drawing once again. "No one knows."

One eyebrow tipped high on her forehead. "No one?"

He shrugged. "We are somewhat near the creation magic in Crystal Thorn, and we are even nearer to a sea. But it is the sea opposite from the one that leads to Swiftsea. Other than that, we only know what we can see."

She stepped forward and then stepped back again. Curiosity plagued her often, but fear usually out won it. Her eyes narrowed at the stream flowing into the shadowy entrance of the nearest cave.

She swallowed hard and hoped it hadn't been too audible. "What's in those caves?"

A puff of air escaped his lips in a dark laugh. "That you must see for yourself."

He stood and put his sketchbook away once again. With it gone, he stepped onto the black soil with pearly pebbles. She stepped back toward the forest.

"Come on." He beckoned her not toward him but toward the nearest cave, the one with the stream flowing into it. "The caves await."

Fear kept her feet planted to the ground, but in her heart, she knew that wouldn't last long. In a magical place like Faerie, curiosity would always win.

10

CHLOE'S HEART BEAT IN FLUTTERS as she stepped toward the black cave. All around her, the air crackled with an unseen energy. It set her teeth on edge, but it also sent her stomach into a tangle of excitement.

The little stream flowing into the cave took up most of the entrance. She had to step at the very edge of the cave just to find a spot of rock large enough to fit her feet. Her cloak brushed against the cave wall as she edged herself deeper inside.

That same crackling energy buzzed inside the cave too—but with three times the potency. Her hand lifted, and she almost expected golden sparks of magic to appear. Of course, as a plain mortal, no magic would ever grace her fingertips.

So why did it feel like it might?

Tiny golden lights were embedded in the ceiling of the cave. There weren't enough to create a true light source, but they almost looked like golden yellow stars. They reminded her of the gold in Quintus's eyes.

Shoving that thought far out of her mind, Chloe glanced back at the fae behind her. "There's something strange about this cave."

She took another step forward, then promptly stopped. Taking in a deep breath, that same strangeness hit her even stronger than before.

"Describe it." Quintus had stepped right up behind her. His eyes alight as he urged her to continue.

Her mouth twisted as she tried to find the words to explain. "It feels like we're in a Faerie door. Like if I take just one more step forward, I'd be transported to an all-new court or land."

A light puff of air drifted from his mouth, sounding too much like a chuckle for her liking.

Her eyes narrowed. "You think that's stupid?"

"No." He raised both hands in defeat. "It feels the same to me too. But try stepping forward."

She went to lift one foot, but then kept it in place instead. Shaking her head, she tried again. Her foot continued to stay planted in place. Now she frowned at her feet. "I can't step forward."

"Neither can I." He spoke the words with such resignation that it was clear he had attempted it many times.

Glancing deeper into the cave, her eyes searched for something beyond the shadows. "Something has to be there," she said. "This stream is flowing through the cave, past where we stand now. If the water flows through, surely there must be something beyond this point."

Her ears pricked, listening intently for the sound of the trickling stream. It *did* flow beyond where they stood. In fact, it even seemed to get faster and maybe larger.

But when she tried to step forward again, her foot stayed as still as it had the other times.

She reached into her leather bag, pulling out her magical book. Hadn't she just read something about a spot in Faerie where feet stayed planted to the ground?

Quintus did nothing to hide his curiosity as he leaned over her shoulder to look at her book. She did her best to ignore how his chest kept brushing against the back of her shoulder.

80

Just as she opened the book and reached for a corner, the pages themselves began flipping on their own. A gasp shot through her lips. Tiny golden bursts sparkled above the pages as they turned.

She went to slam the book shut, but Quintus touched her hand with the very tip of one finger. Despite how she hated him, her body froze in place at the small contact.

"Do not shut it. Let it speak."

If he hadn't been touching her with that tiny tip of his finger, she would have been able to glare at him and tell him how ridiculous it was to think that a *book* could speak to her. But he did touch her, which had worked its own magic on her, rendering her both speechless and immobile.

When the pages stopped flipping, a light glowed from the inner spine, lighting the page. She had no choice but to read the words inside.

A mortal man once lived in Faerie. He walked its paths and made it his home.

Inside Chloe's chest, warmth lit and tingled until it spread out and into her arms. These words hadn't been in the book before. She had read every single page in her magical book at least half a dozen times. Even if she didn't have every bit of information memorized, she certainly knew what she had read before and what she had not.

And she had definitely never seen this story before.

Even without the glowing inner spine and the pages flipping on their own, deep down she still knew what was happening. Faerie itself communicated with her. She hadn't even known it possible until this very moment. But now, her focus intensified. When Faerie itself spoke, she figured she better pay attention.

The mortal man had been in Faerie long enough to learn of its creation. He learned how Nouvel, the first fae, had created the Faerie realm when mortals found him too dangerous and tried to destroy him. Nouvel thrust all his magic into the new realm, which caused him to break apart and form new fae. Brownies formed from his toes. Trolls grew from his arms and sprites grew from his eyes. The high fae who rule Faerie came from his head.

Chloe had heard this story of Nouvel from Queen Lyren when the fae tried to comfort Chloe after Chloe's sister Elora had gone off on some adventure or another. But this story inside the book's pages wasn't just about Nouvel. It was also about the mortal man.

Nouvel left a bundle of creation magic behind after Faerie and all the new fae had been formed. The mortal man determined he would find that creation magic and take the magic inside himself so that he too could have power like the fae.

A single touch of the creation magic gave him abilities like he had never experienced before. He immediately harnessed them for evil, destroying an entire court and killing anyone who stood in his way. Faerie itself could not remove the magic from him, but it did set a block inside him so he could not access the power anymore.

Since then, both mortal and fae have been kept from the creation magic. No mortal has touched it since…except one.

Chloe sucked in a breath as she clapped a hand to her mouth. Even though she had fainted and had been unconscious at the time, her sisters had told her what had happened in that battle Quintus forced her into. *She* had *touched* the creation magic. Well, she'd been forced to touch it while she lay unconscious, but her hand had still made contact.

Elora had touched the creation magic too, but she hadn't been mortal at the time. The words in front of Chloe could only mean one thing.

Her hand trembled as she lifted it to hover in front of her face. And now she whispered. "I have magic inside me?"

Quintus leaned forward, pressing his chest right up against the back of her shoulder. He pointed at the paragraphs she hadn't read yet. "Yes, but you cannot access the magic unless Faerie itself allows it. See, this part here says there is a ritual you have to do to attempt to gain access to the creation magic. The instructions for the ritual must be on the next page."

He probably expected her to turn the page, but her hand trembled too much for it. Not just her hand, her entire body. She suddenly felt as if those glowing lights embedded in the top of the cave were also glowing inside of her. Glowing and bursting and ready to come to life. "I have magic."

Donning a smirk, Quintus angled himself to get a better view of her face. "You cannot be angry with me now, can you? Maybe I forced you into that battle, but that is when you touched the creation magic. Now you might be able to access magic."

The glowing lights inside her flickered out all at once. A glare pinched her features tight as she slammed the book shut. "You never should have forced me into that battle." She shoved him until he stepped out of the cave. Hopefully leaving the glowing lights and the crackling energy behind would help her think clearly again.

Dropping herself next to the fire, she folded her arms over her chest. "Forget the magic. Let's just figure out how to defeat the mortals."

He scowled at her, but he still followed. After he situated himself across the fire from her, he spoke. "The mortals have iron troughs that they lay on the ground or in doorways or windowsills. They pour fuel inside the troughs, then light the fuel—and iron— on fire. Once lit, the iron from the trough gets into the flame, which then sends it into the air. The iron flame is even more dangerous to fae than plain iron because it infects the air around it."

Poisonous flames sounded worse than she imagined. Chloe nodded, almost afraid to hear more.

When Quintus continued, he sighed. "The iron flame acts like a barrier, so no fae can pass it."

Unfolding her arms from over her chest, she picked at the golden cord securing her corset. "But how did the mortals overtake an entire castle? Did the mortals put these iron flames at every single window and door? Bitter Thorn Castle has hundreds of windows."

Quintus raised an eyebrow. "It is called Crystal Thorn Castle now."

She waved off the words. "You know what I meant."

His shoulders hunched forward before he continued. "They put the flames around the entire castle at first, encircling it. Back then, the flames were low enough that fae with wings, like your sister, could still escape the castle. But of course your sister only left to get help from me and a few others. She then flew back to the castle to be with her beloved."

He dug his fingers into his hair, tugging at the soft black curls on top of his head. "After surrounding it, the mortals closed off small sections of the castle one at a time, forcing the fae into a smaller area of the castle than before. They did it little by little, and now they have all the fae trapped in the middle of the castle where there are no doors nor windows to the outside. Even your sister cannot escape."

Cold trickled down the back of Chloe's neck, though it had nothing to do with the gentle breeze around them. She gulped. "If the mortals are so powerful, I don't understand how I can help."

Quintus's eyes focused as he glanced toward her. "I need you to put out the iron flame. You just have to kick the trough over until it is upside down on the ground. Once the iron flame is out, or at least enough of it that I can get past, I can sneak into the castle and kill the mortals responsible for this attack."

The cold trickling down her back hardened to ice. "*Kill* them?"

He tilted his head with a condescending stare. "They are destroying Faerie." When her expression didn't change, he sat up straighter. "The iron poisoning in Faerie gave scurpus to all those people in your town, remember? The mortals are destroying your home too."

"I know."

His face turned gentler. "You do not have to fight them. I will take care of that. I just need you to put out the flames."

She sighed. The thought of knowingly aiding a person's death still formed tension in her shoulders. But what choice did she have? The mortals had captured her older sister, and they had given scurpus to her younger sister. Something had to be done—and letting Quintus do it seemed a lot better than doing it herself. "Fine."

Darkness closed in around them. The dusky light nearly swallowed up their dying fire. But the Court of Crystal Thorn never got too cold, even at night. She knew that from her time in Faerie before.

Quintus reached into his pocket and retrieved a sleeping mat and some blankets that had to be at least ten times the size of the pocket he had taken them from. But Chloe had seen the magic of fae pockets before. They could carry nearly anything inside, no matter how big.

When he arranged his sleeping mat right next to hers on the ground, she didn't say one word about it. Of course she wouldn't tell him she was glad to have him nearby. His already enormous ego didn't need to know that. But secretly, she was glad.

If anything dangerous happened, she'd probably just faint at the worst possible moment. At least with Quintus nearby, he could protect her from anything too perilous.

Now she had the fire on one side of her and Quintus on the other. Pulling her blanket up to her chin, she faced the fire and shut her eyes tight.

It wasn't until Quintus's breathing went slow and even that she finally peeked through her eyelids once again. Her gaze flicked to her fae companion first. He certainly looked to be asleep, but maybe he was only on the verge of sleep.

Regardless, if she waited any longer, she'd probably fall asleep too, and she couldn't have that.

As quiet as a mouse, she reached for her magical book and opened its pages. With hardly any flipping at all, she found the page with instructions for the ritual on how to access her magic.

Just like Quintus had said, the ritual would only give her a *chance* to access her magic. Faerie itself would have to choose whether or not she could wield it. But she'd never know unless she tried.

By the dying light of the fire, Chloe read the ritual three times.

To access fae magic, she just had to hold in her hand, for an entire night, anything that held magic. If Faerie itself deemed her worthy, she would then be able to access her magic, but only when she touched that same object that she chose to hold for the entire night.

It would probably be best if she could find a magical object that didn't require her to get out of bed. Even if asleep now, that sort of movement would likely wake Quintus.

She first settled on the magical book, but then she realized how inconvenient a heavy book might be if she had to grab hold of it any time she wanted to do magic.

Her gaze flitted around the clearing for something else nearby that might work, preferably something that could fit in her hand.

Right in between her and Quintus, a small mossy rock sat on the ground. It would probably work. It was small enough to fit in her palm, and since it came from the Court of Crystal Thorn, it had to hold magic inside it.

Just as she went to reach for it, the glowing embers from the fire finally went out. But she had seen the rock. She still knew where to reach.

A moment later, her hand closed around the object. It was warmer than she expected and softer too, but it also gave off a crackling energy just like the cave had. It was definitely magical.

Afraid to lose grip of it, she kept her hand as still as possible. According to the book, she had to keep the object in her hand for the entire night. Then—if Faerie deemed it so—in the morning, she would have magic.

Magic that could hopefully help her save her sisters.

11

As THE FIRST THREADS OF consciousness wrapped around her mind, Chloe lightly squeezed her fingers. Just as she hoped, she still held the magical object in her hand. Magic pulsed through it, sending a pleasant tingle into her fingertips.

It should have given her relief, but her eyebrows pinched together instead. The object definitely felt warmer than it had last night. Her thumb brushed across the item in her hand. Though it was smooth, it felt like an entirely different kind of smooth than the rocky surface she expected.

Fear knotted in her chest. Now the fuzz on its surface she had noticed the night before felt a lot less like moss and more like something softer. Hair maybe. Had she grabbed another object instead of the rock? Was the object still something small enough to fit into the palm of her hand?

Her heart sped up as she dared to open one eyelid. The moment she caught a glance at the object in her hand, her other eyelid shot open wide.

She ripped her hand away and pulled it close to her chest.

The movement woke Quintus at once, though perhaps he had already been awake.

With her fist curled and her hand pressed against her chest, she glared at him. "You were holding my hand."

How had she failed to notice the *object* had not been a rock, but *his hand?*

He rubbed his eyes as a few black curls tumbled onto his forehead. "You are the one who reached for me."

She jumped to her feet and took a step back, as if that would help. "Why didn't you pull away when I touched you?"

And why had she been so certain last night that she had grabbed a rock and not a *hand?* Had Faerie itself tricked her?

He stood, revealing a shirtless chest. With one hand still rubbing his left eye, he snarled at her. "I cannot keep up with your mortal customs. I thought it would be rude to pull away."

"When have you ever cared about being rude?"

He stepped closer. "I was tired. I did not want you yelling at me while I was trying to fall asleep."

When he stepped toward her again, her feet stumbled back. She tried to get away, but the ash from their previous fire kept her feet in place.

Now he leaned toward her with no shirt on and complete and utter disregard for how it made her heart flutter.

The snarl that had narrowed his eyes relaxed as he leaned even closer. "What is this?"

His bare chest expanded as he inhaled, which she desperately tried to ignore. Now he brushed his thumb across the bone under her right eye.

Heat from his thumb sank into her skin, leaving behind an electrifying tingle.

"Don't touch me." She smacked his hand away, somehow unable to pull her eyes away from his bare chest that he kept leaning even closer to her body.

"You have markings there."

Only then did she manage to force her gaze up to his face. His eyes narrowed as he examined her. But now she had something to examine as well. Quintus had a marking on his face in nearly the

88

exact same place he had just touched on her face, though his mark was on the opposite side. He had a small crescent moon tattoo just under his left eye.

After swallowing, she caught his eye. "Is it a black tattoo?"

His gaze flicked to hers for only a moment before he went back to staring at the spot on her face that he had touched. "Yes. You have three stars tattooed just under your eye here. The center star is bigger and the stars on either side are slightly smaller."

He went to touch the spot again, but she ducked away just in time. Stars? An involuntary shudder passed through her, which she decided to ignore.

"Does it look bad?" she asked.

His hand froze midair as he caught her gaze again. Though his expression revealed nothing, the intensity of his gaze spoke volumes on its own. "No."

She stepped to the side, finally regaining her personal space. Her eyebrow raised now. She hoped her smirk looked as mischievous as it felt. "Does it look good?"

The same intensity in his gaze lasted for another beat, but then he jerked his head away. He bent to begin rolling up his blanket and sleeping mat. "We need to clean up and get to the castle. The sooner we save Faerie, the sooner you can get back to your younger sister."

She got to her knees, rolling up her own sleeping mat. But she did it across from him to make sure she could stare right into his face. "Does it look good, Quintus?"

He grunted in response.

The refusal to answer meant he probably didn't want to admit the truth, since he couldn't lie about it. It took effort to hide her growing smirk. She shrugged. "Yours looks good."

His stared downward as he finished rolling his sleeping mat. "My what? My face? I know it looks good. I am fae."

"Your *tattoo* looks good."

He laughed and stared at her like she was a child who had just suggested the moon was made of cheese. "No fae has a tattoo. Our healing abilities press the ink back out of our skin. Some have attempted it still, but the tattoo fades away almost instantly."

Throwing her leather bag over her shoulder, she shrugged again. "Yours must be a magical tattoo then, because it hasn't faded at all."

He blinked at her, not speaking, hardly even breathing. When she stepped up to him and traced his moon tattoo with her finger, he stepped back.

"I do not have a tattoo. You are using mortal trickery." The words sputtered out of him while his curls bounced on his forehead. "Lying. You are lying."

"It's a crescent moon, which seems to pair with my st—"

"A *moon?*" He spat the word out, but when his eyes opened wide, it was more with fear than anger. "That's impossible."

His hand shoved deep into his pocket until he pulled out a mirror made of polished wood and red gems. The mirror sat in front of his face for a single breath before he threw it across the clearing. It slammed into a nearby tree, and the glass shattered into tiny pieces.

"A *moon?*" Now he threw his hands into the air, shaking his fists. His gaze pointed up toward the sky. "Do you hate me? Is that it?"

Chloe gathered the last of her things as she raised an eyebrow at him. "Do *I* hate you?"

His gaze flicked to her. "You?" He scoffed. "As if you could have the power to mark me with such a demeaning, disgusting…" All the sharpness in his tone deflated when his chin fell to his bare chest. "A moon."

The brown of his skin had more of a reddish undertone in this early morning light. His lean muscles tensed with each of his breaths. Soft dark curls spilled onto his forehead. She struggled to keep her eyes off his chest, but the curls had captured her attention now.

She was almost certain his hair had been straight before. Or maybe it had just been shorter.

Stepping toward him, she spoke in her gentlest voice possible. "What's so bad about a moon?"

Whirling on her, his finger jabbed at the bone under his left eye. He didn't quite touch the moon tattoo, but he came close enough. "*This* is a mortal image. Faerie itself has tainted me with the mark of a *mortal*."

The words jangled in her gut, reminding her of the shudder she had ignored earlier. Her fingers reached up for her own tattoo. "Are stars a fae mark?"

His eyes opened wide in disbelief. "Of course not. Stars are a mortal mark as well. Faerie has no moon. It also has no stars."

"What?" Her hands landed on her hips as she stared at him. "Of course Faerie has stars. And I know it has a moon. I've seen it before."

"No, you have not." He pinched the bridge of his nose as he started to pace the clearing. "You just remember your moon from the mortal realm and always assumed Faerie had one too, but it does not. I am fae. I cannot lie about this, remember?"

As he spoke, he trailed over to his shattered mirror. Ignoring the beautifully polished wood with red gems in it, he reached for one of the broken shards. Lifting it up, he examined his face again. The sight of it caused him to wince.

"Maybe we can undo it." Guilt tugged at Chloe's throat when she spoke.

He glanced at the mirror piece again only to throw it far away. "We do not even know why it happened in the first place. We cannot undo it."

Aches threaded deeper in Chloe's throat as the guilt intensified. She tried to swallow, but her chest just strained instead. "*I* know why it happened."

His muscles tensed, but then they relaxed again. He dug into his pocket and pulled out a soft rectangle blanket with brown and black triangles at the ends and a dark green color at the bottom that faded into a lighter green color at the top. When he put the blanket over his head, she realized it wasn't a blanket at all, but an article of clothing that worked like a shirt and a cape at the same time.

"What do you think happened then?" He ran his fingers through his hair, combing away any tangles. His hair looked even glossier when he finished. Since he went right back to cleaning up their camp and putting things away, he didn't seem especially hopeful that she'd have an actual answer.

But then she opened her magical book to the page she had read last night. Holding it out in front of him, his gaze darted over the explanation of the ritual, of how to access her magic.

The words promised she could access her magic but only after holding an object that contained magic for an entire night.

She saw the exact moment when realization met his eyes. The gold rimming his brown irises flashed with a gleam. His gaze dropped to his hand, the hand she'd been holding all night long. Slowly, his gaze trailed back up to her.

"I thought I was holding a rock. Since I have to touch the object I held in order to use any magic I might have, I thought a small rock would be the perfect size to carry around."

It seemed so ridiculous when she said it out loud. How could she have mistaken a rock for a hand? Then again, last night she'd been more concerned about finding an object that held magic. Maybe it made sense that she hadn't noticed the feel of it because she'd been too focused on the magic in it. And Quintus's hand had certainly held ample amounts of magic.

The gold sparks in his eyes lit one by one as he stared at the book again. "If you can use magic against the mortals *and* resist their iron flame, you will be even more valuable in the fight against them."

Closing the book, she stepped back. "You said I wouldn't have to fight."

"Try it." He ignored her statement and reached out. Only a breath later, his hand laid carefully on top of hers. He didn't squeeze or press his skin hard against hers. He just kept his hand close enough to maintain skin contact. "Try using magic."

Suddenly, it didn't matter what the magic would mean. Curiosity won out again. Taking in a short breath, she tried it.

Magic and sparks burst from her palm in a golden shower. It came out almost exactly as she had imagined it might when she stood in that cave the night before.

Once the moment passed, Quintus pulled his hand away. He looked her straight in the eye. "Try it again."

Her hand still hovered in the same spot, but nothing happened. She pressed her lips together, trying even harder to push magic into her hand. Again, nothing happened.

Stepping away, he kicked a small stick into their fire that had died the night before. "If you must touch me to use magic, you will not be able to use it on the iron flames, since I cannot get close to them. I suppose your magic will not be that valuable after all."

He glanced toward her leather bag where the magical book now sat. "But maybe we *can* undo it."

Just then, a thorny demorog shrieked from the sky. The piercing sound dug deep under Chloe's skin, but fear didn't plague her this time. The prickling under her skin came entirely from concern.

She glanced up at the creature. "Is it hurt?"

"Yes." Quintus stuffed the rest of the items strewn through the clearing into his pocket. "From the iron poisoning. Forget the tattoos. We can try to undo the bond between us later. For now, we need to stop those mortals."

She nodded, knowing exactly what this meant. They were going to the castle.

12

WHEN CHLOE STEPPED DEEPER INTO the lush forest of Crystal Thorn, her heart squeezed at leaving behind those black caves. The forest had trickling streams, and it smelled of crisp rain and wild berries, but she still longed to return to the caves. Something about them felt safer, or maybe they just felt more enchanting.

Her feet stomped harder on the ground at the thought. It did not bode well that she already longed for Faerie when she had only been here for a single day. But she didn't want to stay in Faerie, not really.

She had her job as an apothecary to return to. And her harp. Maybe she couldn't play as beautifully as Grace, but she still enjoyed harp playing more than Elora ever did. And what about Dunstan and the other young men in town? She'd been batting her eyelashes and flashing charming smiles at them for three years now in the hopes of making a good match.

All she ever wanted was a quiet life with a man who'd care for her and protect her. She spent so much time helping and caring for others in hopes that someday it would give her someone she could love and grow old with.

And here she was pining for Faerie and stomping around with a fae who would make it very difficult to appreciate a plain mortal man once she returned. Just for that, she threw her meanest scowl toward Quintus.

He rolled his eyes at the sight. "The castle is not far. I did not want to open a door in case the iron flames sent poison inside it. It is better to walk from this distance."

Typical. He had wrongly assumed the cause of her scowl, reassuring her about something she cared nothing about. But now he focused on the path again as if the entire situation had been dealt with.

Why did she want to strangle him and kiss him all at the same time?

Before she could scowl at him again, he gestured toward a large bush heavy with purple berries. They ducked behind it, then Quintus gestured toward the nearby castle.

Black spires climbed high into the air. Its gleaming black walls had the opulence and shine of the rarest crystal. Moist soil surrounded the castle with bits of moss crawling up its sides. Lush green vines grew in and around windows and doorways. With so many windows, the inside of the castle felt as much a part of the forest as the forest itself.

It looked as beautiful and as magical as she remembered, except for the metal troughs surrounding the castle with hot flames that burned twice as tall as her.

The soil at the base of each trough had turned to a pale, sickly white, as if all nutrients had been stripped from the soil and only the ghost of what it had once been remained.

"We do not want to go in through the front doors. The mortals have that area too well patrolled." He gestured now toward an unassuming door with mossy cracked stones leading down to it. "But this side of the castle they only patrol when day dawns, at midday, and when night falls."

She nodded, but her mind had drifted off to thinking of what Faerie would look like once night fell. Despite Quintus's assurance, she still didn't believe Faerie had no moon nor stars. She had to remember to check once it got dark.

He pulled out his sketchbook and flipped through it until he got to a page depicting what looked like a map of the interior of Crystal Thorn Castle. "If we both enter the door there, I just need you to put out iron flames in two other spots, and then I can get to the room where their leaders spend most of their time."

Slipping her finger under a page of his sketchbook, she attempted to turn the page. "Are you crafting another harp?"

She got just enough of a look to know he had indeed sketched a harp, one that featured ink pots and feather quills carved into its pillar.

He snapped the sketchbook closed and tucked it into his pocket. "Never mind that."

The words would have been more defiant if his pointed ears hadn't flushed.

She smirked at him, ready to tease even more, but then his eyes went wide.

"Here they come." He grabbed her around the middle and tugged her down behind the bush. His grip around her stayed firm. Though she wanted very much to ram her elbow into his stomach, the coming mortals would probably hear him grunt if she did.

Instead, she had to peek through the leaves of a berry-laden bush while Quintus breathed just next to her ear. His proximity had stolen her focus almost entirely until a young woman rounded a corner, a mortal.

The women carried a thin sword and had a thick braid that trailed down her back, ending at the knees. Her light brown skin was about the same shade as Quintus's, though with an olive undertone.

Two other mortals came up behind her, one woman and one man, both several years older than the young woman. The sight of them set fire to Chloe's memories until she was completely certain of what she saw.

Pushing herself lower to the ground, she turned until she could glance at Quintus. "Those are the mortals Elora saved."

"Ansel's mortals. Yes. There are about forty of them still." He barely even spared her a glance, keeping his focus on the castle instead.

Pushing her eyebrows together, Chloe tilted her head toward the patrolling mortals. "But Elora *saved* them. Why are they trying to hurt her now?"

Quintus let out a soft sigh, quiet enough that it didn't even rustle the leaves of the nearby bush. "They believe your sister is just as evil as Ansel was now that she has turned fae like him."

Chloe wanted to smack every one of those mortals across the back of the head. "But Elora was *fae* when she saved them."

He shrugged.

Now Chloe's teeth clenched tight together. "How can they be so ungrateful?"

His eyebrow raised while the tiniest smirk pricked at his lips. "That is what they say about us."

When that answer clearly did not satisfy her, he finally released his hold around her middle. "If it makes you feel any better, only their two main leaders seem to truly hate us. The mortals, Portia and Julian, had high positions in Ansel's household. They were angry they were taken from Ansel's house. The other mortals are too defeated after being manipulated by Ansel for so long that they do not realize they are being manipulated again, just by Portia and Julian now."

Slumping nearer to the ground, Chloe frowned. "That does not make me feel better even a little bit."

Quintus had nothing to say to that. He just looked on, waiting for the mortals to disappear around the other corner of the castle. Such a fae thing to do. How could he not care that these people were being treated so poorly? If she needed any reminder of how selfish and unfeeling the fae were, this was it.

"I remember that girl." Chloe peeked through the bush once again, her gaze landing on the young woman carrying the sword. "She reminded me of a friend I had when I was young. We spoke sometimes while the mortals were still in the castle and I hadn't returned to the mortal realm yet."

Chloe glanced at her fingers now, attempting to rub away a splotch of ink on one finger that had probably been there for a week at least. "The girl said she'd been forced to become a warrior while in the mortal realm. Then, once in Faerie, Ansel forced her to hurt the other mortals when they didn't behave the way he wanted them to. All she wanted was to put down her sword and never have to fight again."

"Stop doing that."

She glanced up at Quintus's face, which had turned surprisingly sharp. The edges of it hardened as he narrowed his eyes. "Do not try to form a connection with her. She is the *enemy*."

Chloe's fingers curled into fists. "Not all of these mortals are enemies. They are just pieces in someone else's game. No one deserves to be manipulated like that."

"If we do not save Faerie from them, the mortal realm will be destroyed too."

"I know." She glared at him even harder than before. "That means our goal now isn't just to save the castle and kill their stupid leaders."

He raised an eyebrow. "I thought you did not want to fight."

"I never said anything about fighting." She sat up ever so slightly, making certain that no part of her moved higher than the bush she hid behind. "We're also going to save the mortals. Again."

Just as the last word left her lips, a loud clanging noise sounded from nearby. On instinct, she ducked even closer to the ground. Her heart started racing so fast, she could barely catch her breath. Even speaking seemed nearly impossible. "What is that?"

"We need to get out of here." Quintus grabbed her by the hand, and for once, she was grateful he took charge without waiting to see what she thought about it.

With danger involved, she couldn't be trusted to do much of anything. But Quintus seemed to have a plan. He held her hand tight.

With the other hand, he waved it in a small circle through the air. A swirling tunnel appeared before them. He had said earlier that opening a door near the iron flames could be detrimental, but apparently, they were in too much danger to worry about that now.

But just before they could step inside the door, a small metal object whistled through the air above them. It flew right inside the door.

The moment the object entered the door, Quintus dropped to the ground with a heavy grunt. His body immediately writhed in agony. She didn't know exactly what had gone through his door, but she had a guess as to what it was made of.

Iron.

13

BLOOD POUNDED IN CHLOE'S EARS. Her hands twisted in front of herself as sweat gathered in her palms. She willed her feet to move, but they were even more immobile than they had been in that black cave. Because now it was more than just a mysterious magic that kept her feet in place. It was fear, thick and prickly.

The feeling coursed through her, flooding each corner of her body. It swelled and ached and paralyzed her no matter how she tried to move. Tears came next. Each one stung in her eyes before it trailed hot and feverish down her cheeks. Soon, her vision blurred with the tears.

Why did she have to be so useless in a fight? Why did her muscles lock up and her heart race when it should have allowed her to run?

Even with tear-blurred vision, she still saw the mortals near the castle running toward her. One of them, the man wearing a blue coat with lace at its sleeves, ripped an object from his belt. A dagger probably.

Quintus still writhed on the ground. The iron object that had been thrown into his door continued to hurt him though it should have been far away now. His pain must have kept him from closing the door because it kept swirling right behind Chloe, giving off that faint scent of mossy earth and fresh parchment.

When the man with the blue coat threw the object he had retrieved, a glint of light reflected off its blade. Definitely a dagger then.

With Quintus on the ground and her body still paralyzed from burning fear, Chloe closed her eyes and waited for the end. At least with her eyes closed, she wouldn't have to witness her own demise.

But then a clang sounded, something like metal against wood. Holding her breath, her eyes flew open.

Quintus held a wooden spear in one hand that had clearly knocked the dagger off its course since it now lay on top of the bush they'd been hiding behind.

His knees shook horribly, but at least he had gotten to his feet. Now he stepped in front of Chloe, ready to block any other weapons that came their way. His head tilted back, pointing toward the swirling tunnel behind her.

"Go through the door. Bring back the ball of iron." He gasped for air as a harder shake of his knees nearly sent him sprawling to the ground. A second dagger flew toward them, but he whacked it off course with lightning speed. The effort forced him to keel over and grip both his knees for support.

His voice came out breathless after that. "When you get back with the iron, I can close the door, and we can get out of here."

Concern wriggled deep enough inside her to cool her heated skin. His words entered her mind, but fear still rattled her too much to let them sink in.

Just as he blocked another small object with his spear, he jerked around to face her. He gestured wildly at the door and shouted a single word. "Go!"

Understanding dawned like the crack of a whip. Her feet could finally move because now she had a job to do. No one expected her to fight anymore. If anyone expected it of her, they'd only be disappointed since all she could do in the face of a fight was stand still and cry. Or faint, which was even less helpful.

But the fight didn't concern her anymore. Quintus would take care of it. Now she just had to find the ball of iron that had been tossed into his door.

Salt dried to her cheeks, but at least her tears had stopped. She jumped into the door, holding her breath as she did it.

The moment her feet touched a sandy shore, she knew the door had worked properly, unlike the door Quintus had opened in the mortal realm. Her blood pulsed so hard she could feel her heartbeat in her fingertips. At least she was moving.

Her boots sank into the soft white sand from the Court of Swiftsea. Leafy palm trees and a sparkling blue sea created the landscape around her. No part of her could enjoy it though. Her gaze raked over the beautiful court, eager to find just one thing.

The ball of iron.

Nothing but pretty white sand and opalescent seashells covered the ground at her feet. She lifted her skirts and took several steps back, then several steps to the side, just in case she had hidden the ball by standing over it.

But that didn't help her find anything.

She darted toward a cluster of rocks. Just as she neared them, her body seemed to slam into a wall. With an oof, she landed hard on the sand behind her. For the briefest moment, shimmery blue magic flickered across the space in front of her.

Reaching out, she tried to extend her hand through the same place she had just tried to run. Her arm only got halfway stretched out before the shimmery blue magic stopped it in place once again.

An enchantment. The Swiftsea fae must have put it up to keep the mortals out. Hopefully that meant their gleaming white castle wouldn't be overtaken the way Crystal Thorn Castle had. They'd be safe from the mortals if they could just keep the mortals away from their castle.

Chloe dusted sand off her backside and darted toward another cluster of rocks. This time, light flashed in a spot that had just looked sandy at first. As she moved closer, she found the ball of iron.

Gripping it tight to her chest, she sprinted toward the swirling tunnel with its lush green vines and star-like golden bursts. Just before stepping inside it, a dagger flipped through the opening and landed blade side down in the sand only inches from her feet.

That same familiar fear coursed through her veins at the sight of it. Cold trickled down her neck, freezing her legs in place. She had to take several deep breaths before she could move again. When she could, her fingers reached straight for the hilt of the dagger. Maybe the weapon didn't have iron in it, but if it did, it probably injured Quintus just as much as the ball had.

The tunnel swirled faster by the time she finally stepped inside it. The smudges forming its walls even flickered. Would it hold long enough for her to get back to Crystal Thorn?

She could smell moss and parchment, but then the scent vanished. In desperation, she leapt forward, hoping she'd land back in her sister's court.

Her shoulder hit the moist soil of Crystal Thorn Forest just as the Faerie door behind her flickered away from view. She let out a deep breath of relief. The relief instantly faded when she glanced around for Quintus. He was gone.

Shaky breaths heated her mouth as she stood. She gripped her leather bag with both hands just to give them something to do. Her feet stumbled backward. A logical thought at the very back of her mind told her to stay calm, to survey her surroundings. But fear quickly squashed all logic before it could fully form.

Quintus was gone. When two women jumped out from behind the bush Chloe had been hiding behind earlier, she screamed. She held the ball of iron and the dagger closer to her chest. She hardly even noticed when the blade of the dagger cut into the golden embroidery that edged the corset front of her dress.

The older of the two women had wild eyes as she leapt forward with a short sword. But then the woman next to her, the one with a thick dark braid that fell to her knees and olive-undertoned brown skin, held out one arm in front of her companion.

"Wait, Ivanna." The young woman's brown eyes narrowed as she glanced at Chloe's hands. Now she gestured toward them. "She's mortal. Look."

The woman—Ivanna, apparently—pointed her short sword straight at Chloe's chest, but she also narrowed her eyes at the objects in Chloe's hands. With a disappointed sigh, she dropped her sword to her side. "So she is."

The young woman with dark skin took another step forward, her eyes thinning with concern. Chloe wracked her brain, trying to remember the young woman's name. She had known it when they spoke in Faerie before. But that had been three years ago for Chloe. Who knew how long it had been for the young woman since time didn't exist in Faerie.

"You can come with us." The ferocity in the young woman's voice melted away until it was nothing more than a lilt. "That cruel fae ran off and left you here defenseless. I'm guessing he tricked you or forced you into Faerie as well."

"No." Chloe raised both her hands, dropping the ball of iron and dagger. "I came willingly."

Her head tilted to the side. "Well, I guess I was unconscious at the time, but that's only because I was drowning. I would have come willingly."

The young woman set a hand on Chloe's shoulder. "It may seem that way now, but once you've been with us for a few days, you'll see how he manipulated you."

Chloe scoffed. "Quintus wishes he could manipulate me." She shook her head. "I do want to be here though, I promise. You have to stop using iron. It's hurting Faerie, but it's also poisoning the mortal realm."

Both of the women stared at her with the kind of looks a mother gave a child after he declared the dead could return to life.

With fists curling, Chloe pressed her eyebrows down over her eyes. "You are the ones being manipulated." The young woman's name finally fluttered to the front of her mind. "Mishti."

The woman's eyes flew open wide.

Chloe gestured toward the thin sword in the young woman's hands. "I thought you wanted to put your sword down for good. I thought you wanted to be free to do what you choose to do, yet here you are participating in another battle that someone else has forced you into. Isn't that manipulation?"

Mishti's grip on her sword tightened as she stared back. Her eyes searched Chloe's face, as if trying to figure out how Chloe knew her name. But even as she tried, she kept getting distracted by the truth in Chloe's words. A truth she seemed eager to tuck into a dark corner of her mind.

The older woman lifted her short sword and pointed the tip toward Chloe's chest again. "How dare you."

Heat and stings crashed in Chloe's chest. If any other weapons entered this conversation, she'd be back to crying while paralyzed in fear.

"Chloe." Mishti whispered the name while her eyes lit with recognition.

Ivanna jerked toward her companion with a question in her eyes.

Mishti gestured toward Chloe. "She's the destroyer's sister."

"The destroyer?" Chloe couldn't help releasing a short chuckle. "Is that what you call Elora now? She saved you."

105

Flashing her teeth, the older woman lifted her sword. "We had a perfect life in that house in Mistmount. With our captor gone, we could have lived happily for years. But your *sister* took us away and forced us into this cruel cunning world of the fae, who know nothing of sisterhood or selflessness. She ruined our lives."

"That house didn't have any doors or windows to the outside. We would have run out of food after only a few weeks." Mishti muttered the words under her breath as she used the tip of her sword to draw lines in the dirt at her feet.

The expression that twisted over the older woman's face could have frozen the lake that nearly drowned Chloe. "Portia and Julian would have found a way to get us food. They've always taken care of us, especially when our captor was still around."

Attempting to take advantage of her clear uncertainty, Chloe caught Mishti's eyes. "I want to help you. I don't want you to be manipulated anymore, not by fae, and not by your mortal leaders who put that sword back in your hand."

The belief in Mishti's eyes glinted only for a moment before it dulled to a darkened stare. "If you really care about us, then bring us bandages and extra wards to protect against fae enchantments. That's what we need more than anything."

"Okay."

Both women stared at Chloe in disbelief.

She tapped her chin, glancing away from the short sword that was still partially pointed toward her. "Bandages should be easy to acquire. I just need some clean fabric. Quintus can probably conjure some for me. I'm not sure about fae wards though. Do any of you have red fabric? A simple red ribbon around a wrist or an ankle gives decent protection. It's not as strong as a fae-made ward, but it still works."

"Listen to this nonsense. She can't get us fae wards. If she's so friendly with that fae, she probably wants to become a fae just like her sister did."

"I do *not* want to become fae." Chloe gagged at the thought. "But I will try to bring you bandages and whatever fae wards I can find."

"Lies." Ivanna spit the words from her lips, releasing a splash of spittle as well. Her sword jabbed out.

Chloe couldn't stumble away fast enough. The tip of the sword sliced across her skin, just next to the invisible fae wards she wore around her neck. It stung as blood beaded from the wound.

"Quintus." The word slipped from her mouth in a tremble. She cleared her throat and spoke it louder. As a fae, he could hear much better than a mere mortal. But maybe that was only if he was listening.

Ivanna reeled her arm back ready to plunge the sword even deeper than the small gash she had just inflicted.

Chloe tried to step away. She tried to duck or shout or do anything. But when the icy hot sludge of fear took over her limbs, she could do nothing to combat it. Tears dripped from between her eyelids. She watched as the sword sliced across the air. She watched as it dove straight for her heart. Watched and could do nothing.

But just before the sword made contact, a whoosh sounded that blew air through the loose strands of her messy bun. The sword clattered to the ground before it could touch her. Only then did she see that a spear had collided with it and thrown it off course.

She barely had enough time to notice the spear lying on top of the sword when another whooshing came from nearby. This one was much louder.

In a flash, strong arms swept her off her feet. Someone held her now and carried her away from the mortals. She could only guess it was Quintus, though he had moved too fast for her to see for sure.

The forest around them seemed to whirl past. Was he running? If so, he ran even faster than a horse. Faster than a bird.

"How are you moving so fast?" Her voice came out breathless.

In another flash, he set her down on the ground. His curls bounced as he shook them off his forehead. His eyes had lost all the light they usually had. He opened his mouth to speak, but he didn't. He collapsed onto the ground in a heap letting out a huff that sounded like all the air in his body had come out in one breath.

Was he hurt?

14

THE AIR, THE TREES, EVEN the scents seemed to close in around Chloe until they suffocated her. Every chirp, creak, and leaf flutter pounded like hammers in her ear. Every bit of magic and wonder edged into something sharp and icy until it needled under her skin and deep into her heart.

The calm had caused her to forget how lethal Faerie could be. Even the fae could be vulnerable here.

She wanted to say Quintus's name. It sat right there on the tip of her tongue, heavy and thick. But it would not come out, not even when she took a step toward him.

His body winced when a twig snapped under her feet. "The iron has injured me. I need…" His eyes closed as he released a heavy exhale. "Rest."

Dropping her knees at Quintus's side, she tried to swallow. Her fingers brushed away the black wave of hair that had fallen into his eyes. "Are you okay?"

"I will be fine." The raspy quality of his voice did little to ease her fears. When his breaths grew even shorter than before, the ice under her skin turned jagged. As an apothecary, the back of her hand almost instinctively rested across his forehead.

109

He had a fever. She examined the rest of him with a quick glance. When her gaze landed on his fingertips, she gasped. She grabbed his hand and lifted it close to her face.

Her voice shook as she forced the words out. "You have—"

"Scurpus, I know." He shook his head, wincing yet again. "It used to take prolonged exposure over multiple days to contract this stupid illness. But there is so much iron in the air now that one simple…"

He trailed off and she couldn't tell if it was from pain, from frustration, or from something else entirely.

"Quintus, I…" Pain gripped her throat in a tight ache. Though she had started it, the end of the sentence eluded her now.

Her thoughts must have been written on her face because Quintus looked her straight in the eye. "It is not the same as when a mortal gets it. I can heal myself."

The fae had incredible healing abilities, which she already knew. But as much as he said, she could tell there was more he wasn't saying as well.

"You can heal yourself, but…," she prompted.

"But it will take a great amount of energy, and I do not want to wait."

She dug into her bag, feeling around for the herbs inside. She still had enough goldenrod, juniper, and the other ingredients to make a poultice, but once again, she was missing a key ingredient. "I know the remedy, but you know I do not have any Swiftsea salt. Do you have fennel in Faerie?"

"I am not sure." He forced himself to a seated position. Dark red splotches covered his neck. His hand pressed against the skin of his face, then he rubbed it across the back of his neck. When he winced, it didn't shake his entire body like it had before. "I do know of a fae who will know about fennel. And if he does not have any already, he will know where to get some."

Now he pushed himself up until he stood. Though he had gotten to his feet, his knees still wobbled. And he hadn't even started walking yet.

Her eyebrow raised, doing her best to keep an even tone that didn't sound *too* patronizing. "Are you certain you can walk?"

He took a step forward, which shook his entire frame. At least he had stayed upright. "For now, yes. Later? We shall see."

He threw her a sideways glance, waiting until she came to his side and started walking too. His knees shook with each step, but her weak muscles couldn't help hold him up anyway, so it was probably better not to suggest it.

"I had to run when they pulled iron weapons on me. The mortal man came after me and threw some iron shavings at my collar. The iron shavings got under my cape."

A shudder passed through his shoulders as he gestured at the blanket-like cape covering his torso. "I ran faster than the man and got away. I needed to rest though. I heard when you came back through my door, but I was so tired."

Now *she* threw a sideways glance his way.

His shoulders hunched forward as he turned his gaze downward. "I could hear them talking to you. I knew you were not in danger. As soon as you called my name, I came as fast as I could."

"You got there right in time." A stinging thread stretched through her throat when she tried to swallow. She wanted to stare at him, to drink in his soft curls and his solid frame. She'd admired the muscles in his arms far too many times already, but now she could only think of how tight he had held her to his body when he saved her from the fight. He had rescued her.

Part of his cape now had a tear from the collar down to his lower chest. The soft wool fabric bounced lightly with each of his steps. The torn portion kept falling a little more, revealing his dark and smooth skin underneath.

She bit her lip, unable to turn away. "How did you run that fast anyway? Is that a new kind of magic you have now?"

He finally caught her staring and glanced down at the tear in his cape. Shaking his head, he lifted both hands to the tear. His fingers moved across the soft fabric while a greenish gold hue glowed out from his fingertips. In a few breaths, the tear had been repaired perfectly. There wasn't even an extra stretch in the fabric or a slightly different color of thread anywhere to suggest a repair. It just looked as perfect as it had before the fight.

Once finished, his hands dropped to his sides heavily. "No. Fae have always had such speed, but we prefer to travel through our doors."

"What happened to your door when they threw iron into it? Can you not close it when there is iron inside?" Her feet trailed closer to his as they walked. If he asked about it, she could easily insist she only worried he might topple over from his weakness, and she wanted to be close enough to catch him, though truthfully, that had nothing to do with it.

"I could have closed it, but..." His face twisted like even the thought of iron could injure him. "It hurts worse that way. It is better to remove the iron first and then to close the door. Still, I will not be able to open a door properly until I have healed."

"Which explains why we're walking." Chloe didn't mind the exercise. The scenery made it even more pleasant.

A thick canopy of lush green leaves towered over them. Tall tree trunks grew from the moist soil. Mossy rocks, trickling streams, and quaint bushes dotted the landscape. Throughout it all, shiny black thorns that had a crystalline surface twisted and stretched. The thorns had once seemed sinister and dangerous. Now they added to the beauty of the court around them.

After a moment, she whirled around toward Quintus. "Was that your way of apologizing?"

His face twisted into a snarl. "What?"

"You said you heard when I came back through your door and then you explained why you couldn't come get me right away. Were you apologizing?"

One side of his lip curled up until it made his eye twitch. "Fae do *not* apologize, not if we can help it. If I had said *sorr*—that word, I would owe you a debt. But I did not say it, so I owe you nothing."

She sighed at his indignance. "Yes, I remember the rules of Faerie. We can't say *please* or *thank you* either."

He glanced around before turning a sharp gaze toward her. "Be careful."

Rolling her eyes, she kicked away a small rock. "I didn't say those words to anyone specific. I know it's fine."

His eyes narrowed at her. Annoyance danced inside them, but maybe he was just annoyed that she was right.

"Where are we going?" She flashed a bright smile at him, which would maybe set aside his frustration. Or even better, it might make him even more annoyed.

He jerked his head away until he faced forward, suddenly refusing to make eye contact. "I know a fae who has a penchant for obtaining difficult-to-find items. He lives in Crystal Thorn, somewhat nearby." His head tilted to the side. "He does not like to be surprised though."

When Quintus glanced up at the air, her gaze followed. Tiny glowing green lights floated up above. They almost looked like tiny pulsing stars that served no purpose except to make Faerie look more magical, though she knew there was much more to them than just that.

Quintus held his hand up with the palm flat toward the sky. With it in position, he clicked his tongue three times.

In a flash, one of the glowing green lights began moving away from the others. It darted down toward his palm. Once it landed, a tiny creature no taller than a thumb stood on Quintus's palm.

The little sprite had velvety dark green hair as wild as a bit of moss. His large blue and yellow eyes had greenish blue eyelashes rimming them. His small shirt and pants looked as green and vibrant as the leaves fluttering on the trees above. In fact, they even had the same veins as a leaf.

Chloe had been to Faerie before. She had seen how sprites were used for communication. Still, the entire sight fascinated her so completely, she had forgotten to walk.

Clearing his throat, Quintus began. "I, Quintus of Crystal Thorn, have a message for Ludo of Fairfrost. Tell him I am coming to visit, and I have a small list of items I need him to retrieve. I will give him the list when we arrive."

The sprite with moss-like hair blinked his greenish blue eyelashes in recognition. Then Quintus dug into his pocket with his other hand.

A moment later, he had a small wood shaving pinched between his thumb and forefinger. The sprite's eyes gleamed at the sight of it. He took the wood shaving into his tiny arms and promptly stumbled to the side from the weight of it.

Did he need help?

Before Chloe could offer, the sprite managed to stuff the wood shaving into his pocket, even though his pocket was at least five times smaller than the wood shaving itself.

With the wood shaving put away, the sprite then flew off. His green glow disappeared almost instantly.

She turned to Quintus now. "I thought sprites required living things as an offering. Things like berries or flower petals."

"No." Quintus chuckled. "Offerings just have to have personal significance to the person who gives them. They can be anything though, a pebble or a thread." His eyes lit with a mischievous gleam. "Even a harp string, if it happens to be important to you."

She sucked in a breath while heat surged into her cheeks. She whipped her head around to stare at the nearest tree. "Good. If I ever have to send a message, I know exactly what offering to give. I can finally get rid of that stupid harp string."

"You have to give an offering when you send a message *and* when you receive one."

Her fingers curled into fists. Of course he had completely missed the point. Maybe a change of subject was needed. Hopefully he wouldn't notice how her boots stomped on the moist soil with a little more fervor than before.

"Can you conjure me some bandages?"

"No."

Her jaw flexed as she let out a small grunt. "Why is fae hearing so perfect? I wish you hadn't heard me talking to those mortals; you wouldn't know the bandages are for them."

He raised an eyebrow. "If I had not heard you, I would not have been able to rescue you."

She rolled her eyes with a groan. "Just conjure the bandages."

"I cannot."

When she dared a glance at him, his gaze had fallen to the mossy path beneath his feet. A light breeze sent a lock of hair across his forehead. The gray tinge along his hairline crawled down toward his eyes.

He frowned. "I am not the best at conjuring." His hand reached into his pocket only to pull out the ghastly dress that had been sitting by the fire when Chloe first got to Faerie.

"This is what happens when I try to conjure things." For a moment, his scowl looked even worse than the dress, which was saying something.

Her nose wrinkled at the hideous dress, but then her eyes opened wide as she considered it. She had never seen such an awful print, but the stiff cotton fabric would be decent for bandages. Taking the dress into her hands, she ran a finger over the yellow and brown pattern. It was clean, which was all it really needed to be. If she could just tear it into smaller strips, it might be perfect.

"I know it's awful." Quintus rubbed a hand across the back of his neck. His knees still shook with each step, but he did seem a little better than before. Now he sighed. "My greatest magic is in crafting. Give me the right materials, and I can work magic on them."

Considering how he had repaired that tear in his cape, she didn't need proof to know he spoke the truth.

He leaned toward her now, narrowing his eyes. "Speaking of which…"

Reaching out a hand, his fingers trailed over the embroidery along the corset of her dress. The embroidery had been sliced away by the knife of that mortal woman, Ivanna. But Quintus just tapped and touched the golden threads while that same golden green magic glowed from his fingertips. When he pulled his hand away, the embroidery had not just been repaired, now it looked shinier and more intricate than ever.

Instead of bringing his hand away though, he just reached for the strap of her leather bag. "This has been bothering me too."

She hadn't noticed it until he fixed it, but suddenly, her strap no longer hung at a tilted angle. The pockets inside must have had their weight distributed unevenly, but after Quintus whirled his hand around, the bag hung evenly.

That alone was wonderful, but his fingers continued to work as they trailed across the brown leather. Another moment later, the bag felt completely weightless. The items inside still sat exactly as they had before, but now, she couldn't feel their weight at all.

Since she couldn't say *thank you* without owing a favor, she threw him an appreciative look instead. But just as her lips started curling into a smile, a loud, horrifying grumble filled the air.

Quintus stepped back while horror painted his features. "What was that?"

15

IF CHLOE HAD THE SUDDEN ability to melt into a puddle, she would have taken it in that moment. Warmth sent pinpricks into her cheeks as she twisted her hands together in front of herself. She stared at them too intently, but she couldn't look at anything else either.

Her stomach grumbled again, just as loud and grinding as before.

This time, Quintus's gaze found the source. He looked right at her stomach as something very much like disgust curled his lip. "That sound came from you?"

Why couldn't she sink into the soil or become one with the nearest tree or even float away with the sprites in the air?

Quintus stepped forward, his eyes still homed in on her stomach. "Are you injured?"

"No."

Another grumble erupted from her stomach, this one sounding like the combination of a creaking door and a dying cat.

He folded his arms over his chest, which rearranged his cape just enough to reveal the sides of his torso. "You sound injured."

"No." She threw her hands into the air, giving up with trying to hide the noise. "I'm just hungry. Don't you fae ever eat? I haven't eaten anything since I got here yesterday, and I've tried to be polite and not mention it, but my stomach, apparently, cannot stand it any longer." She let out a heavy sigh. "I'm starving."

His eye twitched as she spoke. The muscles in his arms twitched too. He wore an indiscernible expression, and though she wanted to find some guilt in it, he looked more confused than anything. He released his arms from across his chest and looked away. "I ate while you were unconscious. And this morning, I had some berries and nuts while you were fixing your hair."

The heat from embarrassment still lingered in her cheeks, but it was nothing to the surge that flared inside them now. "*You* ate, and you didn't bother to get any food for me?"

His gaze turned downward as his lips thinned. "I probably should have thought of that."

She grunted in response.

He ignored the sound completely as he scanned the area around them. Only a moment later, he stepped off the path and toward a leafy bush that had crystal thorns growing throughout it. Plump yellow berries with a pinkish hue grew in thick clumps on the bush.

"Here." He began plucking berries off the branches and piled them onto his palm. "You can eat these."

Stepping forward, she eyed the berries carefully. In the mortal realm, berries with that sort of coloring would either be unripe, or they'd be poisonous. Since the magic of Faerie seemed to keep every berry perpetually ripe, that likely wouldn't be an issue. That did nothing for the second issue though.

She touched a leaf of the bush, examining both the top and bottom of it. "Are these berries poisonous?"

He dropped one of the berries into her free hand. "Not to fae."

The berry bulged slightly as she poked her finger against it. "But is that because they aren't poisonous, or is it because your body can heal you before the poison sets in?"

At least he had the decency to look guilty when he shrugged.

Her stomach grumbled louder as she settled down on top of a mossy rock. She grabbed the magical book from her leather bag and flipped through its pages until she found the section on berries.

The pages didn't glow this time, but they still gave off the same energy they always did. She could feel magic buzzing in each page she touched, in each word she read. The magic called to her in such a tangible way, she almost believed magic would burst from her fingertips if she asked it to.

Since she had done magic just that morning, she believed in the possibility of magic more than ever. But when she tried to make golden sparks shoot from her hand again, nothing happened.

Just as the book had promised, she could not access the magic at all unless she touched Quintus, and that made it basically useless.

Scowling, she focused on the pages again. It only took a bit of skimming to find the information on the yellow berries. She read the paragraphs about them two times, then a third time while she rubbed a thumb across the surface of one of the berries.

"It says they are safe to eat, even for mortals." Quintus stood behind her now. He held the pile of berries in his hand, reaching them toward her.

She slammed her book shut. "I know how to read."

Would he notice how she took her time tucking the book into her leather bag? Did he notice when she stared at the berries without making any move to touch them?

"They are delicious." He nudged his hand closer to her when he said it.

Her gaze flicked up to his for a brief moment before it dropped to stare at the berries again. "Good."

Still, she sat in place, not moving at all.

His knees bent until he was eye level with her. "Why do you not eat them?"

Her arms reached across her stomach until her hands found her opposite elbows. After a swallow, she spoke in a strained voice. "Some foods don't sit well with me."

He looked at her like he didn't even know what that meant. Why would he? If his body could heal itself from every illness, every injury, even from tattoos, why would he know anything about food that didn't sit well?

Maybe it would be fine anyway. She was in Faerie, after all. If Faerie itself could communicate with her through a book, maybe Faerie itself could also make berries that tasted delicious to everyone and that never gave people stomach troubles.

Hunger won in the end. Chloe reached for the entire pile of berries and dropped them into her lap. She popped one after the other into her mouth, savoring the tart and tangy taste.

They really did taste delicious.

"I wish I could have some water too." She spoke as she chewed, which caused a tiny spritz of juice to shoot from her mouth and onto the back of her hand.

"There is a stream right here." Quintus pulled a stone cup from his pocket and filled it with water from the stream.

When he offered it to her, she leaned away. "In the mortal realm, we have to boil our water before we drink it. That ensures it is clean."

He laughed and pushed the cup toward her again. "That will not be necessary."

Still leaning away from the cup, she raised an eyebrow. "But is that because the water is safe to drink? Or is it because your body heals you before it can hurt?"

He didn't have an answer for that. For a brief moment, she considered building a fire to boil the water. But then she noticed the sheen of sweat across Quintus's forehead. Gray spots still splotched across his forehead. His eyes had sunken in too.

Maybe his body could heal him from the scurpus eventually, but he probably needed the remedy for scurpus more than she needed water.

Just when she gave up on the drink, she remembered her little pouch of Faerie things.

"I forgot." She fished through her bag to retrieve a small swirled shell with an opalescent sheen. "I have this shell from Lyren that can cleanse any water."

She dropped the shell inside the cup and let it sit for a few moments. Then she took a sip. Just as the queen of Swiftsea had promised, the water now tasted as sweet as honey. Soon, Chloe drank up the last drops from the cup.

The meal hadn't been much, but it was enough to keep her stomach from roaring. She tucked the shell back into her bag, brushed the wrinkles from her skirt, and then began walking once again.

Everything seemed fine for the first few minutes. Quintus still breathed a little heavier, and his body trembled more than usual, but he could walk without trouble. For now. His scurpus did not seem to be getting better though.

They even rounded a corner and a house made of trees came into view. Branches bent to form the roof. Leaves and clay had been stuffed between tree trunks to fill any spaces in the walls. It was such a beautiful, magical sight. Despite that, Chloe stopped short. Panic rose in her chest, curling her fingers into fists.

She sucked in a short breath and then turned to Quintus. "Excuse me for a moment."

When she tried to step away from him, he followed immediately. "Where are you going?"

Pressing her hand on his shoulder firmly, she looked him in the eye. "Stay here. Right here in this spot. Do not follow me."

If she'd had any more time, she would have waited until he agreed. But she couldn't wait anymore.

Gripping her stomach, she darted behind the nearest tree. The moment she stepped behind it, she vomited.

Her stomach clenched with each heave. She should have known better than to eat berries. Just when more berries spewed from her lips, Quintus appeared at her side.

She turned her face, attempting to hide it from him. "I told you not to follow me."

His eyebrows pinched together, forming a little crease between them. "But the book said the berries were not poisonous to mortals."

With another heave squeezing her stomach, her knees dropped to the ground. "Not to most mortals maybe, but berries never sit well with my stomach."

She coughed and used a nearby leaf to swipe the mess off her lips. "It's my own fault. I should have known better. I just thought maybe Faerie fruit wouldn't affect me the same as mortal fruit. I thought maybe it's magical and wouldn't hurt."

Tears pooled in her eyes while she spoke. Being sick always brought tears to her eyes, though it seemed more of a bodily response than an emotional one. One teardrop slipped down her cheek while her stomach clenched and heaved again.

As the remaining contents of her stomach spewed out, Quintus held back a strand of her hair that had fallen from its bun.

"You cannot conjure bread, can you?" she asked. "Or porridge maybe?"

"No." He kept tucking her hair back, but it would only fall out of place again. "Even among the fae who are good at conjuring, it is rare to find a fae who can conjure cooked or prepared food. That is why so many fae have brownies. Those fae creatures are expert at conjuring meals."

Her body sagged to the ground until her cheek met a clump of lush grass.

"Maybe I can find some nuts or a root vegetable of some sort," he said. "Will those sit better with your stomach?"

She nodded, which rubbed her cheek against the grass clump. "The nuts will, yes. I can only eat root vegetables if they are cooked though."

He stalked away without a word.

At least she wouldn't have to worry about throwing up again. Her stomach had nothing left now, which did not help at all with her hunger. But maybe more water would help.

She forced herself onto her hands and knees. Crawling wasn't the best mode of transportation, but if it got her to the stream, she didn't care.

Just as she started dragging her body forward, something heavy and wooden slammed into her side. Pain burrowed deep in an explosion of spikes.

She didn't have time to be afraid or scream or *anything*. The heavy object just thrust her straight into the ground. It rammed against her again, this time sending a shock through her spine. Dirt filled her mouth when her face pressed into the soil.

A strangled attempt at a scream escaped her lips, but she didn't have the energy for more. Pain coiled in tight ropes down her side and at the base of her back. If that wooden object slammed against her again, it might just snap her spine in two.

Using the little strength she had left, she pushed herself over onto her side. A fae towered over her with an axe in his hand. His fair skin looked nearly white against the green and brown forest behind him. His icy blue and scarlet red eyes were as sharp as a lethal icicle.

He had used the wooden handle of an axe against her so far, but he turned it in his hands until the curved metal end of the axe now stood up. Lifting the weapon, he eyed her chest, ready to strike it.

16

CHLOE CURLED HER BODY INTO a tight ball, bracing for impact. With her senses on such high alert, she could feel when the axe started swinging toward her. Her knees pressed against her chest. Her arms reached across the back of her neck. If the axe had to hit her, it would probably be best if the blade hit an arm or a leg. Her father had taught her that.

Just as the axe came swinging toward her, a shout rang through the branches all around.

"Stop!"

Quintus shrieked with a tightness in his voice she had never heard before. A breeze fluttered the trees, which didn't actually come from a breeze at all but from his body as he ran.

Peeking just above the knees still pressed against her chest, Chloe looked up just in time to see Quintus grab the handle of the axe that had been swinging toward her.

The fair-skinned fae holding the axe wrenched it out of Quintus's grip and stepped around Quintus in another attempt to hit Chloe.

Quintus grabbed the axe handle again and spoke in a low growl. "She is mortal. You will kill her with a strike like that."

The fae's blue and red eyes bulged as he lowered his axe ever so slightly. "Oh." A tremor rocked his arms as he swallowed.

But then his features twisted into a glare. "*Mortals* are destroying our land." He shoved his elbow into Quintus's side and swung the axe at Chloe again.

"Not this one." The curls on Quintus's head bounced as he stepped in front of the weapon.

Baring his teeth, the fair-skinned fae turned his axe on Quintus now. Quintus stepped away in time to keep the weapon from slicing into his chest, but he had to use his arm to block the blow.

A large gash tore through the skin of his forearm, spurting blood onto his attacker.

Tiny spots of blood spattered across the blue-and-red-eyed fae as he flashed his teeth again. "Neither of you should be here. My guests are supposed to warn me before they arrive."

Quintus blocked another blow from the axe, but his arm hit the wooden handle now instead of the blade. "We *did* warn you, Ludo. I sent a sprite."

All the fight drained from Ludo's face in an instant. His arms dropped to his sides, bringing the axe along with them. "You did?"

He let out a small chuckle and lifted his shoulder in a shrug. "That might be my fault then. The sprites are still angry with me for stealing a sword sheath from them."

When Ludo reached a hand toward Chloe to help her up, Quintus used one hand to shove him away. Since blood still oozed from the large gash in Quintus's arm, he offered his other hand to help Chloe up. He continued to glare at Ludo the entire time.

She took Quintus's hand gratefully. When she stood, she pressed the side of her body right up against his. He must have been as wary of this fae, Ludo, as she was because he wrapped his uninjured arm around her waist and closed the little distance that still stood between them.

He flicked his gaze over to her and shook his head. "You are a difficult mortal to keep safe."

"I know." She lifted her chin, letting her gaze follow it up to the sky. "That's why I told you I couldn't help, but *you* seemed to think Faerie needed me. Don't blame me for being exactly who I have always been."

He said nothing to that. He just tugged her tighter still and narrowed his eyes at the fae in front of them. Blood continued to pour from the wound in Quintus's forearm, but he didn't seem to notice it at all. His eyes had sunken in more than ever, and the gray tinge along his hairline was definitely closer to his eyes than it had been before.

"Where is your house?" Quintus asked the fae before them.

Ludo directed them toward the house made of trees that stood only a few steps away. While they walked toward it, Chloe fished out the hideous cotton dress that she'd stuffed into her leather bag earlier. Now she used it to press against the wound in Quintus's arm.

Her eyes were so focused on the wound, she hardly even noticed once they stepped inside the home. Then again, the home had moss for carpet and at least two small trees growing in the middle of the front room. One of the trees had a trunk that had been molded into the shape of a chair. The other tree acted as a partition between the main room and a smaller, very untidy, workroom.

Dozens of small items hung from strings that were tied to the branches of the ceiling. The house smelled of ink and parchment and of boots that had been worn a little too long. The boot stench was far from pleasant, but ink and parchment always made her feel right at home.

Ludo directed them deeper into the house, past the trees and the workroom. He brought them into a large room that felt as small as a closet because so many items filled it. Bookcases were stuffed against every wall and even stood in the middle of the room too. Short and tall piles of items covered almost all the rest of the floor. A few dusty pieces of furniture sat in the very middle, forming something that *almost* resembled a sitting room.

The room held nearly every item imaginable inside it. One tall pile had books, blankets, kettles, and even wooden toys. Capes and cloaks and robes hung from metal hooks jutting out from one wall. There were small decorative items, pieces of furniture, dishes, shoes. Every time Chloe finished cataloguing the items in her mind, she would notice another new item.

No sprites floated in the air, though. Usually, the glowing green creatures floated everywhere in Faerie, even inside of rooms and houses. Then again, Ludo had mentioned the sprites were angry with him, so maybe that explained why the room had to be lit with candles instead.

"You can sit there." Ludo gestured toward a small blue sofa covered in shoes and tall opalescent vases with swirling gold designs.

Quintus slumped onto the small sofa as soon as he reached it. His shoulders sagged so far down, he could nearly drop his head on the sofa arm. Chloe had to shove a pile of vases and shoes out of the way before she could sit on the velvet blue fabric beside him.

But then her gaze wandered to a short table that sat between the sofa and the high-backed wooden chair Ludo now sat in. On top of the table, a white plate with a gold-rimmed edge had been set. And on top of the plate, food.

Her stomach flipped at the sight of it.

Three thin pancake-like pastries sat atop the plate. One had been folded over its filling and half eaten already. The other two pastries laid open, displaying a filling of herbed ground beef and diced *cooked* vegetables. A small dollop of sour cream rested on top.

Chloe's eyes widened. She had reached her hand toward the plate before even realizing it.

"Are you hungry?" Ludo stared with an indecipherable expression, but then he pushed the plate toward Chloe with a smile.

She pulled the plate onto her lap without another word.

"Wait." A raspy cough shuddered through Quintus's lips before he spoke again. "Let me try it first."

One of the pastries had already been folded and was halfway to her mouth. She pinched her mouth into a knot and glared at him. "Why? *You've* already eaten."

He shot her a glare of his own, which was a bit frightening with how sunken his eyes had become. "I can check if it's poisoned."

Staring him straight in the eyes, she stuffed the food into her mouth and took the first bite. With her mouth still full of food, she finally answered. "If it was poison, I doubt he would have eaten some already." She stuffed a second bite into her mouth. "And besides, it wouldn't do any good for you to test the food first since your body will just heal you before any poison can set in anyway."

The glare on Quintus's face eased, but only because his injured arm shifted, and it caused him to wince.

Her fingertips froze at the shoddy work she'd done wrapping his arm with that hideous dress. She still had one bite left of the first pastry, plus the entire second pastry left to eat, but she set them both aside.

Now, she carefully pulled the stiff cotton away from the wound in his arm. Maybe fear could seize her muscles and force tears to her eyes, but at least she could stomach the sight of wounds. Otherwise, the mangled muscle and half-dried blood before her might have emptied her stomach yet again.

Instead, she eyed the wound carefully. Covering her hand with part of the ghastly dress, she pressed her finger lightly on the skin around his wound. After the quick assessment, she dug into her leather bag.

The pockets had all been moved around after Quintus's crafting rearranged them to distribute the weight more evenly. It had been helpful for fixing the angle of the bag, but now she couldn't find anything.

"Do you have any witch hazel?" She pulled out her magical book and set it on the table to make it easier to dig through the other pockets.

A gleam lit in Ludo's eye at the question. His gaze turned toward the towering piles of items in the room.

"Or alcohol." But then she opened a pocket she hadn't noticed at first and found a tincture made of a strong alcohol, some chamomile, and a bit of milk thistle. "Never mind," she said as she plucked out the cork stoppering it.

When she poured a generous amount of the tincture onto Quintus's wound, he hissed. He bared his teeth when she wiped the bits of dried blood from the wound. But when she started smothering honey onto the open gash, he pulled his arm away.

Tilting her head to the side, she held her hand out for his arm. "The honey will prevent infection."

He bared his teeth. "I am fae. I can heal myself."

"Oh." Chloe made a show of closing her little pot of honey back up again. "And did you want to walk around with a half-chopped-off arm that gets infected, which will then take days to heal? I mean, if that's what you want. You are fae and all. I suppose you don't need any remedies at all then."

A vein in his jaw pulsed when he clenched it tight. But after another beat, she knew she had won. He moved his arm back in front of her. Still, he refused to look when she smothered honey over the wound.

With it applied, she then ripped long strips from the parts of the cotton dress that hadn't been bloodied already. The first few strips wrapped around his wound, which had finally stopped bleeding. Using the last few strips, she formed a sling that kept his arm bent and against his body.

He scowled at it.

Ludo, on the other hand, sat so far forward in his wooden chair that he nearly toppled it over. "Fascinating."

His blue and red eyes had looked downright deadly before, but now they sparkled with the same awe that Chloe always imagined covered her own face any time she opened her magical book.

"This is a mortal remedy?" he asked. Before she could answer, he opened a little drawer inside the table between them and retrieved a small notebook and quill. He scratched away at the paper, somehow not needing to fill the quill with ink before writing.

Quintus still scowled at the bandages on his arm, but she was much more concerned with the gray tinge that had nearly spread down to his eyebrows.

Setting her hands neatly into her lap, she turned to the fae across from her. "Do you have any fennel?"

"Fennel?" Ludo dropped his notebook and quill, which fell straight onto the mossy ground. He stared intently at Chloe the entire time. "Fennel from the mortal realm?"

She nodded. "Or some Swiftsea salt will do."

He had already darted behind a heavy black bookshelf with claw feet that dug into the moss beneath them.

"I do have fennel." His voice came out muffled from behind whatever pile of objects he currently was behind. After a bit of clattering, he emerged from behind the bookshelf once again.

A little bundle of dried green stalks sat on his palm. He flashed a wide smile as he dropped into his wooden chair again. "I would love to know more about your mortal remedies. Fae remedies are effective, but they almost always rely on magic, which is not always available if injured or ill."

He chattered as he set the fennel on the wooden table and slid it across the surface toward her. She hardly noticed anything but the dried herb once he revealed it. When he released the herb, she immediately reached out to grab the stalks.

"Chloe." Despite the rasp in his voice, Quintus still infused his words with warning.

She glanced up at him, but that didn't stop her from curling her fingers around the herb.

The moment she touched the bundle, Ludo snatched her magical book off the table and pulled it tight to his chest. His eyes glinted with mischief. "If you take the fennel, I get to keep this book."

The fist she had over the herb bundle tightened as her stomach dropped. Why had she assumed the fae would just give her what she wanted? Of course he would expect a trade. But why did he have to expect the one item that meant the very most to her?

17

THE FEAR THAT PARALYZED CHLOE during a battle had no place inside her now. Her mind buzzed as she turned over the current situation inside her mind, considering a dozen possibilities all at once and how each one might play out. Though her thoughts churned, she bit her bottom lip and pressed her eyebrows together.

"Oh no." She allowed the smallest whine to tighten over her words as she said them. Her gaze darted from her clenched fist, which held the bundle of herbs, to Ludo's arms, which held her magical book.

He grinned openly as he repeated the words he had just spoken a moment ago. "If you take the fennel, I get to keep this book."

But did she have to do what he said? They hadn't made a bargain. She hadn't said *thank you* or *please* or even *sorry*. Still, something in his eyes gave her pause.

She had grown up with stories of Faerie, first told by her father, then stories she had found in epic poems. From what she knew, the rules of Faerie could not be broken. Faerie itself made it physically impossible to break a bargain or a vow. If a promise was made, it could not be undone.

Maybe this exchange was nothing more than some simple spoken words. Or maybe it was some official Faerie bargain that couldn't be broken. If the exchange worked like other fae rules, she would have to give him the book once she took the fennel. Faerie itself would make it impossible to break the terms of the exchange.

Quintus pinched the bridge of his nose as he let out a heavy sigh. "You should have let me negotiate before you told him what we wanted."

Her head snapped toward him, though her hand stayed resting on the table with the herb in her fist. "You could have jumped in at any time."

Except he couldn't have. Not really. His breathing had grown so heavy, it sounded like he was breathing through piles of pillows instead of regular air. Beads of sweat slid down his hairline and then down his neck.

For all his claims about fae healing, he clearly needed the remedy for scurpus more than ever. Did that mean she'd have to give up her book? What if Faerie itself needed to communicate with her again? If she gave up the book, would she give up that chance as well?

Ludo lifted the book to his nose and inhaled. A light smile played at his lips as he took in the scent of the pages. "This used to sit in the Crystal Thorn Castle library. It has more magic inside it than a mortal like you could ever imagine."

Her eyes narrowed to tiny slits, but she didn't glare at Ludo like she wanted. Instead, she brought her face close to the table. Unclenching her fist, she examined the bundle of herbs before her.

The narrowing of her eyes lasted for only a moment before her hand whipped backward. "This isn't even fennel."

Ludo tore his blue and red eyes away from the book just long enough to throw her a skeptical eyebrow raise. "What?"

She pulled both her hands far away from the herb and reached across the table. "Give me back my book. I'm not trading it for some herb I don't even need."

He blinked at her, then turned his gaze to the table. "That *is* fennel."

Letting out a haughty chuckle, she rolled her shoulders back. "Between the two of us, which one has been an apothecary in the mortal realm and has used fennel in a remedy before? Just me?"

The glint inside his eyes dulled as he stared at her with more focus. After another beat, he turned toward Quintus. "She was not truly an apothecary in the mortal realm, was she?"

"She was." Quintus answered without hesitation, but then a cough erupted from his lips. It took several hacks before he could speak again. "She was a rather good apothecary too, from what I heard. Better than any the town had ever had before."

Those words set Ludo's teeth on edge. He dropped the book to his lap and grabbed the bundle of herbs from the table. "But I was told this is fennel."

"Did a mortal tell you that?" Chloe raised an eyebrow. "Because mortals can lie."

After a small sigh, she turned to Quintus. "This is obviously a dead end. Maybe we should go to Swiftsea."

"This *is* fennel. It has to be." Ludo shook the herb toward her, its dried green stalks trembling at the movement.

With a scoff, she jammed her hands against her hips. "You want me to prove it to you?"

He lifted his eyebrows, accepting the challenge.

Her fingers fished through her leather bag until she found a cotton square that held one of her pre-made poultices. It had everything it needed except for the fennel and a little water. Luckily, she had a vial of water in her bag ready to go.

After untying the square and spreading out the other ingredients, she then retrieved a small mortar and pestle from her bag.

"Drop a bit of that herb in here." She gestured toward the mortar. Ludo eyed her suspiciously, but when she shrugged and reached for her book, he finally nodded. He untied the little bundle and pulled a few stalks away from the rest.

"Just a little, mind you, not too much." She began crushing the herb as soon as it dropped into her mortar. By the time she finished crushing it, Quintus had slumped even farther into the blue velvet sofa beneath him. His head lolled to one side, resting half on the arm of the sofa and half on the back of it.

Tingles shot through her veins when she sprinkled the crushed herb into the poultice before her. It only took a moment to add water and combine the ingredients together.

Once finished, she lifted the cape covering Quintus's chest. He made no reaction to the movement at all, almost as if he hadn't even noticed it.

Pounding filled her veins when she started spreading the poultice across his chest. Heat tingled through her fingertips each time she made contact with his skin. The fever heating him had risen much higher than a mortal could bare.

It wasn't too late to save him though. It couldn't be.

She rubbed the last of the poultice onto his chest and then threw a look at Ludo that made it clear she had proven her point.

"If that herb really was fennel like you claim, this remedy would cure the iron sickness affecting Quintus. Do you see that gray tinge across his forehead? It's a result of the illness."

She spread the ingredients out over his chest just to further her point. "This poultice should be healing him already."

Ludo had risen completely off his chair. Now he hovered over the table, leaning as far across it as he could to get a better look at Quintus.

Lifting Quintus's hand into the air, she gestured toward his fingertips. "This gray tinge on his fingers should recede, and yet you can see…"

All three of them, even the heavy-breathing Quintus, leaned forward at the same moment. Their eyes narrowed, staring at the fingers. Shallow breaths filled the space between them as they waited. And waited.

Then, right before their very eyes, the gray tinge began to recede. Light brown with a copper undertone overtook the gray tinge. It crawled over it until even the gray at the very tips of Quintus's fingers had been swallowed up.

Quintus didn't seem to notice how his fevered skin had already cooled. He just stared at his fingers with the utmost confusion. "It *is* working."

With a gasp, Chloe clapped a hand over her mouth. "It is? How can this be?" She brought the fingers closer to her face, donning an expression of shock.

Ludo stared at the pair of them, his gaze jumping from one to the other while his face stayed as still as stone. But then his eyebrows pinched together as he glanced at Chloe. He met her gaze for a moment, then stood up with a nod. "Just as I said, the herb was fennel. Now I can take my book."

He reached for the book, which he had set back onto the table when he had stood. But when he reached for it, she reached for it too. Her fingers closed around it just as his did on the opposite side of it.

"This is mine now," he said with a snarl.

"No." She pulled the book back toward herself. "You said if I *took* the fennel, I would have to give you the book. But I didn't take it. You gave it freely."

His mouth dropped just as he lost his grip on the book. "I…you…" He shook his head. "But I said—"

Quintus smirked as he let out a dry chuckle. "She tricked you." He sat up taller, eyeing Chloe with a smirk. "A mortal tricked a fae."

Ludo would not be happy about being tricked, that much Chloe knew. But right now, she'd take any consequences just to see that twitch in Ludo's eye again. Even if it might be dangerous.

18

CHLOE COULDN'T HELP HERSELF FROM grinning, though she knew it might agitate Ludo more. Across the table, Ludo's eye did narrow, but then he donned a wide smile. "Very impressive for a mortal. I may have a thing or two I could learn from you."

She grinned as she sat taller in the sofa. With Quintus's arm and scurpus taken care of now, she could finally finish the food she had started.

When she reached for it though, Ludo stretched his hand out to touch her book with a single finger. "I do wonder, has Faerie itself ever tried to communicate with you through that book?"

The question may not have had any ill intent behind it, but this was Faerie. She wasn't about to take a chance like that. And on that note, maybe she needed to find a better resting place for her book other than her lap.

"Communicate with me?" She rolled her eyes as she stuffed the book back into her leather bag. For good measure, she put the strap over her head and rested it on her shoulder. Even sitting down, it was probably best to keep the bag as close as possible.

"Faerie itself is just the ground beneath us. I know it can't communicate. Why would you suggest something so ridiculous?"

The finger he had used to touch her book now tapped against his chin. "Then what are those markings on your face?"

Her heart stuttered in her chest as the question sank in. Her gaze darted over to Quintus until it landed on the black crescent moon under his left eye. He stared at her face, right in the spot where her star tattoos sat.

His face started twisting with disgust, which would have told Ludo everything he wanted to know. With a laugh, Chloe waved her hand through the air. "Those are nothing. We were just having a bit of fun with a quill and forgot to clean the ink away afterward."

The wrinkling nose on Quintus very slowly went still until he donned a lopsided smirk that did its best to corroborate Chloe's story. Since he couldn't tell an outright lie like her, she could only hope his expression would work well enough to convince Ludo.

The blue-and-red-eyed fae leaned over the table in front of him. "Are you certain it is not a tattoo?"

"A tattoo?" Chloe laughed out loud and touched her fingertips to her collarbone. "No."

When she glanced toward Quintus, he matched her laugh with one of his own. He played along with her ruse a little faster now.

"Of course." Even Ludo smirked a bit as he stood from his wooden chair. "Our fae healing pushes out any ink that is injected into the skin. It happens almost instantly. It should not be possible for a fae to have a tattoo, unless perhaps it is a magical one."

Chloe nodded at him, but he didn't see since he had just ducked behind an enormous pile of clothing, cups, and jewels. "Luckily," he called out from behind the pile, "I happen to have a very excellent ink remover."

He emerged from the pile with a small cloth in his hand. One end of it had been soaked in some sort of liquid, probably the ink remover. She swallowed at the sight of it, her stomach turning over on itself.

When he reached a hand toward her tattoo, she flinched and leaned backward.

Quintus caught the fair-skinned fae by the wrist, immediately wrenching the hand away. "Do not touch her."

Their eyes locked, and each of their expressions grew more calculating. Lifting the cloth upward, Ludo shrugged. "I can wipe away yours instead."

"Sit down." A feral look blazed in Quintus's dark brown eyes. He bared his teeth, which somehow sent every muscle in his face into a splintery edge. He used his head to point at the wooden chair. "Tell us what you want. And no, you cannot have the book, so make it reasonable or we will be on our way. Since you made no bargain nor earned any favor, we do not have to give you anything if we do not want to."

Dropping all pretense, Ludo nodded. His shoulders shivered when he glanced Quintus's way again. The half-soaked cloth got draped over his hand as he used it to grab something from inside a drawer of his table. After settling into his wooden chair again, he dropped an empty sword sheath onto the table.

"Is that the sword sheath you said you stole from the sprites?" Chloe almost snickered as she asked.

Ludo nodded, but she barely noticed it because now her face leaned in close to the table. "This is my father's." Her fingers traced over a small shield marking at the top of the sheath. "Why did the sprites have it? This metal has iron in it." She shook her head, then pinned a glare on the fae across from her. "More importantly, why did *you* have this? It's my father's."

"He cannot have it back." Ludo spoke through his teeth.

"Obviously." She matched the expression with a wry smile. "He's dead."

The color drained from Ludo's face. His gaze flicked to Quintus, as if seeking confirmation of her claim. Whatever expression Quintus gave him made Ludo shrink lower in his chair.

Her thumb brushed over the shield marking with a chevron pointing upward and a star inside. "This is the sheath Elora used to have. She must have given it to the sprites for some reason."

A cough that sounded more like a strangled word sputtered from Ludo's lips. He mouthed the name *Elora* while his eyes bugged out. Then he stared down at the sheath. "If this belonged to your father, that means…"

Chloe met his eyes, anticipating the end of his sentence. "Elora is my sister, yes. Do you know her?"

"I know *of* her," he said, nearly laughing. "Everyone does."

Before she could ask again why he had the sheath, he hovered his hand over it. When his fingers got close to where hers sat, she immediately pulled her hand away and set it in her lap.

His hand continued to hover over the object, like he wished he could touch it. "The craftsmanship of this sheath is extraordinary. Did you know your father is well known in Faerie, not just your sister?"

She narrowed her eyes at him. "I had forgotten, but yes, I knew."

"It looks like you inherited his eye color. Blue eyes are quite stunning on you."

The desire to grab the sheath and whack him upside the head with it sparked in her belly. But Mother had always taught her politeness worked as a better weapon in situations such as this. So, Chloe donned her sweetest smile and fluttered her eyelashes twice. "Thank you."

Quintus inhaled sharply. "Chloe."

"What?" Her polite expression dropped when she glanced up at the horror quavering in his eyes.

He covered his forehead with one hand and shook his head. "You are supposed to know better."

It took another beat before she realized, but by then it was too late. After being so careful, after tricking the fae already, he had now tricked her. She had said *thank you.*

Her fingers pressed against her lips as she held her breath. When she finally exhaled again, tight words came out. "It slipped out. I wasn't thinking." She shook her head back and forth, which

140

sent several strands of hair out of her bun. "I've been in the mortal realm for too long. I *should* have known better."

Ludo smirked. "You get to keep your precious book, *Chloe*, but now you owe me a favor. And this time, I will get what I want."

Quintus made a fist with one hand, which curled tight enough to make his veins pop out. His knees jutted out and to the side, tucking her own knees behind his. He put his uncurled hand onto his hip, shielding the rest of her body with his bent arm.

His eyes narrowed as he leaned forward. "She is under my protection. Whatever favor you ask, whatever thing you expect to get from her, it will be overseen by me. So watch your words carefully."

Though it was clear Ludo wanted to appear unaffected by the words, his shoulders still drooped a little. He cleared his throat, which only added to his deflated appearance.

Whatever he wanted though never got stated.

Several horns sounded at once, causing all of them to turn toward the noise. Just as they started looking, a thin sword and a heavy axe burst through the front door of Ludo's home. Two mortals followed the weapons, holding them tight.

Chloe recognized the first mortal at once.

Mishti's long braid swung in a wide circle. But once her gaze found Chloe's, she opened her mouth. "We've come to rescue you."

19

ARMS WRAPPED AROUND CHLOE'S WAIST, lifting her off the velvet sofa and behind the nearest bookshelf. Quintus moved in the single blink of an eye, his arms holding her tight but not so tight that it hurt. Once they were hidden from view, he loosened his grip.

With one hand still at the small of her back, he urged her to keep moving. The mortals might have seen which bookcase they had just hid behind, but if they kept moving, the mortals wouldn't know where to look next. Chloe and Quintus had their choice of numerous hiding places with all the piles of objects dotting the room.

After guiding her behind a pile of chairs and upholstered stools, Quintus glanced toward her. He looked straight at her shoulder, probably confirming her leather bag was still draped there, which it was.

Leaning as close to his ear as she dared, she whispered, "Did she say they were here to *rescue* me?"

His jaw ticked as he turned toward her. A whisper left his lips, and it was so soft, it didn't seem humanly possible. "They are lying. They tried to attack you last time you were with them."

Pressing an urgent hand against her back again, he led her behind a pile of napkins, baskets, and candelabras.

Whatever organization—if any—existed in this room, it certainly only made sense to Ludo. The blue-and-red-eyed fae had disappeared from her view, which didn't mean much since Chloe could only see a sliver of the room from behind the pile she and Quintus crouched behind.

A voice called out. "I know Ivanna tried to hurt you, but she is always too hasty with her anger. I spoke to Portia. She agreed that you should be with us. We can save you from the fae who are trying to manipulate you."

Mishti had a way of filling the room with her voice, though she didn't even speak that loud. Still, intimidation seemed to be her greatest asset, even when she wasn't trying.

Chloe glanced toward Quintus for his reaction. He rolled his eyes and immediately scanned the area around them, probably looking for a way out.

His shoulders tensed. "If we can find a window, I will glamour us to be invisible, and we can jump out. The glamour will not mask the sound we make, but it should confuse them long enough for me to open a door. Then we can get away."

Ducking farther down, she raised an eyebrow. "Can you open a door right now? Have you healed enough for it?"

"Yes." His voice came out sure, but judging by the wrinkle across his nose, some doubt still lingered. "As long as they do not use any iron against us before then."

That didn't seem like a bet worth taking. Peeking through a small sliver between a candelabra and a basket, Chloe caught a glimpse of the mortals. Mishti stood there, swinging her sword as she scanned the room. A new mortal had come with her too. The man had golden hair and a mole as big as a thumbnail on his chin.

He reached into his pocket and retrieved a transparent jar with a small metal cup at the bottom of it. Chloe's stomach jolted at the sight of it. Maybe the cup didn't have any iron in it though. Maybe the mortals just intended to use it as a threat.

But then the man lit a match and threw it into the cup. Considering how quickly a large flame ignited, the cup at the bottom of the jar clearly had fuel inside it.

Swallowing over the tightness in her throat, Chloe glanced back at Quintus. Bright red spots broke out across his neck. The copper undertones in his skin flashed with a crimson hue. The iron flame inside the mortal man's jar had already begun to work.

Quintus flinched and eyed the area around them again. When he moved them forward, she followed, but she bit her lip as she did.

They ducked behind another enormous pile of objects. A bit of light shone onto the ground, so there must have been a window close by somewhere. If there hadn't been so many piles of random items scattered throughout the room, it probably would have been easy to find the window. After another hard swallow, she opened her mouth. "I think I should go with them."

A short exhale puffed from Quintus's nose. He didn't even bother looking toward her as he guided them both behind the next pile.

"I mean it," she said in hush.

"And what would you do once they have you?" His eyes narrowed, clearly more focused on the window from which that light came than on what she had just said.

He tried to move forward, but she planted herself in place. She wouldn't move until he looked at her. Once their eyes locked, she raised both eyebrows. "I'll turn over the troughs surrounding the castle while I'm there. I'll make sure to do it to the ones you showed me in front of that doorway. I'll make a way for you to get into the castle, but I'll do it from the inside where they are less likely to suspect me. You'll be able to sneak in even easier than we already planned."

His eyes stayed open so long without blinking that water started glistening inside them. When they started to water, he finally closed his eyes and shook his head. "No."

"You have to consider it." She wrapped a hand around his wrist, which immediately attracted his gaze.

Staring at her hand, he shook his head. "And what if you get frightened? You always freeze up in a fight."

"There won't be any fight if I go with them willingly." Her fingers slid down his wrist until they rested overtop his hand. With a gentle squeeze, she spoke in her most reassuring tone. "I can handle this."

His gaze never left her fingers. He stared at them so hard, she could almost feel it. Warmth from his hand seeped into her skin until it tingled with heat. He still said nothing, but the fact that he hadn't refused said enough on its own.

Her head tilted toward the light where there had to be a window nearby. "You go that way. I'll distract them. Come to the castle tomorrow, and I'll take care of the troughs full of iron flames."

His fingers twitched under hers, but then he twisted his wrist until their palms met. It only lasted for a breath, not even that, but heat surged in her hand at the small contact. His fingers wove between hers for only an instant and then he jumped behind a different pile of objects.

Walking might be more difficult than she expected with the sudden headiness that overcame her. Swallowing, she crawled across the mossy floor until she hid behind a pile in the opposite direction Quintus had gone. After edging herself even deeper in the opposite direction of him, she let out a whimper and quietly called out for help.

Footsteps immediately pounded toward her. Mishti spoke again, even firmer than before. "Can you wriggle out of his grasp long enough to scream?"

Chloe pressed her lips together, not even moving. The longer she stayed silent, the more time it gave Quintus to get away.

The mortal man with the mole on his chin scoffed. "She's probably just trying to trick us. I bet the fae is waiting and ready to pounce."

While he spoke, Chloe shuffled across the floor to hide behind the pile Ludo had gotten that ink remover from earlier. The Fairfrost fae still hadn't made an appearance that Chloe knew of. He had probably run off in fear the moment the mortals arrived.

As she moved, she caught a glimpse of Mishti. The young woman held out her own jar of flames. Her face was stoic as she scanned the room. "That fae couldn't stop us now even if he tried." Her shoulders stiffened as she checked behind a bookcase. When looking behind it didn't reveal anything, she called out. "We are having a party tomorrow night. You can join us if you let us rescue you."

"Yes, a party with food and dancing." The golden-haired mortal rubbed his belly as he checked behind a pile of boots.

The thought of food sent a flip through Chloe's gut. She had eaten most of one pastry from Ludo, but the second still sat forgotten on the table in the middle of the room. The food had been delicious, but it certainly hadn't been enough to fill her up. Now her mouth watered at the thought of a grand banquet with as much food as she wanted to stuff into her mouth.

Mishti drew her sword and stepped across the ground evenly. "And we found the most spectacular dresses. You're sure to find one you love. Mine is blue as midnight and has frosty white pearls that sparkle in the candlelight."

The golden-haired man with the mole threw her a sideways glance. "Why are *you* excited about wearing a dress? I thought you preferred your uniform. It's much more suitable for fighting."

She lowered her eyebrows so much they nearly covered her eyes. "Just because I'm good at fighting doesn't mean I can't like dresses. I'm allowed to have more than one personality trait."

Chloe had to suck her lips into her mouth to keep from chuckling. There had been more than a few times in her life she wished she could have said similar words to the young men in her town. Getting into a low squat, she prepared to knock over the pile of objects in front of her and pretend as if she had just managed a great escape from a fae while doing it.

Before she could enact her plan, all the little strings holding items from the ceiling snapped. Every item came crashing down. Some of the items were simple candlesticks or teacups, but many of them were heavy, like large vases. Some of the strings even held weapons. The strings couldn't have snapped on their own. Magic had clearly been involved.

A barrage of items threw Chloe to the ground, and the pile at her side did indeed topple over her. Judging by the gasps that erupted, Mishti and her mortal companion had been hit by the falling items too.

As she attempted to throw the pile off her, Chloe caught a glimpse of Ludo disappearing through the front door of his home and into the forest. He must have been the one to make the items fall from the ceiling. At least both he and Quintus were gone now. It would be easier for her to reveal herself to the mortals now that doing so posed no threat to any fae.

She shoved the rest of the items off her, but when she did so, something sharp sliced across the back of her hand. Pain clenched her teeth together while a hiss shook through them.

If the mortals hadn't already found her, it wouldn't take them long to do so now. Her gaze darted to the leather bag still hanging from her shoulder. She still had a bit of that hideous cotton dress, which she could use to make a bandage. If she just poured some tincture on the wound and then smothered it with a bit of honey, she could bandage it and be on her way in just a few minutes.

She reached for the cotton dress but caught a glimpse of the other mortals out of the corner of her eye. Both of them had much larger wounds than she did. Mishti even had a small dagger that had been driven into her calf.

And what had Dunstan always said? Selflessness was the most admirable quality a woman could have. Chloe could have taken care of her own wound first, but what kind of person would she be if she ignored the others' wounds for her own? Blood did pour down the back of her hand and onto her palm though. Maybe she should take care of herself first, if only so she didn't get blood everywhere.

With a sigh, she glanced down at the slice marring her skin. It wouldn't take long to clean and dress her own wound before tending to the others. If she did, it would even be easier to help the others afterward.

The thought got flicked away nearly as soon as it appeared. Faerie had clearly gotten to her. Guilt curdled in her gut as she tried to stand. How selfish to think of herself when two other people lay even more injured than her just across the room.

But when she tried to step forward, her foot got caught in some sort of trap. A cloth gag wrapped around her mouth at the same moment, clearly falling into place thanks to some sort of magic. The cloth smothered the screams she tried to release. With one foot hanging from the ceiling and her hair dangling nearly to the floor, she could do nothing except watch the injured mortals writhe in pain on the ground.

Ludo appeared in a doorway and swung his axe. The aim should have split the axe across the mortal man's forehead, except the mortal acted first. Kicking one foot out, the man with the mole threw Ludo off balance before his blow could land. The mortal reached for his jar of flames and chucked it straight at Ludo.

The red in Ludo's eyes flashed with a glow when the still-burning flames hit his skin. An ear-piercing shriek shook the walls of his home. His teeth gritted as he sprinted off into the forest.

The mortal man took off after him, though he ran much slower.

"What about Chloe?" Mishti winced as she tore the dagger from her leg and tightly wrapped the wound with a cloth from her pocket.

"Forget her." The mortal man disappeared through the front door. He called out loud enough to be heard as he ran away. "I told you she didn't want to be rescued. We need to kill that fae before he gets away."

Mishti darted after him, not bothering to glance behind her where Chloe still hung from the ceiling.

In a flash they were both gone. Ludo was gone. And of course, Quintus was gone too. Chloe had caught her leather bag before it fell to the floor, but she had nothing else except one leg tied to the ceiling and no way to free herself.

20

COTTON DUG INTO CHLOE'S TONGUE, pressing it deep into her throat. A rope wrapped tight around one of her boots. It attached to a large branch in the leafy ceiling above. With her leather bag held tight to her chest, her body lightly swung from one side to the next.

Her fingers itched to remove her gag first, but that could cause her to lose grip on her leather bag. Instead, she flipped the bag over until its opening faced the ceiling instead of the floor. Maybe she hung upside down, but the bag didn't have to.

Reaching inside, she retrieved her magical book. The strap of the leather bag got settled into the crook of her elbow, while she carefully tucked the bottom edge of the book against her chest.

Since she swung upside down from the ceiling, the book had a good chance of clattering to the ground if she wasn't careful. Holding it tight against her chest helped to keep it from falling.

Her eyes scanned the pages while blood rushed into her head. She had to give her head a little shake just to keep spots from appearing in her eyes.

Remedies for illnesses along with descriptions of plants and animals stared back at her. Had she been hoping Faerie itself would communicate with her again? That it would give her a way out of this situation?

Though she knew how ridiculous and hopeful such thoughts were, she admitted to herself that had been exactly what she'd been hoping for.

But the pages of the book had no extra magic, no insightful words for her to read that could free her from the rope holding her upside down.

Buzzing tingled at the tips of her fingers. The ribbon in her bun barely held onto her hair as she swung lightly again. Magic. She had magic inside her. Could magic save her?

Closing her eyes, she pushed all her hope, all her concentration, into her hand. Perhaps a shower of golden sparks at her fingertips couldn't help in this exact situation, but if she could manage a little magic, maybe she'd also figure out a way to use that magic to free herself.

But her hand stayed as plain and mortal as it always did.

The gash along the back of her hand even dripped more blood from it, which dribbled through the hairs on her arm. Considering all the items that had fallen onto her, the wound would probably get infected if she didn't treat it soon.

Now, freeing herself from the rope on the ceiling seemed more important. She glanced toward the book again and immediately scowled.

Why had she felt it so important to touch something smaller than her book during that ritual to get her magic? She had tried to use magic twice now and both times she'd been holding the book in her hand. If she'd just bonded to the book, despite its inconvenience, she probably would have been able to free herself in an instant.

Instead, she had bonded to Quintus, which left him with the mortal marking of a moon on his face and the even worse mark of stars on her own. A scowl knotted her muscles until even her fingers had clenched.

Unfortunately, that small movement was all it took.

The magical book in her hands slipped from her grip and toppled to the ground. Her arms flailed as she tried to catch it. Instead of succeeding, she only managed to drop her leather bag along with it too.

A loud *humpf* left her mouth. At least she could remove the stupid gag from her mouth now. Her fingers dug against the cotton until it slipped under her chin and off her mouth. Now it rested against her neck, almost like a choker.

With her voice free again, she shouted as loud as she could. "Quintus!"

After a very reasonable wait time of a single breath, she shouted his name again. This time, she waited a little longer to see if he had heard.

Of course, nothing but thick silence met her shouts. Quintus had obviously gone too far away to hear her. He had probably gotten far enough from the iron flames and then opened a door that led to an entirely different area. Somewhere he'd never hear her, even with his heightened fae hearing.

Blood pounded in her temples. If she didn't find a way out of this soon, she had a very real chance of passing out. Then she might never be free.

Gritting her teeth, she shouted again. This time she simply called for help. Maybe the mortals were still close enough to hear her.

It became clear much too soon that the mortals would not come to her aid either.

Itchy cords of pain stung across the wound on the back of her hand. Why hadn't she just cleaned her wound before worrying about the others? If she had just taken care of herself first, she could have avoided this entire predicament.

Maybe she should have felt guilty for such a selfish thought, but for once, she didn't care. With a large *floof,* her skirts finally fell the rest of the way down. Now they surrounded her head and arms like a tent.

The clasp at her neck had the entire weight of her cloak pulling it down. It dug into her throat. That combined with the blood rushing to her head made it difficult to breathe properly. Her fingers shot toward her cloak and unclasped it.

She had to get out of this mess, and she had to do it soon.

Lifting the hem of her skirts up so she could see again, she stared hard at her foot. A thick rope wrapped around the ankle of her boot. She had no dagger, no knife, and nothing even remotely sharp on her.

If the rope had been wrapped around the toe of her boot or even around its middle, she might have been able to wriggle her way out. But it wrapped around her ankle, where she had no chance of slipping or shaking free.

With a whimper, she let her head hang back down. Her dress billowed around her like a tent again, covering the little view she had of the room. A loud grumble erupted from her stomach. What a perfect thing to remember at a time like this. She was hungry too. Starving.

And now she wished she had just eaten that second pastry before cleaning Quintus's wound and healing his scurpus. If she had eaten first, she could have eaten *and* healed him. But since she had taken care of him first, she had completely lost the chance to take care of herself.

A tight squeeze worked through her chest. She was supposed to save Faerie, not get stuck hanging from a rope inside a random fae's house. If no one came to help her down, would she die up there?

Just when hope slipped away, a tiny spark of it lit again. She threw her skirts away from her face and curled her stomach up until her fingers could reach her boot.

Maybe her boot had no chance of getting out of the rope's grasp, but what about her foot? Her fingers moved nimbly across the laces of her boots. She untied its knot and then loosened the laces as much as she could.

After only a few moments, she had to fall back and let herself rest. The muscles in her stomach ached after holding her upright in such a position. Her arms ached now too. Blood rushed so heavily to her head she could feel her cheeks heating.

One more time. If she tried just one more time, she could do it.

Taking a deep breath, she curled her stomach up again. Her fingers flew across her laces, loosening them as much as possible. Her foot began wriggling downward as she attempted to free it from the rope. When the arch of her foot met the tight spot where the rope wrapped around the outside of the boot, she had to use every bit of her strength to wriggle around it.

She held her breath. If it didn't work, she wouldn't have any energy left to try again. This was her chance. Do or die.

With a strong wrench, her foot finally freed itself from her boot. Her back slammed against the ground beneath her. The moss helped to pad her fall but not by much. Air knocked out of her in a rush. It took several coughs and sputters before she could breathe again.

Once her foot came free, the boot tumbled out of the rope too, falling down beside her.

Tears welled in her eyes as all the aches in her muscles throbbed. Her stomach muscles had never been strained so tight. Her back ached where it had slammed against the ground. Not to mention, bruises still throbbed in her side where Ludo had whacked her with his axe handle.

Darkness seeped into the house, which her stomach took as another cue to grumble. With tears gathering in her eyelashes, she stomped across the floor until she reached the sofa she'd been sitting in not long ago. Dust and broken debris covered the table now.

When she reached for the uneaten pastry, she realized bits of the porcelain plate now stabbed straight through it. The fact that she considered eating around the broken bits of porcelain only proved how serious her hunger had gotten.

But then her gaze landed on her father's sword sheath that also sat on the table. It ignited an idea within her.

Grabbing the sheath with one hand, she also tore off a bit of the pastry with her other. She then gathered her leather bag and book and even donned her cloak and boot again.

With the sheath and pastry still in her hands, she exited the home made of trees.

Darkness had claimed the air outside. Despite the aching in her muscles, despite the tears slipping down her cheeks, she still looked up to examine the sky.

It had no moon and no stars.

If Quintus were there, he would have gloated. If she'd had any smidgeon of strength left in her, she might have chuckled at the thought.

Her eyes focused now on the only lights that did fill the air above her. The sprites. She'd never been given explicit instructions on how to use a sprite to send a message, but she had seen it done a few times before.

She wondered if sprites even delivered messages for mortals like her. Since she had just come from Ludo's house, whom they already distrusted, she might have to work a little harder to get on their good side.

Now it was time to see if her idea would work.

21

AN UNSTEADY TREMBLE PASSED THROUGH Chloe's arm as she lifted it into the air. Only half of it came from fear; the other half came from the complete exhaustion that seized every muscle in her body. With her palm facing upward, she clicked her tongue three times.

One of the glowing green lights from above immediately flew down and landed on her palm. A sprite blinked back. She had a mane of lilac-colored hair growing from her head, but it looked more like actual lilacs than hair. Her brown skin had a lustrous sheen that stood out beautifully against the yellow tunic and pants she wore.

Swallowing hard, Chloe lifted the sword sheath from her side. "I have the sword sheath Ludo stole from you. Do you want it back?"

The sprite's green and brown eyes went wide at the sight of the object. Her lilac hair shook as the sprite's wings fluttered and lifted her into the air. She flew down toward the sheath. In a flash, a whole swarm of sprites joined her until they surrounded the sheath. They touched only the leather belt as they carried it upward.

They flew so fast it just took a blink before the sheath had nearly disappeared from view.

"Wait." Chloe waved her hand at the sprites and then held it out flat again. "I also have to send a message."

She had only given them the sheath in hopes that it would get her on their good side, where Ludo obviously didn't reside. To her relief, the lilac-haired sprite landed with a tiny plop onto Chloe's hand again.

Her gaze caught on the sprite's stunning shimmery yellow tunic before she shook her head and remembered her plan. Pinching the smidgeon of food she had grabbed between her fingers, she held it out to the sprite. That last bite had been the only piece semi-presentable to eat. It hurt when the sprite took it away.

Chloe bit her bottom lip. "Will that work as an offering?"

The sprite's brown and green eyes sparkled as she tilted the bit of pastry back and forth between her hands. After a quick nod, the sprite stuffed the food into her pocket.

Relief flooded Chloe's veins. "I have a message for Quintus of Crystal Thorn. It's from me, Chloe." Her lips pursed as she tried to think of how to finish that sentence. "The, uh…mortal." Once the words left her lips, she looked back at the sprite. "Does that work?"

With a smirk, the sprite bounced her head with a nod.

Nodding to herself now, Chloe continued. "Tell him…" She chewed on her lip and stared off into the forest. "The mortals left me." She tapped her chin. "Oh, and Ludo is gone too." It took another few taps of her chin before she could finally finish. "It's a long story, but I'm all alone at Ludo's house." A gulp pressed against her throat. "Could you come get me?"

By the time she finished, the little sprite was tapping her toe against Chloe's palm. Realizing the message had finally concluded, she immediately flew off even faster than the other sprites had.

Now Chloe just had to wait. She checked the clasp of her cloak and then checked the strap of her leather bag. Whether logical or not, she then checked the contents of her leather bag.

The true fear in her mind came crashing forward now she had too much time to think. What if Quintus didn't come? Without him, she had no idea how to get back to the castle. How long could she survive Faerie alone?

She only had a moment to consider those fears before a swirling tunnel that looked like a blurred forest appeared before her. The golden lights that twinkled among the black smudges of the door gave her a comfort she didn't expect.

When Quintus stepped through the door and onto the path just ahead of her, she was struck with the overwhelming desire to fall into his arms and sob.

Her aching muscles probably would have sent her straight to the ground in a heap if she had tried to run toward him though. She praised the pain that managed to hold her back.

Something about his face seemed tighter than usual as he stepped toward her. His pointed ears were pricked a little higher. His cheekbones gleamed with an extra sharpness.

He walked straight up to her. For a moment, it seemed like he wanted to take her by the shoulders, but his hands stayed at his sides instead. He swallowed loud enough for her to hear it. "What did you give the sprites as an offering?"

She held his gaze for three full blinks before a chuckle tumbled from her lips. "That's what you're worried about right now? You're afraid I gave away the harp string?"

Pink tinged the tops of his pointed ears as he stepped away. He scoffed and did a half shrug that was the opposite of convincing. "Why would you assume that?"

Raising both eyebrows, she stood on her tiptoes until her eyes came right up to his chin. "Say you don't care then. Say you weren't worried I gave away my last reminder of you."

His entire body tensed as he glanced down at her. His gaze darted from her eyes to that spot just under her eyes where her star tattoos rested.

She could feel his gaze under her skin in a warm tingle that brought heat to her cheeks.

After swiveling his gaze between her eyes and her tattoo, his gaze suddenly dropped lower. To her lips. His eyes immediately slammed shut as he shook his head. When he opened them again, he stared straight into her eyes and nowhere else. "Did you?"

"No." She stepped back and brushed a blonde strand of hair away from her face. Heat flushed in her cheeks while her heart hammered. Getting close like that was supposed to get *him* bothered. It was not supposed to make her react in the same way. Judging by the blood pounding in her veins, her body had clearly not gotten that message.

She turned herself toward the forest, desperate to look anywhere but at him. "I gave away a piece of food that I would have much rather eaten."

He did nothing to hide the deep sigh of relief that slipped through his lips. Only then did he examine their surroundings. "What happened?"

Her fingers found the bottom edge of her sleeve, which normally drifted just above the ground. She scratched a thumbnail over it to give herself something to do. "Just when I went to join the mortals, Ludo attacked. He ran off, the mortals followed, and then my foot got caught in a trap, which I only barely escaped."

She rubbed her eyes then, which felt itchy and sleepy after such a long day. Her belly rumbled, though it sounded slightly quieter than it had earlier that day. Once again, the urge to fall into Quintus's arms flooded through her.

He gestured toward the tunnel still swirling behind him. "This door will take us back to the black caves. We should be safe there. No one ever seems to linger in that area except for me."

Pain burst down her spine when she stepped forward. Every muscle in her body ached and moaned at her for moving. If she hadn't been worried what he might think of it, she would have taken Quintus's arm and leaned on him as she walked.

At least the door didn't do anything funny this time. One moment she stood deep in Crystal Thorn Forest right next to Ludo's home, and the next she stood in a small clearing with the black caves on one side and the lush forest of Crystal Thorn on the other. A little fire crackled at the center of the clearing, exactly as it had when she woke up after drowning.

She would have collapsed right there except then she noticed a hunched figure sitting beside the fire. Ludo's light brown hair hung into his icy blue and scarlet red eyes as he dropped small pinches of black soil into a glass vial.

Her face twisted at the sight of him. "What are *you* doing here?"

The slightest flinch passed over Quintus's features as he dug into his pocket. "Until your favor is paid to him, I want him close by." He pulled out the sleeping mat and blankets Chloe had used the night before and set them down at her feet. Then he turned toward the fair-skinned fae. "It will be better than having him show up unexpectedly. And I'm hoping he'll claim his favor sooner rather than later just so he can leave our presence."

Ludo laughed "I won't leave if you continue to bring me to parts of Faerie with items never seen before. I've already gathered opalescent pebbles, this magnificent black soil, even some of the black cave rock."

Quintus stepped toward him with his chest puffed out. "Which you only get to keep if you do your part."

Rolling his eyes, Ludo tucked the vial of black soil into his pocket. "Fine. I suppose you are hungry."

Chloe had just finished shaking out the blankets over her sleeping mat, but now her head jerked toward Ludo.

160

"He can conjure food," Quintus said as he pulled his own sleeping mat from his pocket.

Her mouth watered as she dropped herself onto the sleeping mat. She caught a glimpse of the wound on her hand, which looked even more awful than it had earlier. It had dust and grime on it now, but since it had stopped bleeding, she chose to ignore it. "I thought only brownies could conjure food."

A sly smile danced across Ludo's face. "The brownies taught me how." Once the words left his mouth, he started coughing. Was this what happened when a fae lied? After the third grinding cough erupted from him, he shrugged. "Well, I got the knowledge from them anyway."

He pulled a large porcelain bowl from his pocket.

Rolling her eyes, Chloe brushed away the wrinkles in her blankets. "Did they give you that knowledge as willingly as you gave me the fennel?"

He chuckled. "Something like that."

His blue and red eyes shifted to stare at his hands. His eyes narrowed, looking even more carefully than before. "I cannot conjure *any* food, mind you. It has to be something I have made before, something I have made often. The process has to be so deeply engrained in my mind that I can make the food without any recipe before me."

He brought his hands together until the palms faced each other. "You see, when you conjure food, you still have to make the food, you just do it in your mind instead of with your hands."

With that, he shut his eyes. His fingers twitched and so did his closed eyes. He breathed in and out steadily. Each breath seemed to cost him more than the last.

But then a thin line of steam wafted into the air above the porcelain bowl. Chloe leaned forward to get a closer look.

Rich stew with floating meat chunks and boiled vegetables sat inside the bowl. She breathed in to capture its spicy and sour scent.

After another moment, Ludo's eyes flew open. He glanced right at her, probably trying to gauge how impressed she was. He had turned toward her too fast for her to school her expression, so he had probably seen amazement etched all over her face.

When he retrieved a small bowl and spoon from his pocket and scooped stew inside the bowl, she took it gratefully.

The first bite warmed her mouth perfectly. Not too hot. Not too cold. The meat was so tender it fell apart in her mouth. The boiled vegetables had the perfect combination of soft and crisp. The herbs flavored the broth in a wonderful way, blending perfectly with the sour and delicious aftertaste.

Based on how he described the magic, Ludo must have been an excellent cook. If he weren't, the stew never would have turned out so delicious.

Instead of saying so, she kept that particular piece of information to herself.

Quintus got his own bowl of stew and stared across the fire at Chloe as he ate it. He said nothing. He just stared with those rich brown eyes that had a way of sending flutters into her stomach.

Maybe talking would ease some of those flutters. She swallowed another bite of soup, then glanced off into the forest. "The mortals are having a party tomorrow."

Even with her gaze turned away, she still saw how Quintus arched an eyebrow.

Shrugging, she scooped more stew into her mouth. "I don't know much else about it, but I thought it might be a good time to sneak into the castle and save the fae inside."

Quintus's gaze turned even more intense. "Will the party last all day? Will it begin when day dawns or after night falls?"

"I just said I don't know." If he would just stop staring at her like that, she would have been able to think more clearly.

Slurping up the last of her stew, she crawled into her bed with her dress and cloak and even her leather bag under the covers with her. She turned away from Quintus and Ludo and hugged the leather bag tight to her chest.

For all her anger toward him, she hadn't realized how much she trusted Quintus until now that a less trustworthy fae sat among them. Ludo's presence did not make the space seem safe enough for sleeping. She didn't have much choice now though.

Hopefully the Fairfrost fae wouldn't try anything while she slept because she couldn't keep her eyes open even if she tried. In only a few breaths, sleep overtook her.

22

HEAT BURNED AT THE BACK of Chloe's hand while pain throbbed through it. That stupid cut had turned into a gash so bad it woke her from her sleep. The dusky light above had the soft whisperings of morning rising from its edges, so dawn would probably come soon.

Sitting up, she first checked that she still had her leather bag held tight to her chest. After confirming that, she checked the items inside. They appeared untouched. Now, she examined her hand.

Inflamed red skin surrounded the cut that went from her knuckles down past her wrist. The skin was tight and hot. Dried blood caked the inside of the cut. Some of it had turned black. Dust and other debris must have gotten inside it too for how infected it had gotten overnight.

Despite the pain, a part of her found gratitude for that cut. It allowed her to test something she had thought of just as sleep clouded her mind the night before.

Putting the strap of her leather bag over her head, she got off her sleeping mat to find Quintus's. He lay even closer to her now than he had the other night. He had also positioned himself between her and Ludo, which she was annoyingly grateful for.

164

Once at his side, she shook his shoulder. His whispered name flitted from her lips.

Deep breaths rose and fell in his chest, but the moment she said his name, his eyes flicked open. When he caught sight of her at his side, he jolted upright. "What happened?" His gaze raked over her entire body. "Are you hurt? Are you in danger?"

She shushed him and glanced over at Ludo's sleeping mat. The Fairfrost fae continued to sleep without stirring. "I'm fine. Just sit still for a moment. I probably didn't even need to wake you up."

Quintus ran a hand through his hair, which tossed the soft curls across his forehead. Ignoring it as best she could, she reached out for his hand.

She very specifically touched him with just one finger on his wrist. That position had been the least romantic one she could think of. Still, when she pressed her skin against his, a heartbeat pulsed under her fingertip.

The small touch froze Quintus until he barely breathed. After a swallow, he glanced into her eyes.

Why did he have to look at her like that? How could she possibly concentrate now?

Closing her eyes, she thought back to Ludo's explanation about how to conjure cooked and prepared food.

Her mind now focused on her hand, the one with the gash in it. With her eyes still closed, she imagined golden sparks shooting from her fingertips. She had no idea if the magic actually shot from her fingertips like it had the day before since her eyes were still closed, but magic definitely seemed to be buzzing inside her.

Now she thought of the same tincture she had used on Quintus's arm the day before. In her mind, she imagined pouring the tincture over her wound, then using a clean cloth to wipe away any dried blood or other grime. The skin around her wound tingled as she thought.

After the tincture, she imagined smothering honey over the wound, along with an extra herb that would help with the inflammation and infection.

Now for the last part, which she feared the most, she imagined the wound healing. She thought of how the muscles and skin would stitch back together, how they'd scab and itch but slowly heal. Then she imagined a tiny scar that eventually faded away completely.

Holding her breath, she opened her eyes. Despite her fear that it wouldn't work, her gaze still darted straight to the wound on the back of her hand.

But now it was gone, *completely* gone. Not even a trace of a scar stretched across her skin.

"Remarkable," Quintus whispered. "You have magic, and you already know how to use it."

"Let me try it on your wound now." She pulled away the cloth that covered the wound he had gotten from Ludo's axe the day before, but it had already healed, except for a thin scar that would probably be gone before midday.

He waved his arm and got to his feet. "Forget that. I have something better to test your magic on."

Leading her into the forest, he gestured ahead. "I have some iron buried nearby in case I ever need to test anything with it. I have tried to create devices that could turn the iron against the mortals, but of course, none of them have worked since mortals are immune to iron."

By the time he finished speaking, he stopped in front of a small dirt mound that had been marked with a sprinkle of wood shavings. Did the wood shavings come from the same project as the wood shaving he had given the sprite? Did it come from the harp he had a drawing of inside of his sketchbook?

"What are we testing?" Chloe tried to tuck a loose strand of hair back into her bun, but her hair had become so knotted and tangled, it wouldn't stay in place.

Kicking the mound away, he dug into the dirt until a large iron candelabra sat before them. He flicked his wrist and lit a fire in each of the spots a candle would go. As soon as the flame burst to life, bright red spots broke across his neck and climbed up to his face.

Though the iron clearly caused him pain, his eyes still danced with mischief. "If you can use your magic to heal yourself, then maybe you can use your magic to create an enchantment that will protect against iron. I cannot create such an enchantment, but I think it is because iron is harmful to me."

She nodded, already reaching for his arm. Her fingers wrapped around his forearm as she considered what to imagine. "I can try. Since I am naturally immune to iron, I can still use magic without a problem. So maybe I *can* create an enchantment around you that will protect you from it."

His eyes went alight, clearly believing in her more than she believed in herself. The splotches of red on his neck had grown so numerous they now covered his entire neck.

Whatever she tried, she needed to do it quickly. Squeezing her hand, she imagined an enchantment hovering just outside Quintus's skin, all around his body. The enchantment encased him, not in a bubble, but in a shield that was the same shape as his body, just ever so slightly larger. For good measure, she turned the enchantment invisible.

She had seen a burst of golden light surrounding him exactly as she imagined, and it even went invisible when she directed it, but did it keep him safe from the iron?

A grin curled his lips upward as the red spots across his neck receded. "It is working."

She let out a sigh of relief, then kicked the candelabra over to put out the flames. No reason to keep the air filled with iron when it didn't need to be.

He leaned toward her. "Remember how you told me about the party the mortals are having today? I spent all night trying to think of how to use it to our advantage, but now, I have a plan better than any I thought of last night. If I glamour myself to look like a mortal, and you use magic to keep me safe from the iron…"

Her eyebrows darted upward. "We won't have to sneak into the castle at all. I can tell them I finally escaped my fae captor, and I'll tell them you're another mortal who got captured too. We'll be able to enter the castle and wander the halls with no one suspecting a thing."

The grin on his face grew. "Exactly. And once we're inside, we can kill the mortals."

Her lip curled as she finally pulled her hand away from his arm.

He must have seen the thoughts in her eyes though because he leaned closer. "We must do something to stop them. We cannot let them continue to poison our land."

"What if we rescue the fae hostages instead?" Chloe chewed on her lip, thinking of Mishti and how she was nothing more than a victim. Almost all the mortals were the same. "What if we find Elora and Brannick and help them and other fae escape? Then, once they are free, we can devise a strategy to beat the mortals without having to kill them."

"There you two are." Ludo stumbled toward them, scratching his chin. He glanced between the two of them as one eyebrow raised higher and higher on his forehead.

"What were you doing? Some bonding ritual that has to do with your tattoos?"

"I need fabric." Quintus made no attempt to answer the question as he began stomping back toward the clearing with the fire.

Ludo trailed after him. "I can get you fabric. What sort do you need?"

Quintus pulled a sketchbook from his pocket and scribbled across it with a pencil. After a few moments, he shoved the sketchbook under Ludo's nose.

The fae's blue and red eyes narrowed at the page. "If I get you the fabric, what will you give me in return?"

A twitch shook Quintus's left eye, right by his moon tattoo. "I will let you stay by our camp and gather whatever items you can find around the black caves. I will even let you attempt to get inside the caves, though that might be impossible."

Chloe cocked up an eyebrow. Impossible? She and Quintus had gotten inside the caves without any trouble. They didn't get far before the magic stopped them from moving forward, but they had gotten inside.

With a nod, Ludo tore the page from the sketchbook. "That is good enough for me. I will stay by these caves as long as you will let me."

His hand whirled in a circle, which opened a swirling door ahead of him. The snowy white color of it seemed to have opalescent clouds hanging throughout it. The tunnel smelled of wet leather and icicles. He disappeared through it a moment later.

The moment he disappeared, Chloe threw a sideways glance at Quintus. "It might be *impossible* for him to get inside the caves?"

"Yes, because I put an enchantment over their entrances." A smirk tilted one side of his mouth upward. "I did not tell him that part, of course. I thought it might be better if he assumed the magic came from Faerie itself and not from me."

She chuckled. "He will probably give up faster that way, just like we did when we tried to step deeper into the cave."

They had reached the clearing again. Chloe went to roll up her bedding, though she glanced toward Quintus before she got there. "What are you going to do with the fabric?"

He shrugged. "If we plan to attend that party, we need suitable clothing."

Her eyes definitely went a little too wide before she could hide it. "That is sweet, but that other dress you made…"

The ghastly thing was so hideous it barely worked as bandage, but was it too cruel to say such a thing out loud?

"I conjured that other dress." Quintus pulled out his sketchbook again, scribbling his pencil across its surface. "This will be different. I am going to craft our clothes."

He only got a few scribbles in before he glanced up at her with a calculating stare. "We need to do something about your hair."

Heat rushed to her cheeks as she stared at the ground. "It's like a rat's nest. I know it." Her cheeks prickled with warmth as her chin fell to her chest. "Maybe if just undo the ribbon and try another bun, it might—"

"I can fix it." Quintus tucked his sketchbook away and produced a wooden brush from his pocket. The bristles looked soft yet sturdy. He gestured that she should sit down in front of him.

Without a word, he removed the ribbon from her bun, and began gently tugging the brush through her knotted hair. The bristles clearly had magic in them because the brushing didn't hurt at all, not even when he worked through the biggest knots.

Her heart leapt in her chest each time his fingers came near her neck or trailed down her back. She had to remind herself to breathe at least a dozen times. But he worked so methodically, he didn't seem to notice the hitches in her breathing. His fae hearing normally would have picked them up, but her hair held his full attention now.

By the time he finished, her blonde hair fell in thick, shiny curls all the way down past her waist. She put her fingers through it, admiring how beautiful it was, especially since it had never been so beautiful ever in her life before.

His own fingers combed through a small section near her face. His eyes focused completely on the blonde strands, still oblivious to how her heart pounded in her chest. He brushed the hair away from her face. "I know the perfect flowers to put in your hair, but we will do that after you've put on your dress."

Ludo arrived not long after. He held two bolts of fabric, one rich and red and more luxurious than anything Chloe had ever felt before. The other fabric was a dark green, almost black, that felt like a mix between leather and velvet.

Quintus shooed Chloe and Ludo away as he got to work. Ludo went straight to scouting the area. He gathered all sorts of small items like bark and stone fragments that Chloe never would have noticed on her own.

Every time she tried to catch a glimpse of Quintus's work, he would position his body to block her view. Finally, she opened her magical book and skimmed its pages to pass the time instead.

Just as a passage about castles caught her eye, Quintus stood. "It is done."

He held up a magnificent red dress with wide sleeves that fluttered all the way to the hem. Gold embroidery patterned every edge of the dress. Even the bottom edge of it had thin golden curlicues along it. At the waist, a golden belt crisscrossed a few times before it tied in a knot with the rest of the belt hanging down the front of the dress.

The belt seemed to be made of golden chains, but each chain link looked more like metallic fabric than like actual metal.

In all her life, she had never seen anything so stunning.

He held it out to her. "I made it slightly too big on purpose. It has magic inside it that will shrink it to fit your body perfectly once you put it on for the first time."

Once she took the dress into her hands, Quintus grabbed Ludo by his collar and yanked him toward the forest. "We will go and gather the flowers for your hair while you change."

When Ludo tried to glance back at her, Quintus shoved his elbow into the Fairfrost fae's gut. Only after they had completely left her view did she begin to change.

The soft fabric of the new dress glided over her skin like a soft, warm rain. It felt loose, but after only a breath, the fabric molded to fit her body perfectly. It had just enough give for movement and for filling her belly with food, but it was also fitted enough to show off her figure.

She felt like a princess. It was truly the most spectacular dress she'd ever worn, and she'd even worn Faerie dresses before.

She was still admiring the dress when Quintus and Ludo returned. Quintus wore new clothes now too. He had crafted the dark green fabric into long pants and a coat that wrapped around him. An ivory cloth belt held the coat wraps in place. Small leather strings that matched his belt fell from each shoulder seam down over his biceps. That same leather formed crossstitching down the sides of his pants.

In his palms, he held a cluster of red roses with lush green leaves still attached.

His eyes gleamed with golden sparks as he grinned at the sight of her.

Now they just had to sneak into the party and rescue the fae stuck inside the castle. And she'd have to keep an enchantment around him the whole night that would protect him from the iron flames. It would have seemed a lot easier to concentrate on the task at hand, except she knew she'd have to touch him the entire night no matter where they went.

The whole, entire night. How could she manage it without losing her heart?

23

GLOSSY, CRYSTAL THORNS EDGED THE path leading to the castle. Chloe kept brushing a hand across the smooth red fabric of her sleeve. She'd never felt something so slippery and luxurious before. Though the quality of the fabric did nothing to soothe the collapsing tangles in her gut.

Quintus ran a hand through his black hair, tumbling his curls in perfect gorgeous waves. He glanced back toward the black caves, but of course they had walked too far away now to see them. His nose wrinkled. "I do not like Ludo sitting there alone while we are gone."

She shrugged. "I'm just glad my leather bag and cloak fit into your pocket so Ludo can't steal anything from me."

The nose wrinkle on Quintus's face immediately shifted into an arched brow. "I can fit anything into my pocket."

"What about a castle?" She threw the question at him just to get him to stop talking. It hurt a little when it worked.

Reaching out his arm, he gestured to a small opening in the sleeve of his coat. It trailed from the crook of his elbow to halfway down his forearm. "This will make it so you can take my arm and touch my skin without being suspicious."

Neither of them knew for sure if she had to maintain contact with his skin or if her magic would still work if she touched the outside of his clothes, but neither of them wanted to take the chance either.

"I can repair the holes easily once we are finished taking back the castle." He said this as he formed a matching slit down the sleeve of her dress.

When she wrapped her arm around his, their forearms now brushed against each other. The contact brought a tingle to the surface of her skin that not even a hard clearing of her throat could dispel.

The black spires of the castle came into view only a moment later. Vivid green vines grew over its surface with as much sparkle as the crystal thorns that wove through them.

She glanced toward Quintus. "You need to glamour yourself to look like a mortal."

"Right." He nodded and whirled his hand in a circle. After a flash, his eyes appeared less brilliant. His ears were no longer pointed. Even his facial features looked simpler and plainer.

But the sight still caused her to shake her head. "No, that won't work. Mishti and a few of the others already know what you look like. You have to change your face entirely."

The words sent his jaw into a tight clench, but he whirled his hand around anyway. After another flash, the body of Dunstan Bennett now stood at her side.

Quintus shrugged with very Dunstan-looking shoulders. "He is the only mortal I could think of who no one would recognize."

Her gut swirled in all kinds of flops at seeing Dunstan's face in Faerie. It didn't feel right. But if she looked ahead and focused on the arm wrapped around hers, she could forget the face and know that Quintus stood with her.

She released her magic then. It formed an invisible enchantment all around Quintus that would protect him from the iron flames around and inside the castle. Once at the front doors, they simply walked right in.

They didn't get very far before two mortals holding maces stopped them in the hallway. "Who are you?" The first mortal spat the words out.

The other mortal eyed both Chloe and Quintus up and down before stepping closer. "How did you get in here?"

"Can you not see our ears?" Quintus's voice still sounded like his, even though he currently wore Dunstan's face. He glanced back at the iron flames they had just passed through. "And what about the flames we walked past? Would a fae be able to do that?"

"You are mortals?" The first mortal in front of them cocked his head to the side.

"Obviously." Chloe brushed a wrinkle from her skirt. "Mishti told me about this party. She said I could come."

Both guards flicked their gazes toward each other. One of them shrugged and began stalking off. "I'll go get her, and she can decide if they should live or not."

The remaining guard continued to eye them with the sort of look that one would give to a deer on a rooftop in the middle of summer.

Since the spikes of his mace pointed toward the ground, her breathing still flowed like normal. As long as they continued to use words instead of weapons, she feared nothing. Her tongue had always been a little too sharp for her own good.

Luckily, Mishti appeared before Chloe had to say a single word. The young woman wore the midnight blue dress with a white pearl encrusted bodice just like she said she would. But she still wore her sword at her side as well.

Chloe wanted to rush toward her old friend and possibly embrace her, but doing so would force her to lose skin contact with Quintus, and then the enchantment protecting him from the iron flames would vanish.

Instead, Chloe settled for a wide smile. "We got away. We escaped the fae who manipulated us."

Mishti's eyes roamed over Quintus suspiciously. "Who is this?"

The smile stretching Chloe's face never faltered as she turned toward Quintus. "This is…" Her hesitation lasted only for a split second. She took that split second to come up with a story that she probably should have thought of earlier.

But why think of it earlier when the perfect explanation jumped right to her lips just when she needed it? Yes, her tongue had a sharp edge, but it also worked as the best weapon she'd ever wielded.

"He is my betrothed." Her lips dipped now into a slight pout. "That fae, Quintus, he took both my betrothed and me. He said he would give us money for our wedding, even a brand-new house, but—" She stopped long enough to lower her frown even more. "You were right. He only wanted to get rid of my Dunstan and keep me for himself."

The sour flinch that curled over Mishti's face said she not only understood but was well acquainted with a fae who had done the same type of thing many times. Her previous captor, the fae Ansel, had certainly been as disgusting as fae came.

Her eyes brightened as she led them down the hallway. "I'm glad you came then. The main party is in the throne room, which is just down this way."

Each step took them deeper inside Crystal Thorn Castle, but each step also felt less like the castle Chloe had known during her previous time in Faerie. Vines grew along the stone castle walls, but they didn't flutter with a magical breeze. It smelled like stone and stagnant air instead of like the lush forest outside.

Even the trees that grew from the stone floor looked wilted and feeble. The castle no longer had its same spark. Now it just felt dull and flat.

Once they arrived in the throne room, all worry for the castle leapt from Chloe's mind. A table full of plates and plates of divine-smelling food sat at both ends of the room. Her mouth started watering before she had even taken her second step inside.

Mishti wandered off almost immediately once someone approached her and called her away.

Letting out a soft chuckle, Quintus lowered his head toward Chloe's until his words whispered across the top of her hair. "I know you will not be able to even think until you get some food. We can eat first, then figure out how to leave the party to find the captured fae without looking suspicious."

Whipping a sheet of blonde hair behind her shoulder, she nodded. "I'm glad you understand my priorities. Food should always come first, except *maybe* when it's up against books."

Another soft laugh drifted from his mouth, this time leaving a skittering heat across her forehead where his breath had touched.

Her tongue swelled at how his bare forearm acted like a sizzling blade across her own. At least the searing tingle had a softness to it that a burn never did.

Just as Chloe grabbed a plate of herbed garlic bread knots and white meat with a cranberry sauce, a small group of girls started giggling at her side. Heat burned her cheeks before she realized the girls hadn't been laughing at her. They stood with their heads tilted together, and they all stared longingly at a young man across the room.

Their giggles rang out again when the young man extended both of his arms out to the side in a very unnatural stretch that just happened to show off his muscles.

Shaking her head, Chloe smiled as she began to eat her food. Quintus got his own plate as well. He had a harder time doing it one handed than Chloe had. But since they had to keep touching for her to keep the enchantment up, he didn't have much choice.

While the girls continued their whispers and giggles, a woman with brown hair in a tight bun sidled up to the girls. She wore a stunning teal dress with rippling layers of chiffon that flounced with each of her steps. A sharp jawline and pointed chin seemed at odds

177

with the saccharine smile on the woman's lips. She looked older than Chloe, but probably no more than ten years older.

The sweetness in her eyes multiplied as she addressed the young girls. "I always love to hear your cheerful laughs."

At the sound of her voice, the girls each sucked in a breath. They stood a little taller and unsubtly tried to get a little closer to the woman.

Seeming oblivious to this fact, the woman scanned the table. She reached for a garlic knot, but her hand hesitated before it took the food. Then she reached for a bowl of candied carrots. That didn't seem to satisfy her either though because her hand pulled back again before she could scoop some of the carrots onto her plate.

Her gaze trailed over the table and then she turned to eye the plates each of the girls held. Most of their food had already been eaten, but a few items remained along with the remnants of the food they'd eaten.

The woman with the tight bun suddenly let out a heavy sigh. She stared longingly at the plates and then turned toward the table at a now empty plate that had once held frosted pastries of some sort.

After her sigh, the woman's saccharine smile resurfaced. "It's wonderful that all of you managed to get one of those orange-glazed pastries before they were gone." Another sigh blew out from her mouth that seemed like it would never end. "I just wish I could have eaten even a bite of one before they were gone."

Every eye turned wide as the girls glanced down at their plates. A sugary orange glaze graced each of their plates, proving they had all enjoyed the exact pastry the woman had spoken of. Only one girl at the middle of the group still had hers left. Her brown eyes shimmered as she pulled the plate closer to her body.

It seemed very much like the girl had been waiting to eat the pastry and was very much looking forward to savoring it. The other girls stared at it when the girl with brown eyes snatched it off her plate and brought it toward her mouth for a bite.

Just before the pastry could touch her lips, the woman touched the girl's arm. "I don't mind if you get some, and I get none. You know I'd sacrifice anything for you, even an orange-glazed pastry."

The pastry hovered just in front of the girl's mouth for two whole breaths before she finally sighed and handed it to the woman. Her entire face wilted when she did. "You can have it." The light that had sparkled in her eyes when she giggled about that young man had gone out completely.

"No, no, I couldn't." The woman brushed a hand across her hair, checking that the tight brown strands were still in place.

A frown overtook the young girl's face now. Her chin even lowered as she muttered. "But we are mortals. Our selflessness is what sets us apart from the fae."

After a somewhat believable expression of pride, the woman touched a hand to her chest. "That is so true, my dear Mila. Thank you then. I thank you immensely."

The exchange had little sincerity to begin with. But then the woman moved only a handful of steps away, just out of the young girls' hearing, and joined a man with golden hair and a large mole on his chin. The woman glanced back at the girls as disgust filled her face. "Those girls have the most atrocious laughs. The shrill sound is going to shrivel up my ears one day, I know it."

She gobbled down the orange-glazed pastry in two bites while the golden-haired man at her side puffed out a snide cackle. "Just don't let them know you think it, Portia, or they won't be so eager to gain your approval."

A knot twisted in Chloe's stomach at the name. Portia. *That* woman was the leader of the mortals? The one who wanted the fae dead. The golden-haired man with her had to be Julian, the other leader. He had also been at Ludo's house when Mishti arrived.

Tightening her arm around Quintus's, Chloe stuffed the last bite of meat and cranberry sauce into her mouth as she edged them closer to the door of the throne room. She still had half a garlic knot to eat once she'd chewed the rest of her food. As delicious as the food was, the exchange between Portia and Julian took all joy of eating it straight from her mouth. Now she only cared about finding the captured fae and getting them out of the castle.

She eyed the doorway of the throne room as she finished the last of the garlic bread. "How do we sneak out without being suspicious?"

Quintus's arm shifted beneath hers. Using his free hand, he reached across her for *her* free hand. Her skin ignited with that same electrifying intensity that still buzzed where their forearms met. Except then he used the arm that had been around hers to wrap around her waist.

They maintained skin contact through their touching hands, and now his arm sat low on her back. Even as it lowered, he pulled her tight against his body.

His head dipped until his lips brushed the soft skin just below her ear. A shiver rocked through her when he whispered. "I can give them an unsuspicious idea of what we intend to do in the halls."

Did his lips have to be so soft when they brushed her skin?

Her body melted against his, even knowing it was only a ruse. She became intensely aware of her shoulders sliding closer to his chest. He still held her by one hand, but her free hand somehow found its way to his upper arm. Her fingers begged to curl over his muscles, though he'd probably read into that more than she liked.

Flutters filled her veins, skipping as fast as her thumping heartbeat. It had started as a ruse, but the desire to get closer to him quickly drifted to reality.

But when her gaze darted up to his eyes, she flinched. "I can't." Every muscle in her body went rigid as she leaned away from him ever so slightly. "Not while you look like Dunstan."

180

Instead of pulling away, he just trailed his thumb across the back of her hand in soft twirls. "Ah, so you prefer *my* appearance to his, do you?"

No matter how much she wanted to glare at him, she could only huff and look away. "I never said that."

His thumb stopped twirling just long enough for his fingers to squeeze around hers. "Your face did."

The overwhelming desire to kick him in the shin was matched only with the desire to dig her hands into his hair and bring his lips to her mouth where they belonged. But how could she do such a thing when she wouldn't even get a glimpse of his rich brown eyes first?

At least her gaze latched onto something just intriguing enough to drag her attention away from Quintus. Mishti had wandered over to their side of the throne room, but she wasn't alone. She and Portia spoke in low whispers. Judging by the heat rising in both their cheeks, it wasn't a friendly conversation.

Since the two of them stood close to the doors which Chloe and Quintus were trying to sneak out of, this seemed like the perfect excuse to get closer and try to hear.

24

EVEN WHISPERS WERE HARD TO disguise when they were spoken in sharp tones, which would make it easier to overhear this particular conversation. Chloe used one hand to drag Quintus closer to the doorway where Mishti and Portia stood arguing. Now that Chloe had been in the castle for some time, it got harder to maintain the enchantment around Quintus that kept him safe from the iron in the air.

If the enchantment failed, the iron would get to his skin and then the glamour hiding his true appearance would probably fail too. If he had a difficult time with opening a door while iron hung in the air, it was likely he'd have difficulty with any type of magic, including a glamour.

All the more reason to sneak a quick listen to the conversation between Mishti and Portia and then it would be time to leave the party.

"Why does it have to be me?" To her credit, Mishti didn't whine the words. She spoke them with as much solemn ferocity as her face exhibited.

Portia's eyes flashed, showing off her anger much more openly. "Without you, the fae will slaughter us. After everything I've done for you, how could you argue about this now?"

Standing taller, Mishti set her jaw. "I'm not trying to hurt you. I just don't want to do it."

Portia raised a pointer finger and shot it forward. "I helped you through our hardest times in that house. I cleaned your wounds and dried your tears, just like I did for everyone else. You'd forget all of that just to leave us when we need you most?"

Her head shook side to side as she folded her arms over her chest. "I never thought a mortal could be so selfish."

"I'm not selfish." The first glimpse of frustration surfaced when Mishti clenched her jaw. "What you ask is too much."

"It's too much to save your own people?" Portia turned back toward the throne room now. Her gaze pointedly trailed over every person in the room. Men and women ranging from about Grace's age to Portia's age stood in clusters, happily eating and dancing. Living.

A certain deadness still faded their eyes, but they looked much more alive than they had when Elora rescued them from Ansel's house. Seeing how far they had come, imagining that being taken away, it felt like a knife twist to the heart.

"If you turn against us, Mishti, if you become my enemy..." Portia turned just to glance sideways. Her lips curled into a sneer. "I know your weaknesses, and I know where you sleep. *Never* forget that."

Mishti blinked, but a bead of sweat still broke out across her forehead.

Nodding, Portia plodded off toward the throne made of trees on the opposite side of the room. Black crystal thorns wove through the branches that formed the throne, giving it a little sparkle. The thorns may have brightened the throne, but the trees forming it didn't. They had lost nearly all the vibrancy in their leaves. Even the bark seemed to sag.

Once she reached the tree throne, Portia climbed on top of it. Standing, she called out to the entire room.

"My family, the time has come for the announcement this party is being held for." Her hands brushed over the chiffon layers of her teal dress as a frightening smile graced her lips. "Starting tomorrow, we are going to behead every single fae inside this castle."

The room rippled with gasps and exclamations, but none of them could hold a candle to the way Chloe's heart completely stopped. She gripped Quintus's hand so hard, she feared her bones might turn to dust.

Behead?

Her throat soured with the taste of bile. The herbs from her garlic knot that had been so delightful not long ago now dug into her throat like a snake burrowing into a hole.

If she allowed herself to dwell on the news, she would have lost all the food she had just eaten. But Portia wasn't finished speaking yet.

She gestured across the room to Mishti's stoic face. "Our beloved Mishti has the great honor of beheading those fae for us."

Grabbing Quintus's hand, Chloe edged close enough to Mishti to speak to her without others overhearing.

"The great *honor?*" Chloe said with a whispered scoff. "I thought you never wanted to take another life."

Mishti's eyes had a lifeless quality when she turned toward Chloe. "If we do not take Faerie for ourselves, the fae will turn it into our grave."

The words left her lips with such practiced ease that they were clearly something she had repeated a dozen times, maybe more. No trace of emotion twitched across her expression. She stood still. Her eyes were as dead as the fae would be after a beheading.

Perhaps it should have been a comfort that she spoke such words with a complete lack of conviction, but her stiff appearance made comfort impossible.

Chloe's heart faltered then, truly faltered. Her fingers squeezed and her stomach clenched. The little concentration she had holding Quintus's enchantment in place faltered.

Only one short moment, but the consequences were immediate. Her enchantment protecting Quintus from the iron in the air failed and then his glamour shimmered. For a breath, maybe only half a breath, his true appearance flashed.

She gripped his hand tight again and focused on the enchantment, which went right back up. Soon he looked just like Dunstan, like he was supposed to.

Attempting to hide any sign of surprise or fear, Chloe glanced at Mishti to gauge her reaction.

The young woman's eyes narrowed for a moment even shorter than the shimmer in Quintus's glamour. Her stoic features made no other change. Had she seen? Did she know Quintus was really the fae Chloe had claimed to escape and not the mortal he appeared to be?

Just when Chloe opened her mouth to say something—anything—to distract from the moment of weakness, Portia raised her voice again.

Her arms lifted high above the tight bun in her hair. "Tomorrow, the beheadings begin! We will kill every fae, and we will do it without guilt because if we do not take Faerie for ourselves, the fae will turn this land into our grave."

She spoke the same phrase Mishti had spouted a moment ago, but Portia's words dripped with a terrifying level of conviction. Even worse, many of the mortals in the room exhibited that same conviction when they let out great cheers.

Chloe held tight to Quintus's hand, ignoring how much she needed it for comfort. After a hard swallow, she spoke. "Mishti, where is my sister?"

Mishti's long braid shifted as she turned slowly. "I would never tell you that."

Portia had climbed off the throne. Now she trailed back across the room toward them. Whatever Chloe thought she might get from her old friend her chance was fading fast.

Portia wore a cruel smirk as she placed a hand on the shoulder of a woman who was singing under her breath. "Oh honey, I'm only telling you this because I care about you, but…" Portia's face twisted into a grimace. "Never sing again."

That was it. Chloe's jaw clenched as she turned to Mishti. "You can't possibly want to live like this. You know she's manipulating you. All of you."

"What choice do I have?" Mishti's words reeked of a palpable pain.

"Come with us," Chloe said. "We'll protect you. We'll rescue anyone who wants to get away from them."

Even with the words spoken in a rush, Mishti didn't have time to respond. Portia had reached them now and wrapped her arm around Mishti's. "Come, my dear, everyone wants to hear how excited you are about tomorrow."

Mishti nodded. But just before she stalked off, Mishti turned back to Chloe. "You were right. The library is the largest room in the castle, even larger than the throne room. But the throne room had all the iron when we got here, so it made more sense to take control of it first."

Without another word, she and Portia disappeared in the crowd.

Cocking his head to the side, Quintus frowned with Dunstan's face. "Why did she say that? We were not even talking about the throne room."

But the words went wild in Chloe's head. They darted and flipped until she sucked in a breath. "They're in the library."

His eyes narrowed. "What?"

Blood pulsed at her fingertips when she squeezed his hand even tighter. "Elora and Brannick are in there, maybe all the fae are. Why else would she mention the library like that?"

Realization hit his expression just as she stepped closer to him.

"Do it." With his hand still tight in hers, she settled her other hand onto his shoulder. "Pretend you're stealing me away to the hallway to kiss me or whatever it is you wanted to do. We need to find my sister."

Her body reacted when he pressed her body closer to him but not the same as it had before. His arms didn't seem as hungry as they had before anyway. They had a mission now that just happened to require their arms to be around each other.

Neither of them could enjoy anything about the moment. They only had one thing on their minds and that was getting to the library.

Once in the hallway, they separated all but for their clasped hands. Now they flew down the hallways until the golden doorknobs of the giant library doors came into view. Breath rushed into Chloe's lungs at the sight of them.

This was almost over.

Elora was behind those doors, and Elora would be able to save everyone, just like she always did. Chloe might need to use her own magic to create an enchantment that would protect her sister and the other fae from the iron in the air, but she could do that from the edge of the fight.

Once she opened those doors, Chloe's part would mostly be finished.

Her heart skipped with each pound of her boot against the stone. Just a few more steps. Just a few more moments, and this nightmare would be over.

But just as she reached the door, a golden-haired figure stepped out from behind a tree that grew against the wall.

"Thought you could slip out unnoticed, did you?" From behind his back, Julian revealed a small box with a tiny rope coming out of it that almost looked like a candle wick. His other hand came out next. This one held a bowl of flames.

Gritting his teeth, he chucked the bowl of flames right at Chloe's dress.

Even though she didn't have to fear the iron in the bowl, flames could still burn her. All thought of magic vanished from her mind when the flames landed on the golden embroidery of her hem.

The fuel from the bowl soaked her hem, giving the flames plenty to burn through. She wanted to collapse, to fall into a heap and give in to the tears that pricked at her eyes.

Quintus wouldn't let her. He held her steadily, one hand still clasping hers and one arm around her waist.

When Julian lit a match that set the wick-like rope aflame, Quintus stepped back. A smirk slithered across Julian's mouth, which stretched the mole on his chin. "Beheadings are great fun, but I have an even more delightful end planned for the fae. If they happen to live through it, we'll just behead them tomorrow as planned."

Quintus's hand whirled through the air, forming a door behind them. The iron in the air probably made it painful to keep the door open but staying would clearly be worse.

He dragged Chloe back toward the door when her feet refused to move. Fear slid like ice down her spine, clawing at every vein.

"But the fae. We have to save them first." Her voice trembled over the words.

Quintus's grip on her tightened. "If we stay, we will die. We are leaving."

She had probably lost control of the enchantment protecting Quintus again, but maybe it didn't matter now if they were about to escape.

As they reached the edges of the door, Julian set the strange box right at the doorway of the library and he ducked behind the thick tree trunk beside it.

Just as Chloe and Quintus stepped into the door, the small box exploded with flames. Bits of metal burst from the box, smashing straight through the library doors.

The entire hallway, even the entire library, blasted with fire and metal.

But then her feet landed with a hard thud in a darkened area that was certainly not the castle.

She and Quintus had made it out safe, but that explosion...

Those flames, the bits of iron. All of it burst into the library.

Chloe couldn't catch her breath as the consequences became clear. That explosion could have killed them. Every last one of the fae inside.

25

DARKNESS CREPT INTO CHLOE'S STOMACH, clenching it into a cord of jagged shards. Her feet had landed on something solid, and Quintus held her in his arms, but beyond that, she perceived nothing. She didn't know where they were, but she didn't care.

She couldn't breathe. Every time she tried to suck in a breath it got caught somewhere at the back of her throat. Air gathered like bile, filling her throat with a thickness that scraped her tongue raw.

It felt right to close her eyes, but the moment she did, all she could see was that explosion. Flames and bits of metal shredded through the library door, crumbling it even easier than a dried herb.

Burying her face in Quintus's chest, she forced words from her lips so painful they felt like knives on their way out. "She's dead. What if Elora is dead?"

With her head on his chest, she felt when he swallowed. His voice came out steady, but just a little too steady to be natural. "Fae have remarkable healing abilities. We can heal from almost anything."

Her head shot up to meet his eyes. "You saw that explosion. If your body gets blown into little pieces with bits of iron digging into your skin, wouldn't that kill you?"

He said nothing, which said everything.

Burying her face in his chest again, she tried to swallow that rock in her throat. "Will they survive? Will Elora and Brannick survive?"

For her entire life, she had always seen the fae's inability to lie as one of the small advantages mortals had over them. It was one thing that partially balanced the fae's enormous power. But right now, she wished he didn't have to speak the truth. She wanted him to lie. She wanted to hear that everything would be okay and that Elora and Brannick would be just fine.

But Quintus couldn't lie.

His arm slipped across her back, tugging her tighter. "They are the strongest fae Faerie has ever known. If anyone can survive, they can."

The words held a surprising amount of comfort compared to what she had expected. He did speak the truth, yet he also managed to say what she wanted to hear. The tightest knot in her chest began to unravel just enough that she could take in a deep inhale.

They had to go back to the castle, of course. They couldn't stay hidden away while the mortals killed their fae hostages. But maybe they had just enough time to catch their breaths first.

For the first time, she glanced up and caught a glimpse of their surroundings. The black, crystalline walls of a cave towered above and at their sides. Golden lights embedded in the ceiling twinkled down on them.

Quintus swallowed. "I thought you would want a moment alone before we went back to the clearing where Ludo is." His gaze darted away. "I thought this would be a better place to open my door."

She had never wanted to thank anyone so much in her life, but she couldn't just say *thank you* while in Faerie. Then again, maybe Quintus deserved an actual favor for such a thoughtful gesture.

Her eyes narrowed as her gaze turned upward again. "Does it seem like there are more golden lights above us now than there were before?"

"Yes." He pulled away just enough to gesture toward their feet. "And look where we landed."

They stood on a small island in the middle of the stream that flowed through the cave. The twinkling lights above reflected in the water below.

Quintus's nose twitched as he stared at his feet. "We are deeper inside the cave, and I am certain this rock island wasn't here before."

If the circumstances had been any less dire, she might have considered the curiosity even more. Instead, she looked into his eyes. After only a moment, her gaze slid down to the moon tattoo under his left eye.

When he caught her staring, he flinched.

Her gaze flicked away immediately. "I hate my tattoo as much as you do."

From the corner of her eye, she watched him arch an eyebrow.

It took great effort to swallow after that. "It feels like a mockery to have stars on my face."

The hand at her back shifted as Quintus ducked to meet her eye. "You wish you were not mortal?"

"No, it has nothing to do with that."

Slivers seemed to dig into her fingers, but it was a little easier to ignore them when she rested her hand against Quintus's chest. "When I was a child, only eleven, my friend got it in her head that we needed to go stargazing in this one specific meadow that was a little too close to the road leading out of town."

"Stargazing?" He failed to hide the scoff in his voice.

"Don't laugh. Stars can be quite spectacular. Maybe they are not as pretty as the golden magic above us, but they are still breathtaking."

His voice came out gentler now. "Did you go then?"

She inched closer to him, trailing her fingers across the soft fabric of his dark green coat. "My parents forbade it. The road could be dangerous, and it was summer, so the stars didn't come out until very late at night."

He stared at her, almost holding his breath while he waited for her to continue.

Shrugging ever so slightly, she stared at the top of his coat where the collar opened to his chest. "I decided to defy them and sneak out to see the stars anyway. My friend was insistent, and my parents' refusal seemed silly to me. We giggled the whole way there."

"I cannot imagine you willingly going into danger of any kind."

Her gaze snapped up to his as she gritted her teeth together. "Why do you think I fear it so much? Obviously, something happened that cured me of my naïve bravery."

His throat bobbed with a hard swallow as realization lit in his eyes. The hand at her back pressed into her just a little closer than before. "What happened?"

She sniffed. "A man found us. It wasn't hard with how much noise we made. We were right by the road, and only charlatans traveled at that late hour."

Fire seemed to blaze in Quintus's eyes as his nostrils flared. "What did he do to you?"

She tried to turn away, but Quintus held her fast, looking deeper into her eyes with each moment that passed. She had to take a deep breath before she could continue. "He tried to kidnap us. I fought him, but he was stronger. Faster. He…"

The unfinished sentenced hung in the space between them until it wrapped memories around her that she'd always done her best to bury.

"I can still feel his sweaty hands on my arms." Her fingers reached for her upper arm just to flinch away. "Sometimes I wake up in a sweat, and I feel…"

She couldn't finish. No words could explain the anguish that had crippled so many of her dreams. Even in waking hours, that same fear could grip her, and it would freeze her body until she cried. Anytime weapons or danger closed in, she'd freeze. She'd be brought back to that same moment when she was eleven and nothing could pull her out of it.

Quintus brought her close. He held her gently but with a grip firm enough to make her feel safe. That slimy ice trailing up and down her arms immediately receded.

It took another breath, but then she could continue again. "He tied us up in the back of his cart, then got back on his horse. To this day, I don't know how I managed it, but I got out of those ropes and then I freed my friend next. We jumped out the back of the cart and ran for our lives."

Her heart stuttered. "It wasn't until I started sneaking back into my bedroom window that I heard the screams."

Quintus's hand went rigid at her back.

"My friend." She had to close her eyes just to get the rest of the words out. "He had caught her again. I would have gone after her, but then the screams stopped. I assumed she got away from him."

She swallowed. "But the next morning, she was gone."

Her eyes finally stung, heralding in the tears she'd managed to keep back so far. "She was gone, and I never told a single soul why. I never told them it was my fault."

A sob wrenched from her mouth taking a piece of her heart along with it. "I never should have left her. I should have gone back to help her."

After a quick sniff, she forced herself to say the next part. "I learned two things that day. First, that fighting won't ever save me, especially against someone who is stronger and faster, which pretty much everyone is. And second, that when I am selfish, people get hurt. That's part of why I became an apothecary. To make up for my past mistakes. To help people instead of hurt them."

Her last few words got swallowed up by more sobs. Tears sliced down her cheeks in icy lines. She buried her face in Quintus's chest, grateful that he held her tighter each time another sob ripped from her throat.

Neither of them spoke for a long time after that. Quintus just held her and let her cry. She cried for her friend, but now she cried for Elora too. Elora and all those fae were stuck in the castle while iron and flames rained down on them. If Chloe tried to fight, she would just fail.

Eventually, Quintus did speak. His voice came out as soft as the fabric of his coat. "What would have happened if you had gone back to help your friend?"

Her bottom lip trembled, but for once, she felt strong enough to face this truth. "I could have helped her get away."

"But you said the man was too strong, too fast."

With eyebrows pinching together, she glared up at him. "What's your point?" Did Quintus take pleasure in her pain?

His face was soft though. Soft and careful. "If you had gone back, you would have met the same fate as your friend. Maybe you could have helped her get away, but you probably would have just sacrificed yourself in her place. At the very least, one of you would have been captured, but more likely, it would have been both of you."

Heat seized Chloe's heart. "But she got kidnapped—or worse—because of me."

"No." Quintus's expression hardened with resolve. "She got kidnapped because of that man. It was not wrong for you to save yourself."

She turned away with a scoff. "Of course you say that. Fae are selfish. You'd never worry about others unless it benefitted you in some way."

After a deafening silence, he spoke even more quietly than before. "I worried about you when I left you in Ludo's house. I trusted you to take care of yourself, but I worried too. I was glad when I got your message to come get you."

His fingers lifted just enough to slip into her hair. He twirled his fingers around, encircling them with her blonde strands only to release them again.

The weight of his confession poured over her, hot and engulfing.

When he met her gaze, she couldn't help how her body leaned into him. But when his face started to lower towards hers, she shook her head.

"We can't stay here. We need to figure out how to get back to the castle and save my sister."

Instead of pulling away, he just pulled her closer. His lips pressed against her forehead, leaving a soft kiss behind. Her heart skittered when his lips touched her. It beat even faster when he dropped his hand from her waist and intertwined his fingers with hers.

"I agree. It is time to make a plan."

26

AFTER TRAVELING THROUGH ANOTHER DOOR, Chloe stepped into the clearing where she'd slept the past few nights. Ash and blackened wood sat where their fire had once burned, but it had clearly been out for the entire day now. Her head tilted as she scanned the clearing and the surrounding area once more.

"Where is Ludo?"

Quintus's eyes narrowed as he too scanned the area. He even ambled into the forest and then popped his head inside a few of the caves.

"He is gone."

Unease settled in her chest as she bit her lip. "Do you think he finished collecting everything he wanted and just went back to his house?"

Quintus's nose twitched before he answered. "Yes, I think you are correct. I wanted him nearby until he collected on your favor, but I suppose I can go find him again after we…"

The sentence lingered unfinished. Chloe could guess what words he was playing in his mind to finish the sentence. After we fight. After we save the fae. After we win.

But all of them seemed far too optimistic after that explosion Julian sent into the room holding all the fae.

Saving him the trouble of trying to finish the sentence at all, Chloe stepped toward him. "What can we do? How do we get back into the castle and save everyone?" She did mean *everyone*, both mortals and fae. Well, everyone except Portia and Julian. They could meet the next explosion for all she cared.

Quintus's gaze turned downward as he dug a black-booted toe into the soil at his feet. "I do not think I can convince any fae to fight in a battle against the mortals. Many have already tried and failed. No more fae will sacrifice themselves when they have no chance of winning."

She watched as his foot trailed across the spot where the brown Crystal Thorn soil merged into the black pebble-filled soil that surrounded the black caves. Her lips twisted into a knot. "There has to be a way to defeat them *without* fighting."

The words didn't seem to give Quintus any sort of confidence. In fact, the scowl that twitched his nose kept twitching harder. He dug into his pocket and pulled out her leather bag, her cloak, and even her other dress.

Seeing the dress, she glanced down at the hem of the dress Quintus had made her. Most of it still looked as beautiful as ever, but at the very center near the bottom, a burn mark singed through the velvety fabric. The golden embroidery was black and gloppy at the hem, weighing the dress down. The black singe marks stretched across the fair fabric like shadowy tendrils.

Maybe her already heightened emotion caused it, but the sight of those burn marks sent tears to her eyes. She had to swallow just to keep her chin from trembling.

It was such a little thing that the most beautiful dress she had ever worn was now ruined. But sometimes those little things were the only things that got her through tragedy. To have that joy ripped away now seemed more than unfair.

"Maybe we can steal their iron. They cannot defeat us without it." Quintus had pulled his spear from his pocket. He stared at the feather tied to its staff, more intent on it than on the words he had just spoken.

Crouching low to the ground, she trailed a finger across the gloppy burned embroidery at the bottom of her dress. The delicate swirls and bends of the golden threads now just limped weakly. Her throat ached at the sight of it. "But they have piles and piles of iron. I remember seeing an entire roomful of iron objects just off the throne room. And where would we put all the iron if we stole it?"

If she remembered correctly, the iron room in Crystal Thorn Castle had protections around it to keep the iron poisoning from getting into the rest of the castle. Even without protections, though, plain iron usually wasn't harmful to fae unless they touched it. The mortals' weapons only worked because they combined iron with flame.

That thought struck hard in her mind. It buzzed and flickered until her head snapped up to look at Quintus. "What if we steal their fuel? Or even better, what if we burn it until there's no fuel left?"

Shaking his head, he stuffed his spear back into his pocket. "But the fuel is in so many different places. The troughs, in those glass jars they carry around."

"Some of the fuel maybe, but there must be a place where they store most of the fuel. They probably have barrels of it sitting somewhere inside the castle."

He nodded, but his gaze had fallen to the hem of her dress where her fingers still trailed over the blackened and singed embroidery.

Silence broke when a low rumbling filled the air.

His eyebrow tipped upward. "How are you hungry already? We just ate."

Her arms wrapped around her stomach as she stood from the ground. The position made it easier to confirm what she already knew. "That wasn't me."

Except, if the rumbling didn't come from her stomach, that meant it came from somewhere else. But where?

They both scanned the area around them. A tight clench worked its way through Chloe's stomach. She imagined men with sharp knives jumping out from behind the trees. Then she imagined women with jars of flames throwing them onto the parts of her dress that hadn't been ruined.

The thoughts shivered inside her, causing her to look down. Her gaze landed on the spot where the brown and black soil met. The sight held her gaze in place, though she couldn't tell why. At least not at first.

After another moment, the soil began shifting. Tiny waves lifted the soil in various spots. At first, the movement was minimal like a tiny pebble dropping into a pond. But then the black soil started moving faster until it shook like the waves of water in a lake when a drowning person thrashed inside it.

She would have stepped back toward the lush forest of Crystal Thorn, except then the land split apart. It happened so suddenly she had no time to prepare. With a gasp, she tumbled into the pit that had just formed.

"Chloe!"

Quintus shouted her name right as she disappeared inside the pit.

Her shoulder landed with a thud on the soil beneath her, but it was soft enough to not cause any injury. Back up on the surface, the shadow of Quintus's body shifted. He was probably about to jump into the pit after her.

But then another jolting rumble filled the air, and Quintus let out a heavy grunt. Had he fallen into his own pit?

Getting to her feet, she glanced up. The surface towered much too high above her. An entire tree probably could have been inside the pit, and the top of it still wouldn't have been tall enough to reach the surface.

Would she have to climb the walls of the pit to get back to the top surface? She scowled at the thought. She'd never been good at climbing.

Darkness flooded the pit, making it difficult to examine the soil wall she might have to climb. Up above, Quintus let out another grunt that almost certainly had more pain than surprise inside it.

The ground rumbled again. Thoughts of climbing fled as the pit she stood in grew. The opening split wider and the ground stretched horizontally until the closet-sized pit grew into a throne room-sized one.

What was happening? Why? Thousands of questions flipped in her mind, but her surroundings only brought up even more questions. Her eyes narrowed as she leaned closer to the soil wall before her.

She plucked a pinch of soil from the wall and rubbed it between her thumb and forefinger. Did darkened shadows fill the pit or did it just seem darker because the soil had turned black?

Bits of the soil left black streaks on her fingers. She was almost certain this part of the soil had been brown when she fell, but it was definitely black now.

In a flash, golden lights appeared, floating in the air around her. They glowed and sparkled the same as those golden lights embedded inside the ceiling of the black caves.

Pearlescent pebbles started to appear in the black soil beside her and all throughout the pit. They sparkled with such beauty, they almost looked like jewels.

Her long hair ruffled as she shook her head. This was not the time to get distracted by beautiful things.

Digging her fingernails into the soil wall at her side, she made her first attempt at climbing up the wall. She had only lifted herself a few inches before her fingers lost grip and ripped right out of the soil wall. After a snarl, she attempted another climb. It ended the same.

But then the ground beneath her rumbled and waved. Her feet stumbled, trying to catch her balance. Failing, she stumbled until her palms slapped against the ground.

Before she could attempt to stand up again, the ground shook. And then, it started rising.

With her hands still pressed against the soil, the surface above got closer and closer as the ground rose up to meet it.

Apparently, she wouldn't have to climb at all because soon the bottom of the pit became level with the surface above. Her eyes widened once she could see the surface again.

Quintus was exactly where he had been before except an enormous black cave had grown up from the ground underneath him, and he now sat atop it. His arms and legs gripped the cave at strange angles as he attempted to climb off it. Each time he made a little progress, the cave stretched even higher into the sky.

He finally managed to scramble off it once he noticed Chloe stood back on the surface again. Just as he got off the cave, the side of it molded and shifted until it joined the other caves. Now it was part of the network of caves instead of standing on its own.

Small golden lights continued to float in the air, but they were less numerous than before. The lights drifted until they landed on the crystalline surface of the black caves. The moment they made contact, they burst with golden sparks and then became one with the caves. They left behind sparkles in the surface of the cave wall.

One last rumble sounded as the land did its final shift. After a groan, the movement stopped completely.

A quiet breeze fluttered around them, but everything else stood silent. Still. With the shifting complete, it looked and felt as if this was how the land had always been.

Of course, it wasn't the same at all. The caves stood much closer to Chloe and Quintus than before, and there were more of them. Plus, their feet stood fully in the area covered with black soil and pearlescent pebbles, whereas before, they had stood right on the border where the brown soil met black.

Her gaze drifted to the lush forest nearby. The Court of Crystal Thorn didn't look shrunken or smaller. It looked the same as ever. Now her gaze turned to the other side. It seemed more like the crystal caves grew, expanding Faerie itself along with them.

With a swallow, her gaze flitted back to Quintus. The bewilderment on his face perfectly matched the emotion bubbling inside her. Had Faerie truly just expanded? If so, what did it mean?

At any other time, the questions could have held her attention easily, but now, they both had more important things to worry about.

She shrugged.

Quintus nodded at her shrug, lifting one of his own. "I suppose we will have to ignore that for now." His eyebrows pinched together, clearly turning his mind back to the greater conflict at hand. "Ludo's greatest magic is in finding things. He has likely gone back to his home like we already discussed. If I can convince him to do it, he can help us find the fuel inside the castle."

Tremors inside Chloe's chest begged to worry more about the land and what it had just done, but this really wasn't the time. They had an entire castle full of fae to save, after all.

27

GETTING HELP FROM A FAE would always be easier said than done. Chloe chewed on her lips, thinking of all the ways things could go wrong after asking Ludo for help. Maybe he didn't have ill intent toward her, but like any fae, he only cared about himself.

Holding her old dress out to her, Quintus lifted his eyebrows. "We should probably change."

After she took the dress from him, he reached into his pocket and pulled out his old clothes as well. The green cape had an ombre design with dark green at the bottom, which faded to a lighter green at the top, but had it gotten darker since last time she saw it?

Shoving that thought away, she shook the wrinkles out of her old dress. "How will you convince Ludo to help us?"

Quintus removed his coat and its belt with absolutely no care toward how revealing his upper body might affect her. "The mortals want to kill every fae in Faerie, including him. I hope that fact will be persuasive enough, especially since we actually have a good plan to stop them now. Although…"

Trailing off, he turned toward her and stared just a little too intensely. His broad shoulders had just enough definition to cause her to bite her bottom lip.

For once, he didn't seem to notice. He just threw the cape over his head and continued. "You already owe Ludo a favor. It is probably not wise to put you in a situation where you might owe him another one."

Once he had the cape on, he reached for the tie fastening his pants. At least that made him falter. Just before his fingers untied the knot, his gaze snapped toward her, and he dropped his hand away.

She swallowed. "What do you want me to do then? Just stay silent and let you do the talking?"

Whenever he looked at her now, she felt the press of his lips against her forehead. Heat prickled at her cheeks, which she hoped he wouldn't notice. Luckily, he glanced around the space, his eyes focusing on the forest for a few extra moments. "You should stay here."

She arched a brow, but he didn't notice. Or maybe he just pretended not to notice.

He gestured toward the dress still in her hands. "You can change as soon as I leave. I will not be gone long."

She wanted to be upset with him for even suggesting that he leave her alone anywhere in Faerie, but she couldn't. Despite the rumbling and shifting that had taken place not long before, she still felt safe in that spot by the crystal caves. It felt safer to her than any other place in Faerie ever had.

His hand waved in a circle, which opened his swirling tunnel of forest greens and smudges of black. The black definitely seemed to occupy more space than it had previously. And the little golden lights inside of the black smudges looked suspiciously similar to the golden lights that had floated in the air while Faerie expanded.

With the door open, he tipped his head toward it. "Fae cannot open doors directly inside a home unless they have been invited inside. This door leads to just outside of Ludo's home." Something skittered in his eyes then. A glint that shimmered just as he turned in her direction, though he never made eye contact. He cleared his throat. "Once I enter the home, I will not be able to hear your voice if you call out to me."

Tension floated off him then. It wafted through the air until it clenched around her neck. The space had felt safe only moments ago. It still mostly did, but his nervousness was currently scouring up some nervousness of her own.

Her fingers found the edge of her sleeve, which she rolled between her fingers. "Should I come with you and just stay outside Ludo's home then, instead of staying here?"

A crease formed between his eyebrows as he pushed them together. His gaze continued to dart around the clearing, landing on anything and everything except for her. After a few moments of idle wandering, his eyes turned more focused.

He glanced at the path leading into Crystal Thorn Forest. Then he glanced at her, but only for a breath. His gaze finally landed on his swirling door.

Lifting his hand, he swirled it in a circle once again. But the door didn't disappear. Instead, showers of pearlescent sparks burst from his fingertips only to enter the door. The moment they went inside the swirling tunnel, they glowed and pulsed and then disappeared.

His shoulder lifted, pointing to the tunnel. "I will leave my door open, but now there is extra magic inside it too. Once I go through the door, only one other person can go through it and then it will automatically close."

She felt her eyebrows lift up her forehead as his plan became clear. She gestured toward the path to the forest. "So if anyone comes down that path or if I'm in danger in any other way, I can just jump through the door? Even if you are inside Ludo's house and cannot see me or hear me, the door will still close just in time to make sure no one can follow me."

"Precisely." He locked eyes with her just long enough to send her stomach into a mess of flutters. Yet again, he made the space feel even safer than it had before. Why did he have such a knack for that?

The rules of Faerie mocked her while the words *thank you* sat heavily on her tongue. For someone who was supposed to be selfish, Quintus had a way of thinking of her quite frequently.

At least he disappeared through his door so she couldn't forget herself and thank him anyway. But once she began changing out of his carefully crafted red dress, pain curled around her heart. She refused to look at the dress until she had donned her old dress again.

The underdress slipped over her easily, fitting against her like a soft pair of well-worn boots. The familiar feel of it fit just right, but it didn't have the magic Quintus's dress had. Her overdress went on next, and she tied the corset, even though her fingers fumbled through it.

She slipped a hand into her hair to finger comb through the curls. If they were about to enter the castle again, she probably should have put her hair up and out of the way. But she didn't. She even left the roses among the blonde strands.

Her gaze dropped down to the silky, velvety dress Quintus had crafted. Such an exquisite dress, and even more poignant, he made it just for her. The singe marks looked even worse when she saw them up close. Her eyes had only watered up to this point, but now a tear slipped through her eyelashes. Once it fell, another followed soon after.

She hated herself for crying over a dress when her sister might be dead. Then again, maybe she wasn't really crying over the dress at all. Maybe it just acted as the catalyst for all the harrowing fear and sadness inside her.

More tears streamed down her cheeks. When she closed her eyes, the memory of that explosion filled her mind. The flames and metal pieces shattered into the air. Her stomach clenched at the thought of it.

She had to grip her stomach just to force herself to breathe. Why? Why did the mortals have to hurt the fae? Why did her sister have to live in Faerie? And why did those innocent mortals who had already been through so much with their previous captor have to start the cycle again with just as manipulative leaders?

Her shoulders hunched forward as a sob wracked through them. At least Quintus wouldn't be able to hear her crying again. He had already held her through all those tears inside the cave, and now they had returned.

These feelings were awful, but why did they have to be so well deserved? Chloe had left. Again. She had abandoned Elora just like she abandoned her friend all those years ago. Now Elora would die, and it would be Chloe's fault for being selfish. For not saving her when she had the chance. For not sacrificing herself when someone else needed her.

All her life, she had tried so hard to help others. She had done her best to be selfless because—like Dunstan had said—it was the most admirable quality a woman could have. Maybe that wasn't true in Faerie, but it was certainly true at her place in the mortal realm.

And she was good at helping people. She found joy in it. She could heal illnesses and ease suffering. She could lend a listening ear and offer encouragement. So why did this conflict constantly remind her of the one way she couldn't help people? In a fight.

In a madness, she tore her magical book from her bag and threw it onto the ground. Once there, she stared at it. Stared and stared and wanted to kick it for failing to give her the courage she needed to rush straight back to the castle and free her sister before things got any worse.

When glaring at the book no longer helped, she slammed her boot against it. A fresh footprint of black soil now dug into its leather cover. Flashing her teeth, she slammed her foot against the book again. Why did she constantly have to be reminded that no matter how she helped people, it would never be enough?

She'd sacrificed so much of herself along the way. She hardly ever played the harp anymore, even though she loved it. Her dream of writing epic poems that would always be remembered died years ago once her neighbors made it clear they found her imagination too eccentric for their taste.

Only once she reached that deepest part of her grief did the sourest truth sting in her throat. They only loved her because of how she helped them as an apothecary. Without her service, they found her useless and strange.

Did her life only matter because of what she could do for others? Did her own desires matter to no one?

Her boot slammed against the cover of her magical book so hard that it tore part of the cover away from the spine. One glorious moment passed while she relished in destroying the item that had given her the means of forgetting herself in the pursuit of others' needs.

But then her stomach twisted into a knot that yanked straight through her heart. She slumped to the ground, her shoulders heaving with sobs. Her fingers reached for the book, hovering over the spot where the cover had torn away from the spine, afraid to touch it. Tears poured from her eyes as she clutched the book close to her chest.

Stomping on the book had felt cathartic in the moment, but she regretted it now. Her one link to Faerie had been damaged, and maybe nothing could ever repair it. Even though she did feel used and unappreciated by her neighbors sometimes, she still found joy in helping others. She still wanted to help when she could; she just wished it didn't have to take so much out of her every time she did it.

Sniffing, she gingerly opened the book, eager to see if doing so would destroy the book even more. She opened to a random page, but it ended up being the page exactly where she had left off before. The page about castles.

It is impossible to build a castle unless Faerie itself gives aid. The same is true for crowns. Each ruler has only one crown, which Faerie itself helped High Queen Winola create when she divided Faerie into its ■ separate courts.

Chloe's eyes narrowed as she touched the words she had just read. Curious. A little smudge blotted the page right between the words *its* and *separate*. Was there another word written there that had since been blotted out? Even after bringing the page closer to her, she still couldn't tell. If another word ever had gone there, it was probably just *six* since there were six courts in Faerie.

Some fae claim the high queen did not even build the castles, that Faerie itself created them while all of Faerie slept.

A sigh dropped from Chloe's lips as she closed her magical book. The cover hadn't torn away from the spine any more, even after she opened it. So at least her hasty anger hadn't ruined the book completely. Maybe she could find some way to patch it up, if she ever found a way to save Faerie that didn't require her to fight.

She dropped the book into her bag, then stuffed the dress from Quintus in as well. Draping it over her head, she then took her cloak and clasped it around her neck.

Why hadn't Quintus returned yet?

The question flitted away almost as soon as she thought it. He hadn't been gone that long. Plenty of time still needed to pass before she truly had to worry. But anxiety still clipped at the edges of her mind.

Even when she started pacing back and forth along one side of their ashy fire pit, her stomach wouldn't sit still. It hadn't been strictly intentional, but she noted that she only paced on the black soil, not on the brown soil of Crystal Thorn.

Aches stretched through her throat when she tried to swallow. It wouldn't be long now. Quintus would return with Ludo and then they'd attempt to get into the castle again. If they snuck around and never met anyone with weapons, Chloe would be able to help.

With that thought filling her mind, she almost didn't hear the snap of a twig. Even when she did process it, her mind just tossed it away as less important than the upcoming plans involving the castle.

But then she realized. The twig snap had come from the forest. Sucking in a breath, she jerked her body toward the path. Someone had found her.

28

CHLOE HAD NEVER BEEN ONE to pay much attention to sounds. If she had, she might have noticed the sound of footsteps stalking toward her. After the twig snap, her mind focused in at once. Several pairs of footsteps, maybe even a dozen came toward her. Or maybe her anxiety just multiplied a single set of footsteps into several.

This was why she wasn't good in a fight. Her mind always whirled too much to discern anything useful with so much danger all around.

Gasping, Chloe stood up straight and gripped her leather bag against her chest. A figure stepped out from behind a tree then. Mishti revealed herself and then, with a beckon, another young woman with brown eyes stepped out from the same tree to stand at Mishti's side.

Mishti no longer wore her midnight blue gown encrusted with white pearls. Now she wore tan pants and a tan tunic several shades lighter than her brown skin.

Her long braid that usually trailed down past her knees had been pinned up in a bun that towered high above her head. She had her sword, just like she always did, but the sword hung loosely and pointed downward.

The young woman at her side wore similar clothes. Her expression had the same hardened exterior as Mishti's, but her eyes looked a little less dead than many of the mortals. Even more interesting, Chloe recognized the girl. She had been among that group of girls who had been giggling at the flexing young man. And this girl was the one who had given her orange-glazed pastry to Portia.

Why did it have to be that girl who had come? After seeing how Portia manipulated the girl, Chloe just wanted to help her. The girl had done exactly what her leader had asked, yet she also seemed to recognize the manipulation. If Chloe had perhaps a little too much sympathy for any of the mortals, it was for the two standing in front of her now.

Though both Mishti and the girl had lowered eyebrows and firm expressions, they didn't seem on the verge of attacking. If Mishti hadn't raised her sword yet, maybe Chloe could talk her way out of this mess. Her limbs still shook, though. After a careful swallow, she lifted her chin. "How did you find me?"

Tilting her head in a slightly condescending way, Mishti answered. "The same way I found you at that other house. I followed your tracks."

Now she and the girl shared in a sideways glance that only barely masked identical smiles.

"Tracks?" Chloe rested her hands on her hips, narrowing her eyes as she did. "But we left the castle through a door." Once the words left her lips, she pantomimed opening a doorknob. "Not a *door* door, but a Faerie door." She now gestured toward the swirling door still open beside her.

Mishti nodded slowly, which only added to the air of condescension. "You *left* through a door, but how did you arrive?"

The words sent pinpricks across the back of Chloe's neck. She swallowed hard, realizing how careless she had been.

"Are you alone?" Mishti took a step forward, eyeing the clearing without hardly moving her head at all.

"I'm…" Chloe wanted to claim Quintus stood just inside one of the nearby caves and that he would attack the moment Mishti or the other girl did anything threatening. Unfortunately, the tunnel swirling just beside her probably called out that lie.

Letting out a short sigh, Chloe shrugged. "Yes, I'm alone. For now."

Mishti's dark eyes narrowed as she eyed the clearing again. Her sword still hung at her side, as unthreatening as possible, but Mishti's resting face had a way of being frightening all on its own.

It didn't help when another snapped twig made the younger girl whirl around and draw a serrated dagger from a strap hidden inside her sleeve. After a moment, the girl turned back to Mishti and shrugged. "It must have been one of those flying thorn creatures or a dryad or something."

Mishti nodded and tapped her thumb against the top of her sword. She focused in on Chloe. The young girl continued to grip her serrated dagger as she did the same.

Ice drizzled down Chloe's spine. The little hairs at the back of her neck stood on end, just waiting for the sword and dagger to raise into the air. Her muscles hadn't seized yet, but tension still wriggled under her skin until it felt thick and foreboding. Would Mishti and the girl attack or not? Chloe probably should have ignored that question. She did have something else on her mind anyway.

"Did you know the fae were going to be attacked by that explosion the way they were? Is that why you sent us to the library?" She hadn't meant to fill her tone with so much accusation, especially since doing so might invoke anger from these two people she definitely didn't want angered.

But fury never churned in Mishti's eyes. Her chin just lowered until it nearly touched her chest. "No. Even Portia didn't know that would happen. She was angry that Julian acted without speaking to her first."

"Right." Chloe pushed out a huffy chuckle. "She wasn't angry about the attack, just that one of her mortals dared to do anything without her permission. Why would she be angry about an attack on the fae?"

"She was angry about the attack too." The young girl's voice came out a little too fast, but a clear intelligence gleamed in her eye. Maybe she wasn't old enough to control her every action, but she obviously knew what she was talking about still. The sight reminded Chloe so much of Grace that Chloe nearly started crying right there.

Mishti shrugged, giving confirmation of the girl's words. "Portia had her heart set on the beheadings."

The longer those two young women stood in the clearing, the more Chloe felt comfortable with their presence. Mishti's thumb kept tapping the top of her sword, treating it more like an accessory than a weapon. The young girl kept eyeing the caves, her eyes opening wide with wonder every time she glanced at them again.

Getting comfortable with their presence could be dangerous though. It *would* be, if Chloe had to guess. They hated the fae, and they hated Chloe for trying to help the fae. Sliding her feet just a little closer to Quintus's door, she narrowed her eyes at the two young women.

Mishti's thumb tapped on her sword even faster now. "Luckily for Portia—and for you I suppose—none of the fae were fatally injured in that explosion. The beheadings will proceed tomorrow morning as planned."

She spoke the words with the same solemnity as she gave to everything she said. Despite the heaviness in her tone, a weight immediately lifted off Chloe's shoulders as the words sank in.

No fatal injuries. That meant Elora was *alive*.

Of course she was. She could survive anything. Chloe almost chided herself for believing her sister might have died, but too much relief flooded her to feel anything else.

Mishti's face scrunched up tight as her gaze turned weighted. "The fae have been moved though. There's now an ambush waiting for you in the library if you attempt to free the fae before the beheadings tomorrow."

With her hand still on her hips, Chloe laughed. "That's why you're here? To intimidate me?" She jutted her chin forward. "I have a tendency to do the opposite of what people ask just to spite them, so I'd be careful what you say."

"No, that wasn't..." The slightest grimace forced a twitch across one of Mishti's eyes. Her face was usually so stoic, it was strange to see any sign of discomfort. "I came to *warn* you about the ambush."

The girl at her side glanced over, biting her bottom lip as she did.

Mishti's gaze dropped downward. "And..." She swallowed. "You said I could come with you, right? You said you wanted to rescue me from Portia, and I wouldn't have to be a victim of her manipulation anymore."

She gestured toward the young girl. "That's why Mila and I are here. We want to escape."

It took just one breath before the words sank in. Mila glanced toward Mishti but then looked back to Chloe. She still bit her bottom lip, and suddenly, the fear and hope in her eyes became clear as day.

"Yes." Dropping her hands to her sides, Chloe immediately took a step forward. "Of course." Her fingers twitched, not sure if she should reach out and embrace them or if she should just nod. Maybe a smile would help. "I'm so glad you came. Of course you can come with us."

It only lasted for a moment, but a twinkle glinted in Mishti's eyes. She didn't have the kind of face that gave way to smiles easily, but the ghost of one still settled across her features. A slightly less timid one danced over Mila's mouth as well.

Joy blossomed in that small clearing, warming up the bits that fear had frozen. But it only took a moment before that blossom shriveled back into nothing again.

Portia herself stepped out from behind a tree still wearing her teal dress made of silk and chiffon. Once she revealed herself, at least a dozen other mortals followed. They all wore tunics and pants similar to Mishti's and Mila's. Each of them wore the same expression.

They wanted Chloe dead.

29

CHLOE'S FIRST ASSESSMENT OF HOW many footsteps she heard had been right after all. Over a dozen mortals stood before her now, each of them glancing toward Portia, waiting for orders. Chloe's arms wrapped around her stomach. The mortals held weapons and pointed them straight at Chloe. Fear didn't trickle into her limbs, it crashed in like a blizzard.

Her muscles seized, planting her feet to the ground. Even if she wanted to move, she couldn't. Fear had rendered her limbs completely useless while they seized under her skin. It took everything in her just to remember to breathe.

This was a trap. How had she been so naïve again? Why was she *always* so naïve?

But just as she berated herself, she caught a glimpse of Mishti. The young woman's eyebrows had flown up to her hairline. Her jaw clenched tight. She even lifted her sword, but she pointed the blade toward Portia.

Mila had stepped behind Mishti. Her shoulders shook as she too raised her serrated dagger toward Portia.

The woman just laughed and rolled her eyes. "I know your weaknesses, remember? It's useless to raise those weapons to me."

Tremors passed through Mishti's arms as she gripped the sword tighter. She took in a breath and stepped farther in front of Mila. As she moved, her free arm reached out. A single arm couldn't do much, but it was clear the action was meant to keep Mila safe.

Portia just rolled her eyes again. "Calm down, Mishti. I can forgive you for this slight error in your judgment. There will be consequences, of course, but you'll be forgiven."

Those words only caused Mishti to grip her sword tighter. She glanced back at Mila and then at the woman. Portia said nothing. She didn't react in any way, even though she must have known Mishti wanted to ask after the young girl's consequences.

When the other mortals stepped into the clearing, Mishti widened her stance until she looked truly ready to fight. The shaking in Mila's shoulders had calmed. She now wore an angry face nearly identical to Mishti's as she held out her dagger.

Portia's eyes narrowed to tiny slits as her gaze slid over to Chloe. "*You* cannot be forgiven."

At least she looked at Chloe and not Mila when she said it. Portia's lips curled with a sneer. "Usually, I try to save all mortals no matter what they've done, but you deserve to die along with the fae for your grotesque crime."

A vein across Mishti's jaw pulsed as she gritted her teeth together. "What has she done?"

Ice and shadows flashed in Portia's eyes. Her voice came out as severe as the tight bun on top of her head. "She planted the seed of selfishness deep in your heart. You used to put our people first, no matter the cost, but now you keep thinking of how you don't want to kill the fae who would happily kill us in return."

"It's hurting me." Mishti's voice broke. Her mouth hung open as she tried to calm the sudden hurried breaths that tumbled out. "Each life I take, each battle I fight, it's like a little piece of my soul crushes into dust. I'm afraid if I keep killing, I will lose the little of me I still have left."

Behind her, Mila's chin quivered as she nodded in agreement.

The words dove into Chloe's heart, splitting it open like a raw husk. If Portia said anything else, Chloe might just overcome her fear of fighting and pounce on the woman. But even as she thought it, Chloe knew that wasn't true.

Her muscles tensed so tight she might just pass out. Ice-cold tears formed in her eyes, slicing like lethal icicles down her cheeks.

It only took a nod from Portia and the attack began. Chloe's eyes slammed shut completely against her control. Weapons clashed and bodies whirled. She could hear the fight but couldn't see it. If her eyes had been open, the anxiety in her probably would have just turned her vision black anyway.

Tears continued to stream down her cheeks, but now they came from self-loathing. Why did she have to be so useless in a fight? Why couldn't she just throw a kick or tackle someone?

Instead, her past clawed under her skin, into her veins, into her bones. It coiled tight around every muscle, every hair. Memories flashed in her mind now. The sweaty hands. The screams. Her entire body shook so hard she almost lost her balance.

But soon that didn't matter anyway. Someone slammed against her and threw her to the ground. The deepest part of her heart wished it was Quintus, or Mishti, or maybe even Elora. But when Chloe opened her eyes, a mortal with bloodthirsty eyes stared back at her.

Her muscles seized when he touched her arms. He wrenched them behind her back, which left her gasping for air. A metallic rope with prickly needles coming out of it was wrapped around her wrists. The tiny needles pierced her skin, drawing blood as the rope tightened around her wrists. Still, the sensation of the man's hands on her arms hurt worse than the needles. It felt like a hundred knives stabbing her from every angle.

If the man hadn't stepped away at that exact moment, she would have fainted. In fact, the only reason she probably hadn't fainted yet was because the needles in that horrible rope kept her alert.

Tears blurred her vision, but she could still see just enough to know what had happened. She never needed to look anyway though. There had been over a dozen mortals against Mishti, Mila, and Chloe. Since Chloe had been more than useless, that left Mishti and Mila with seven to deal with each.

They never had a chance.

Four mortals writhed in agony on the ground due to the wounds Mishti and Mila had inflicted upon them, which was honestly more than Chloe expected. But the two young women now suffered the same fate as Chloe.

They sat near her with needle-covered metallic ropes tying their arms behind their backs. A stake had been driven through their ropes and deep into the soil, keeping them stuck to the ground as well. A quick tug confirmed that Chloe had been staked down as well.

"Let us go!" Mila shouted the words with the fury that only someone who very nearly experienced freedom could show.

Portia looked down her nose at the girl before glancing at the man who had tied Chloe up. Portia gestured toward Mila. "Kill her."

The man gave half a nod before he realized the woman gestured toward Mila and not toward Chloe like he had clearly assumed. His step faltered. "But…" The grip on his short sword tightened as he swallowed. "But she's one of us."

Mishti's jaw had dropped open. The realization had left her speechless.

Despite the man's hesitation and despite Mishti's disbelief, Portia just rolled her eyes. "Never mind, I'll do it myself."

She snatched the short sword from the man and slammed it up underneath Mila's rib cage. After a single gurgling breath, the young woman collapsed to the ground with her arms still pinned in place by the metallic rope.

"No!" Mishti shouted. Her arms yanked, attempting to free herself from the rope holding her down. The needles inside the rope sliced across her skin. It left tiny scratches at first, but the more she moved, the scratches turned to gashes, which turned to raw and bloodied skin.

It didn't help. No matter how Mishti yanked and fought, she stayed in place. And Mila was still dead. Chloe dropped her gaze to the ground, fighting to stop herself from vomiting. Another person she had failed to save.

Mishti kept yanking and screaming until her arms were more blood than skin.

"Hold still." Chloe whispered the words so the other mortals wouldn't hear.

But when Mishti whirled around to glare at Chloe with ferocious eyes, she almost wished Mishti hadn't heard either.

But Mishti didn't understand. Each time she thrashed, she only tightened her bonds. A metallic rope with tiny needles poking out of it would already be nearly impossible to untie. But if she kept moving, only a sword that could cut through metal would be able to free her.

When Chloe said nothing in response, Mishti just screamed. Her head pointed toward the sky as she let out a shriek that shook the ground beneath their feet.

Portia winced as she finished wiping the blood off her hands with a small handkerchief. She glanced toward the man whose weapon had killed Mila. "Gag her, will you? Gag both of them in case the other one starts screaming too. I cannot stand such shrill noises."

Fear flashed in his eyes as he checked the thick gloves he wore. The gloves must have protected his hands from the needles inside the rope. He then got more rope and gagged both Chloe and Mishti.

The needles sliced across their necks, cheeks, and tongues. Seeing it only made Portia grin. "I told you."

222

Now that the blood had been wiped from her hands, she trailed across the clearing toward Mishti. Using one finger to lift the young woman's chin, Portia tilted her head to the side. A mock look of concern lit in her eyes. "I told you there would be consequences for your attempted betrayal. Look at what happened to poor Mila because you refused to help us when I asked."

Chloe's stomach lurched, ready to lose its contents. She probably should have worked harder to control it, but her entire focus had been stolen by an idea.

Now that the fight had ended, her mind could work again. And even more important, so could her fingers.

The other mortals stood in front of Chloe and Mishti, standing in a half circle behind Portia. Maybe they didn't think any of them needed to stand behind the young women, since who in their right mind would attempt to untie a rope that had needles poking out of it?

But none of them knew Chloe well enough, apparently. Years of harp playing had made her fingers strong. She had never found a knot she couldn't untie. Her fingers pressed against the rope, letting the needles slide into her skin. Once in place, she'd then wriggle the rope looser little by little.

If her gaze ever darted over to the dead body in the clearing, her fingers would freeze, and tears would blur her vision again. So she tried to focus on what she could. The rope could be untied. It *would* be untied.

After a hard swallow, one of the other mortals gestured toward the Faerie door that still swirled at Chloe's side. "What should we do about this? Throw some iron in it?"

The grin that slipped across Portia's face looked as slimy as the hands that woke Chloe from her nightmares. "No. The fae who left that door open must intend to come back through it eventually. We will wait here until he returns." Her shoulder lifted in a shrug. "And then we will kill him."

Chloe didn't bother to wonder why they hadn't killed her yet. Portia probably just wanted to behead her along with the fae. She'd be a lesson of what might happen to any mortals who tried to defy Portia.

Blood dripped from her fingers as she worked. She had nearly freed herself and now she started to figure out how to untie Mishti's rope too. Her fingers faltered then. Suddenly she realized what she had failed to consider before.

Only one of them could go through the door.

The door would close automatically once someone jumped through it. If both of them tried to jump through it at once, the magic inside would probably just close before either of them could get through.

Chloe *couldn't* save both of them.

The realization hit her as her gaze landed on the body she'd been avoiding. Mishti had thrashed so wildly, the chance of untying her bonds now was nearly impossible. But if Chloe left, if she went through the door, maybe it didn't mean abandoning Mishti.

In that moment it finally clicked. Quintus had tried to explain in the cave, but she hadn't understood then. She'd spent so much time blaming herself and hating that she hadn't saved her friend when she should have. But trying to help in that particular instance only would have gotten herself kidnapped along with her friend.

And if Chloe tried to save both her and Mishti now, the numerous mortals would just stop them immediately. Chloe would certainly be killed. And if she did nothing, Quintus would return and be ambushed and then he would die too. And with no one else to save them, the fae would die in the beheadings just like Portia had planned.

With a clench of her heart, Chloe finally understood. Taking care of others was good, important even. But if she didn't take care of herself first, there wouldn't be enough of herself left to help anyone else.

She had spent so much time helping and sacrificing, and it always left her feeling haggard. But maybe if she bothered to take care of herself, then maybe helping others wouldn't drag her down so much. Maybe then she could experience the joy and peace it gave her to help, but it wouldn't suck the life out of her in the process.

And hadn't Portia said Mishti wouldn't be killed? Between the two of them, Mishti was much safer staying here than Chloe was. And since only one of them could go through the door, Chloe finally accepted what she had to do.

It still felt like abandoning Mishti. It still hurt as much as losing her friend to a kidnapper all those years ago. But now Chloe realized, Mishti would meet a worse fate if Chloe sacrificed her own safety to stay. But if Chloe left, she could come back and rescue Mishti properly.

One of the mortals noticed when Chloe slipped out of her bonds. The woman's eyes went wide. Her body moved to lunge.

But it was too late.

For once, Chloe focused on herself first so that she'd still be alive to save everyone else.

She jumped through the door at her side.

30

MOSS PADDED CHLOE'S FALL WHEN she stumbled through the Faerie door. If she had used her hands to catch herself, it probably would have resulted in fewer bruises. But since that needled rope she untied had turned her fingers into a raw, bloody mess, she went with landing on her shoulder instead.

Her heart clenched as soon as she met the ground. The scent of rain and wet tree trunks filled her nose. Such a pleasant scent should have been calming, but all she could think about was the look on Mishti's face when Chloe jumped through the door.

Red had splotched over Mishti's face. Her eyes had been bloodshot. The expression had been clear. She felt betrayed.

Curling her knees to her chest, Chloe played the moment over in her mind again. She had left Mishti, abandoned her. But it wasn't a betrayal. She couldn't have saved Mishti even though she wanted to. Not then.

The door would have closed if Mishti tried to go through. And Chloe never would have been able to untie the young woman's bonds before one of the mortals stopped her anyway. Still, Mishti didn't know any of those things. She just knew Chloe had left.

Why did guilt have to sting Chloe so much in moments like this?

All her life, she'd helped and helped, and no one ever seemed to notice or care when all the helping drained the life out of her. And if they did notice, they praised her for it. They complimented her for being selfless, for ignoring her own needs when others needed her. And if her actions garnered praise, then they had to be good, didn't they?

But then why did it hurt so much? Why did it pain her to constantly wear herself down in the pursuit of meeting everyone else's needs but never her own?

Surely, if it was wrong, someone would have stopped her. Someone would have told her that no one needed her care as much as herself. But no one ever said that. Instead, they told her selflessness was the greatest quality a woman could have. So no matter how her heart withered away each time she ignored her own needs, she had always believed it was right to help others first. It was good.

To think of herself was selfish. Wrong.

But sometimes it left her feeling so empty she could barely breathe. And she was sick of gasping for air. Sick of drowning.

No one knew her own needs better than herself, so why should it be someone else's responsibility to take care of her when she was in need? What was so wrong about taking care of herself? What was so wrong with putting herself first just long enough that she actually had the energy to take care of others?

Sucking in a breath, Chloe forced herself to her feet. She moved carefully to avoid getting any dirt into the wounds on her fingers. Without even knocking first, she shoved her way into Ludo's home.

Her feet marched across the ground, rounding a corner before she found Quintus and Ludo sitting on either side of the same table they had been sitting across before.

Ludo's blue and red eyes flashed at the sight of her. He sat higher in his wooden chair and jabbed a finger toward her. "You cannot just barge into a fae's home without permission. Faerie itself will punish you. I expect my visitors to…"

His words trailed off when he realized absolutely no one listened to him. Quintus had already jumped up from the sofa and sprinted across the room. A heavy exhale blew from his nose. He clenched his jaw, reaching for the gag keeping Chloe silent.

His thumb trailed along her cheek while his eyes narrowed to the tiniest slits.

"Who did this to you?" Though the volume of his voice was low, it came out as deadly as scurpus itself.

He reached for the gag, attempting to remove it. But once he touched it, his hands snapped back. At first, she assumed his fingers had discovered the tiny needles coming out of the metallic rope, but the steam sizzling off his hands proved it was more than that.

Iron.

Of course she hadn't realized it before because iron did nothing to her. But why else would the mortals have metallic rope? *Of course* it had iron in it.

Quintus grunted at his hands and immediately reached for the gag again. "Whoever did this is dead."

A hiss of steam erupted from his fingertips when he touched the rope again.

Shaking her head, Chloe stepped away so he couldn't reach it anymore. The flashing in his eyes made it clear he had no intention of giving up, no matter how much the iron pained him. Luckily, she had a better idea.

Blood and gashes covered her fingers and wrists, but the palms of her hands were still untouched. She grabbed his nearest hand with both her forearms, attempting to keep the blood off him, then she carefully placed the palm of her hand over the knuckles of his.

Now that she touched him, she could just heal the wounds herself. Understanding dawned on his face a moment before she could close her eyes. He immediately jerked his hand away, even taking a step away from her. The skin contact got ripped away in that same moment.

Clenching his jaw, he whirled around to face Ludo. "Why are you just standing there?" He gestured toward the blood dripping down her arms. "Get something to wipe away this blood."

Ludo stalked off, but he rolled his eyes first.

The moment he turned his back, Quintus stepped close enough to set his mouth directly next to Chloe's ear. His breath rustled her hair as he whispered. "Ludo does not know what you can do." Even in that whisper quieter than a mortal could have managed, Quintus still must have feared Ludo might hear.

Pulling his head back slightly, Quintus looked pointedly at Chloe's hands. Only then did she understand what he meant. Magic. Ludo didn't know she could do magic.

Quintus's lips pressed closer to her. A shiver melted into her shoulders at the feel of him. He whispered again. "Until Ludo claims his favor from you, we should try to keep that secret."

She wanted to nod, but the feel of him had a way of rendering her immobile.

He whispered a little louder now, just enough that he probably meant for Ludo to hear the words. "Are you sure you are all right?"

Warmth pressed into her skin when Quintus squeezed her shoulder. His hand trailed down her arm until it came just above the torn and bloody skin of her wrist.

By then, Ludo had nearly reached them again. He held a cloth out to Chloe, but he also threw an annoyed glare at Quintus. "If you keep asking me for things, you will have to make another bargain with me to make up for it."

The cloth had only barely touched Chloe's fingertips, but the pain was nothing to the words just spoken. She sucked in a breath and shot a look at Quintus.

His eyebrows knitted together. "Do you need help? I can do it instead."

He took the cloth, but she saw straight through his intentions. He wanted to pretend that she had no idea how significant and dangerous making a bargain with a fae could be. A mortal making a bargain with a fae always ended badly, but a fae making a bargain with another fae was almost just as bad. Why had Quintus done it then?

When he attempted to wipe a line of blood from the back of her hand, she jerked both her hands away and burned him with a glare. He knew exactly why she was angry, and she would not let him avoid it any longer.

But he just threw another pointed stare at her hands. "This first," he whispered.

If her mouth hadn't been full of a needled rope, she would have gritted her teeth together. He was probably right. She wanted every detail of that bargain, but getting the gag off and cleaning her wounds was slightly more time sensitive.

He attempted to wipe away the blood, but he didn't have the apothecary training she did. Instead of dabbing at the wounds, he wiped across them with a heavy hand, which only opened her wounds even more.

Pulling her hands from his grip, she reached for the gag tied at the base of her neck. Her arms flinched when the needles in the rope dug into her skin. Each gash split just a little deeper as she worked to loosen the bond.

Color drained from Quintus's face as her fingers tugged at the rope. Each time she winced, his entire body would tighten. After only a few moments, he looked ready to vomit. At least four times, he attempted to move her hands and finish the job. But each time, she just slapped his hand away.

Faerie already had enough iron in the air and ground. He didn't need any more exposure to iron than absolutely necessary.

By the time she finished, he stood close enough that his fingers brushed over her waist. He might have reached an arm all the way around her, except he kept flinching too much for it.

Once the rope fell away from her mouth and dropped to the ground, she opened her mouth wide and stretched out her tongue. At least the needles in the gag hadn't scraped across her skin multiple times. With only small punctures inside her mouth and along her cheeks and neck, they would heal faster.

Could she talk without drawing blood though? That was the real question.

"Who did this to you?" Quintus had finally allowed his hand to make contact with her waist. His teeth clenched while fire flared in his eyes.

Instead of answering, she just held her hands out to him. "Dab the wounds instead of wiping across them. And use a gentler hand if you can."

He blinked once before the anger on his face dropped away. Nodding, he raised the cloth back to her fingers and did as she instructed.

While he worked, Ludo stepped up on the other side of Chloe. His gaze trained downward. "What a curious rope. I have to admit, it took genius to decide to have needles piercing through it."

He bent to grab it.

Chloe cleared her throat loudly. "The rope also has iron in it, so unless you enjoy burned and poisoned flesh, I suggest you don't touch it."

His eyes flew open wide. He nodded, but only to himself as he stalked off across the room again.

"I cannot get any more blood off. The rest of it has dried." Quintus's words came out tighter than usual.

Since touching anything could cause any number of pollutants to get into her wounds, Chloe just gestured toward her leather bag. "I have a tincture that will help to get the rest of the blood off. The herbs infused in the alcohol will help to clean the wound as well."

Ludo shuffled through the items on a bookshelf at the edge of the room. He kept moving objects and lifting them. While he did seem to know where to find things, the room clearly didn't have perfect organization, even for him."

"Is this it?" Quintus held up a little bundle of cloth that had the makings of another poultice that would heal scurpus.

Pinpricks from the needle wounds stung in her mouth when she pressed her lips together to keep from smiling. "No, a tincture is liquid. It should be in a vial with a cork stoppering it."

It took a few more guesses, but he found it eventually. While he poured the liquid over the wounds in her fingers and wrists, Ludo came back. He now had a thick piece of fabric that looked similar to leather, but it was much thicker.

With the fabric wrapped around one hand, he plucked the iron rope from the ground. As he studied it, he spoke. "Do you still want to go through with this plan when your mortal is in a state like that?"

His gaze lifted from the rope just long enough to glance toward Chloe.

Her eyes narrowed. If her hands had been free, she would have clenched her fists. "I am not *his* mortal. I belong to no one."

Quintus followed her words with a definitive nod. "And she is more than capable. You just worry about your part. We will take care of the rest."

"And anyway." Chloe lifted her chin in the air. "Portia plans to behead all the fae inside the castle tomorrow. We need to enact this plan as soon as possible."

Now her gaze slid over to Quintus. Her voice turned soft as she caught his eye. "How soon can we leave?"

Despite where she looked, Ludo answered the question. "We cannot leave now."

Chloe let out a small huff. "Clearly. I still have to get my fingers and wrists bandaged. But we should leave soon after that. Portia is away from the castle right now. This might be our best chance to save the fae before she can get involved."

"Wrong again." Ludo tossed the little bundle he had made with the iron rope and the thick fabric. It landed with a soft thud on a pile of picture frames and textbooks. "I still have something to find before we can enact our plan."

Her eyes twitched at his audacity, but when she attempted to get Quintus on her side, he just nodded in agreement with Ludo.

The blue-and-red-eyed fae gestured toward a slightly less cluttered spot on his mossy floor. "You two can sleep here. I should be back before day dawns, but my quest will take most of the night at least."

Quintus finished cleaning her wounds with the tincture. She would have walked him through the next steps of applying honey and bandages, but if Ludo was leaving, she could just heal the wounds with her magic soon enough.

He must have had the same idea because he dropped the empty vial into her leather bag and then reached into his pocket to pull out their sleeping mats and blankets.

"I don't want to sleep here." She had whispered, but without fae abilities, she wasn't able to whisper in a voice soft enough that Ludo couldn't hear. Not that she cared about whether he'd be offended or not.

She took a step closer to Quintus anyway. "Why can't we go to your home in Crystal Thorn to sleep? Then we can meet Ludo at the castle tomorrow morning when day dawns."

Ludo's steps toward his swirling door of snowy white and opalescent clouds faltered when Chloe mentioned Quintus's home. Or maybe he faltered for some other reason.

Quintus turned away from both of them. "I have no home."

Those words seemed to satisfy Ludo. He nodded and promptly disappeared through his door, which immediately closed behind him.

Chloe would not be appeased so easily. "What do you mean you have no home? I've been there before. In fact, I've been wondering why you took me to those crystal caves instead of your home. We stayed in your home for much of the time that I was here before."

Each word from her lips twisted his features into a tighter knot. "I do not wish to discuss it."

She felt one eyebrow raise up high as she dropped a hand on her hip. "Well, that's interesting because I didn't want to come to Faerie, and yet, here I am."

Something almost like a chuckle puffed from his lips. "I will tell you later."

She leaned in closer to him. "Or you could tell me now."

"Not now." He hadn't raised his voice at her, but the sharpness in his tone still caused her to shrink back. He let out a sigh and reached for her hand. He settled his palm under the back of her hand where they still had ample skin contact but without him touching the wounds in her fingers and wrists.

"With Ludo gone, there is no danger in using your magic to heal yourself."

But she didn't heal herself. She just stared at him, hoping the gaze needled its way under his skin until he said what she wanted to hear.

His shoulders shuddered, indicating her gaze had made him at least slightly uncomfortable. "I will tell you about my home later."

She raised both eyebrows and pulled her hand away from his touch.

"Chloe, I will. I just…" A light flickered in his eyes as an idea seemed to dawn on him. "I *vow* that I will tell you what happened to my home."

A gasp momentarily stole her breath away. A vow meant more than just a spoken promise. In Faerie, a vow could not be broken. Faerie made it physically impossible. Quintus had already made some sort of bargain with Ludo, the details of which Chloe knew nothing about. And now he had made a vow to her?

Desperation had truly gotten to him then. Nothing else could have caused him to behave in such a way.

234

He slipped his hand under hers once again. "I will tell you after we rescue the fae and recapture Crystal Thorn Castle. But right now, I want you to tell me what happened."

A vein in his jaw pulsed as he looked at her wounds. "Who did this to you? That girl? The one you used to be friends with?"

"No." The memory ached inside Chloe. After focusing on the wounds, she'd been able to forget for a little while. But now she could see it all again. The hope in Mishti's and Mila's expressions. The mortals attacking. Blood dripping down Portia's arm. Mila's cold and dead eyes.

Chloe sniffed and forced herself to close her eyes and heal her wounds before tears made it impossible to think clearly.

And then she told Quintus everything. He made up their sleeping mats and they both got into bed. She talked the entire time.

He never interrupted except when asking for clarification. Explaining the events hurt almost as much as living them the first time.

She had to remind herself at least twice that she hadn't abandoned Mishti. She still had every intention of rescuing her. And now that she stopped Quintus from meeting the ambush that would have waited for him in that clearing, they both had a good chance of going back to the castle and saving the fae inside.

Just as sleep curled in around her mind, she asked one last question. "What did Ludo leave to find?"

"A distraction." A long yawn tore from Quintus's mouth. "Something the mortals will not be able to ignore."

31

THE NEXT MORNING STARTED IN a blur. Chloe barely had enough time to roll up her sleeping mat, pull on her boots, and don her cloak and leather bag before Quintus ushered her through a swirling door.

She'd been hoping for a chance to ask him about his bargain with Ludo before they met up with the Fairfrost fae again, since she had fallen asleep before she could ask last night. But soon all three of them stood next to a pile of mossy boulders in a small clearing near Crystal Thorn Castle.

"Is it ready?" The slightest tremor shook Quintus's voice as he stared at Ludo.

The blue and red eyes before them flashed with a frightening sort of delight. Ludo glanced over his shoulder just as an enormous roar shook several leaves off the trees around them.

Chloe hadn't even noticed jumping behind Quintus and digging her fingers into his upper arm until he placed a hand over hers. He glanced back too, probably intending to offer words of comfort or maybe just to tell her to calm down.

He never got the chance to do either, though, because a dragon with a head as large as a desk and a body as large as a house stepped into the clearing. It had golden eyes and golden horns. Its large wings sparkled blue like sapphires.

It jerked one of its enormous legs, but it didn't move very far since several thick ropes tied the creature to the ground.

Ludo sighed at the creature, as if he was presenting a delicate rose for them to admire. A shimmer even passed through his eyes that looked suspiciously like tears. "Is it not beautiful?"

Dropping her hands away from Quintus's upper arm, she scrunched up her nose. "Beautiful? I think the word you were looking for is *deadly*."

Quintus shrugged. "That is what makes it a perfect distraction for the mortals. They will not care so much about keeping the fae captured when their own lives are in danger."

"And what about *our* lives?" Her face would start to ache if she kept it scrunched up like this for much longer.

"Here." Ludo pushed a plate of food into Chloe's hands, which definitely felt like an attempt to distract her.

She didn't even have time to glance at the plate before Quintus ripped it out of her hands and shoved it back toward Ludo. "I told you, no berries."

Ludo rolled his eyes and pushed the food back toward Quintus. "You eat it then. I will conjure something else for the mortal."

The plate had a fluffy scone with a pile of fresh berries, a thick berry syrup, and even a sprig of mint on the side. It certainly looked delicious…for someone who could stomach berries.

Quintus glared without moving until Ludo pulled another dish from his pocket and conjured a bowl of oatmeal that still had a visible drizzle of honey on top. He dropped in a silver spoon. Chloe snatched the bowl away immediately.

Only once she started shoveling the food into her mouth did Quintus begin eating his berry scone. Food always had a way of calming her belly, but it was more difficult when a dragon's golden eyes followed her silver spoon each time it left the bowl and entered her mouth.

After the third bite, the dragon's complete attention struck less as frightening and more as a sign. "Is the dragon hungry?"

Quintus stopped mid-chew while his eyes opened wide. Ludo just laughed. "Finish your food and then we can use this dragon to distract those mortals."

She stuffed two more bites into her mouth before scowling at Ludo. "Aren't all dragons wild now? I vaguely remember Severin and his beloved, Tindra, mentioning something—"

"Yes, all dragons are wild except for one, and it is not this one." Ludo lifted an eyebrow. "But I know how to train dragons."

That seemed doubtful, especially since only one trained dragon lived in all of Faerie. Maybe it wasn't a lie if Ludo believed he could do it, but Chloe didn't believe he could.

A smile curved onto Ludo's face, brightening the red in his eyes. "I just need something *special* to do it."

The glaring red in his eyes was far from delightful, but the tone of his voice felt like nails on a chalkboard. And why did he have to look at her so intensely when he spoke?

Ludo took a step forward. "Since you took my sword sheath—"

"My *father's* sword sheath." Chloe turned her nose up and swallowed another bite of food. "Which you stole from the sprites."

Her moment of confidence faded when she noticed her retort had done nothing to make him falter. In fact, the dark look casting a shadow on his eyes only added to his frightening expression.

"I am ready to collect the favor you owe me."

A frosty rope seemed to squeeze around her heart. She gulped.

When the dragon let out another roar and attempted to yank itself free from the ropes holding it, Ludo offered no reaction. He just took another step forward and continued to stare at Chloe in a way that made her stomach writhe. "I believe you have a harp string of some significance."

The silver spoon dropped from her hand and clattered into the porcelain bowl. It was a miracle she hadn't dropped the bowl as well. "How do you know about that?"

She hated that the words came out wispy. And why had she even asked? He only could have learned about the harp string from one person.

Her gaze drifted over to Quintus. He stared at his now empty plate, stared a little too hard.

"Why?" The word came out in a breath as she gripped the bowl in her hand.

Ludo gestured back at the dragon. "I need something with great emotional significance to calm and control the dragon. Objects owned by fae usually do not have enough emotion in them since our connection to the mortal realm is still somewhat new."

Of course Ludo had assumed she directed her question at him, when really she just wanted to know why Quintus would ever tell anyone else about their harp string. How stupid of her to assume it actually mattered to him the way it mattered to her. He had simply tied off her braid with a harp string once, and even though she claimed she wanted nothing to do with him after that, she had still never been able to get rid of the accursed object.

Holding one hand out, Ludo's eyebrows raised. "I request the harp string as payment for your favor."

Her teeth gritted together as her gaze shifted to Quintus again. He still stared at his plate with far too much interest. If he didn't care, then why should she?

It only took a moment to locate the harp string inside her leather bag. Instead of handing it over gently, she threw it as hard as she could. Ludo seemed completely unconcerned when it landed without fanfare only an arm's length away from the dragon.

He sauntered after it while she turned away from Quintus completely. She should have known this would happen eventually. This was what she got for needing help one too many times. Quintus had gotten her Swiftsea salt when she needed it, he rescued her from attacking mortals, he came and got her when she was in Ludo's house all alone. He had saved her over and over again. She should have known it would take its toll.

Apparently all men, even fae, would only admire her for her selflessness, for her ability to help others. But once she needed too much help herself, the admiration would eventually float away.

After retrieving the harp string, Ludo handed it to Quintus. Setting his plate down, Quintus worked his magic to craft the string into a more useful item. In only a few moments, the thin metal string had now been turned into a long thick string that would fit over the dragon's mouth and work like reins.

The blue in Ludo's eyes flashed bright. He took the harp string reins into his hands and eyed them greedily.

Folding her arms over her chest, Chloe turned away from Quintus even more. She couldn't decide if it hurt worse that he refused to apologize or that he refused to be frustrated by her anger. His frustrating, even calm dug into her heart with far more bite than an angered retort would have.

After five attempts, Ludo managed to throw the reins onto the dragon. If Chloe had been watching more closely, she might have known if the reins themselves kept the dragon under control or if Ludo simply used them in conjunction with some other training method.

But aches screwed at her heart each time she turned her head even slightly toward Quintus. And what did she care about how dragons were trained anyway?

She only noticed when Ludo drew a knife and cut the ropes holding the dragon down. With the reins in his hands, the dragon had turned completely docile. His foot tilted, as if ready to kick the dragon into action.

Instead, he turned toward Chloe. "One more thing." His lips curled into a snarl that was probably supposed to look like a grin. "I get to keep the dragon *and* the harp string when this is over. It is part of the favor."

"But…" She dropped her hands to her sides and even took a small step forward. Maybe he had taken the harp string, but he had made it sound temporary. Or maybe she had just assumed that because that was what she wanted. "I never agreed to that."

"Just do it." Quintus finally spoke, and the words edged under her skin like tiny shards.

She immediately turned away from him again, folding her arms over her chest. "Fine. Keep it. The stupid thing means nothing to me anyway. I just thought Quintus might be sad about losing it, but I suppose I was wrong about that."

Sparkly sapphire wings spread out from the dragon's back and began flapping before she had even finished her sentence. Ludo had long since stopped listening, though her words hadn't really been meant for him anyway.

But just as the dragon lifted into the air, Ludo jumped off the enormous creature. The dragon continued flying straight for the castle.

Her lips parted in awe as she touched a hand to her collarbone. The dragon's size should have prevented it from entering the castle through any of the windows, but its large claws took care of that problem almost immediately. Stone crumbled away from the castle walls as it pushed its way inside.

Screams rang out only a moment later.

Ludo smiled as shrieks and the sound of crumbling stone rang through the air again. He turned straight to Quintus. "I will enter the castle as agreed—but not until you cover me with that enchantment that will protect me from the iron."

Chloe's jaw snapped shut. How had she already forgotten about this part? To create the enchantment, she would have to touch Quintus.

A shudder trickled down her spine.

Quintus nodded, not sparing a single glance toward Chloe. "But once we are inside, you will be able to locate the fuel and then the fae who have been captured?"

"We may have to get close enough, but yes, I will locate them as we agreed in our bargain."

"Come on then." Quintus still refused to look at Chloe as he started toward the castle.

"What about the enchantment?" The first tendril of fear wrapped itself around Ludo's words.

"It will be ready when we enter the castle."

Even though Quintus refused to look at her and made absolutely no mention of her, she suddenly understood his actions. He had one arm out, ready for her to take it. But he held it in such a casual position that Ludo probably wouldn't even notice.

Quintus was still trying to keep Ludo from finding out *she* was the one who could create the enchantment that protected against iron. Even though her favor had been collected, Quintus still protected her.

Or maybe keeping that knowledge from Ludo protected Quintus in some way too. After callously forcing her to give up the harp string, she knew better than to assume Quintus's motives had anything to do with her.

But whether he liked it or not, Quintus needed her to get inside that castle. And he'd have to touch her to do it.

Never before had the thought of touching him disgusted her so completely. Unfortunately, the necessity of it had never been stronger either.

32

CRYSTAL THORN CASTLE LOOMED AHEAD. Its black stone walls and vine-covered spires usually had a magical and exciting appearance. Now they did nothing but fill Chloe with dread. That castle had iron inside it now. Both Ludo and Quintus needed protection from it, or they'd never be able to enter the castle with her.

For a moment, her mind whirled with a few lines of an epic poem that she made up right then and there. The heroine left her companions behind and entered the castle alone. The enemies shook with fright at the sight of her and immediately fell to their knees.

In that epic story, the heroine saved the day without hurting a single person and without getting hurt in return. But even if such an unrealistically perfect ending was possible, the rest of it never would be.

Chloe couldn't be like the heroine in her made-up epic poem. She was the one who shook with fright and fell to her knees in the face of danger. If she had any chance at all of saving her sister, she needed Quintus.

Stomping forward, she wrapped her arm around his until their bare forearms met. The feel of his skin caused the same flip in her stomach it always did. It would have felt so much better to shove Quintus away just to prove how little he mattered to her.

But she didn't have time for that. Her eyes narrowed as she called forth her magic. It tingled at her fingertips as she started to direct it into a large bubble of enchantment that would protect both Quintus and Ludo.

Before the bubble got finished, the red-and-blue-eyed fae tilted his head at her. Not just at her, but at her arm and how it was draped around Quintus's. "I thought you were angry at him."

"I am, but I'm also scared." Her head snapped toward Ludo where he could clearly see how tightly she clenched her jaw. "And you know what? Mind your own business from now on, or after this is over, I'll go to your home and rip apart every page from every book you have inside it."

It was a good thing mortals could lie because she certainly never would have destroyed so many priceless books. She'd much sooner steal them for herself than destroy them.

But her tongue had done its usual job of shutting someone up right when she needed it.

Ludo's eyes went wide. He didn't say another word as they stalked toward the castle. Screams erupted from the upper windows. The dragon clearly did its job of distracting the mortals inside. But how much of the castle would be destroyed before Chloe and Quintus found the captured fae?

Perhaps it was better to not think of such questions.

Focusing on the enchantment again, Chloe threw all her magic into the bubble that would protect Quintus and Ludo from the iron inside the castle air. Once certain the magic worked as it should, she turned the enchantment invisible.

Just as Quintus reached for the leather strap that acted as a doorknob on a small door leading inside the castle, she looked over to him. "You better keep me safe."

He'd done such a good job of avoiding her eyes since the harp string incident that she almost forgot how his gaze felt. His eyes

244

locked onto hers now though. The golden star-like flecks inside them gleamed as every part of his face hardened. "I will."

Her heart pounded at the way his voice had been etched with emotion. When she inhaled, her chest expanded too much. And then she scolded herself for reacting at all.

Why did he have to be so infuriating? He had kissed her on the forehead. He had held her while she cried. Why did he do either of those things when he also forced her to give up the one reminder of her past with him that she had allowed herself to keep?

Once inside the castle, the sound of crumbling stone shook the walls around them. Screams punctuated the air. The dragon might destroy the castle completely before they ever got to the fae.

She shook her head at the thought. If she ever had to take back a castle from angry mortals again, she would *not* let two fae make all the plans. They clearly needed someone who could think of strategies that didn't involve so much destruction, something she happened to be very good at. But it was a little too late to offer input on their plans now.

They entered a hallway, which had no mortals in it. At least the dragon had done its job of distracting them.

Ludo trailed a few steps in front of them. He reached both hands out with the palms down. Light blue and shimmery white sparks shot from his fingertips. The magical sparks hovered in the air until Ludo flicked his wrist to send them on their way.

Would the mortals notice his magic as it searched for the fuel and the captured fae? Just as that question entered Chloe's mind, the blue and white sparks disappeared.

In all likelihood, the magic hadn't actually disappeared at all. It had probably just turned invisible, just like her enchantment that protected the fae next to her from the iron.

Biting her lip, she eyed the shaking walls of the castle. The sound of stone scraping against stone filled the air. "How long—"

"This way." Ludo interrupted and stomped toward another hallway. He could have had the courtesy to let her finish the question first, but at least his magic of finding things had worked.

They trailed down several hallways. Despite her fears, they never once ran into any mortals. Each step deeper into the castle showed off more of how the castle had become dilapidated and wilting, even since they'd been there the night before.

Soon they reached a part of the castle she had never been to. Since she'd been creating a little map of the hallways inside her head, she estimated that this area of the castle was on the opposite side as the library, yet still somewhat close to the throne room.

"We are near the fuel." Ludo held his hands out in front of him. His fingers twitched every few moments, usually right around the time that he changed directions.

After a few more steps, he gestured toward a wooden door that had mostly rotted into black. "The fuel is just through there. Can we go find my dragon now so I can get out of here? Then the two of you can do whatever else you planned."

Under her fingers, she felt Quintus's muscles tense.

His nose wrinkled as he gestured toward himself and her. "*We* are going to go in that room to burn the fuel, and then we will rescue the fae. If you want an enchantment to protect you from the iron, I suggest you stay close to us."

Those golden flashes in his eyes turned sharp like daggers. Even his exhales were more heated than usual.

Ludo tugged at his collar and took a step back. "Fine. I will stay nearby, but only until the dragon comes close enough that I can reach it. Then I'm using it to fly far away from here."

"Good." Quintus turned away from him and stomped toward the rotted door with much more vigor than before.

"Where are the fae hidden?" Apparently, Chloe would have to ask these things herself. Quintus may have been good with a weapon and good at being brave, but he didn't always use his head during a crisis.

246

Ludo closed his eyes as soon as she asked. His fingers twitched again. Just when she was ready to ask if the magic would only lead them there and not reveal the location from so far away, the fae's blue and red eyes snapped open.

"They are nearby." One eye narrowed as he gestured toward the rotted door. "That room has a few different entrances. One of them leads to a long hallway going in this direction." He moved one hand forward to indicate the direction. "Then it turns to the right and opens into a much larger room. That is where the fae are hidden."

Touching his chin, Quintus stared at the fae's hands. He tilted his head and then he nodded. "I do not know this area of the castle well, but I believe the room you described is the kitchen. It is a large enough area to fit the captured fae, and it has no windows or doors to the outside."

Ludo raised one finger. "Not all the fae are in that room. Most of them are, but there is another room, a smaller room, that has a few fae inside it as well. I would guess that smaller room has greater chains or other protections keeping the fae inside."

Quintus nodded. "The cellar. The most powerful fae are likely inside."

The ground beneath their feet shook so hard that Chloe lost her balance. Her arm would have slipped right out of Quintus's grasp if he had not held onto to her so tight. The collapsing stone and mortal screams weren't just loud. They were getting closer.

"Let's go." She clenched her jaw and pulled Quintus toward the rotted door. The leather strap nailed to it hung limp and holey like a moth-eaten tunic.

A dragon roar and a fresh bout of screams moved her feet inside the room a little faster. A tree sat in one corner of the room. It had probably once looked as lush and mossy as the trees in Crystal Thorn Forest, but it was all shriveled up now. Its branches were as thin as fingers. Its leaves were as small as thumbnails.

The poor tree only stole her attention for a brief moment though. Now she focused on the large wooden barrels filled to the brim with a dark liquid.

The fuel.

Seeing it might have caused a greater reaction, but then her attention got stolen yet again.

A young woman with a long braid and a sharp sword jumped out from behind the nearest barrel. Mishti's knuckles had turned pale from how tight she held her sword. Her eyes flashed as she glared at Chloe. "You left me."

Chloe couldn't help how she squeezed Quintus a little tighter. She hated it, but her hands reacted without her permission. "Mishti, I…" Her voice hitched before another word could come out.

But the ache in her voice clearly did nothing to persuade Mishti. The young woman lifted her sword, pointing it out threateningly. "Mila died because of you and then you *left* me."

"I told you not to move so much." As soon as the words came out, Chloe scolded herself for starting with an accusation. She shook her head. "Even if I had tried, I never could have untied your bonds. I had to get away so the other mortals wouldn't kill me, but I'm back now. You can still come with us and escape Portia."

A throaty chuckle rumbled inside of Mishti. Her eyes flashed with an even thicker anger. "This is exactly what Portia said would happen. You pretend you want to help me, but only when it benefits you."

The castle walls shook again. The dragon's roar sounded closer than ever.

Heat singed Chloe's fingertips. The hairs on the back of her neck stood on end.

Fear hadn't affected just her, though.

Ludo flicked his gaze toward Quintus. "We need to hurry this along."

Without another word, he pulled a small, curved axe from his pocket and threw it straight at Mishti. His fae speed sent it flying before Chloe even had time to process what she had seen.

But Mishti was considered a necessity to the mortals for a reason. Her sword slashed through the air, throwing the axe off course long before it became a threat to her.

Despite the quick action, Chloe still gasped.

Her arm that was tangled with Quintus's pulled tight when she whirled around to face Ludo. "Do not hurt her."

She had to tug Quintus forward a bit, but she managed to get close enough to kick Ludo in the shin.

His eyes had already grown wide after Mishti blocked his attack so easily. Now, Chloe's swift kick caused him to let out a yelp.

For a moment, she considered letting up on the enchantment that protected him from the iron in the air. But since she had only created one enchantment that surrounded all of them, doing that would hurt Quintus too.

Throwing Ludo another hateful glare, Chloe then turned toward Mishti. "I had to leave you so I could come back. Portia would have killed me otherwise. I didn't abandon you, and I always planned to rescue you still."

An ice-cold calm fell over Mishti's expression. She said nothing. Her body stood still. Her face looked as stoic as ever. The lack of actions filled the room with more tension than if she had lifted the curved axe that now sat near her feet.

Another moment passed in silence.

Then Quintus pulled something from his pocket. He moved so fast, Chloe had no time to react. Plus, with one arm draped around his, she only could have reached him with the arm farthest away from her anyway.

She had never appreciated how much she used both arms until one of them was no longer available.

At least Quintus didn't draw a weapon. He simply conjured a fire and lit each barrel of fuel on fire. Once again, someone capable of thinking even amidst danger definitely should have made their plans. She wanted to shout at him for not noticing the barrels were made of wood.

They would burn along with the fuel, possibly releasing all the fuel onto the ground at once. Then the hallways would be flooded with fire.

Before she could say anything though, Quintus tugged her toward the door on the opposite side of the room. "We can convince her afterward. Right now, we need to find the fae."

His strength prevented her from resisting, but Chloe still glanced back at Mishti. "I want you to come with us."

Instead of nodding or calming down, the words caused Mishti's face to contort and snarl. She let out a raging scream and then shoved the nearest barrel to the floor.

Fuel poured onto the stone. Fire chased after it.

And right on cue, Chloe's feet froze in place.

Flames rose all around them, but Quintus just lifted her by the waist and ran across the room. Ludo probably followed, but Quintus had moved too fast for Chloe to know for sure.

But even once they left the room, Chloe knew the danger had only just begun.

Mishti's footsteps sounded right behind them. Another scream erupted from her lips as she lifted her sword.

Maybe she was just a mortal, but she had too many tools at her disposal.

A weapon, flames, and even worse, revenge.

Their chances of surviving this fight had just gotten extremely thin.

33

ICE AND HEAT CRASHED AGAINST each other as they dove down Chloe's spine. Quintus held her tight around the waist as he and Ludo charged through another rotted door and into a long hallway.

Just as Quintus set Chloe back on her feet, the flames from inside the other room licked toward their feet. Quintus slammed the door shut, but the rotted door wouldn't hold back the flames for long.

"Where is the enchantment?" Ludo's shoulders quivered. He stared down at his hands, which had large red splotches across the back of them. Red splotches broke out across his neck, spreading up to his face as well.

It only took a single glance toward Quintus to see that identical red splotches marred his dark skin as well.

Her arm wrapped around his at once. She wanted to close her eyes to concentrate on the magic, but that might give away where it really came from. Instead, she looked through her eyelashes and up into his eyes. "Go on. Create the enchantment again before the flames get out here." Hopefully the words would convince Ludo that the enchantment came from Quintus and not from her.

Magic coursed at her fingertips as she spoke. When a bubble of enchantment appeared around them, she turned it invisible right away. The red splotches on their faces started to recede, but the ones on their necks were still as bright as ever. Maybe those would need more time to heal.

If they'd had any more time, she would have insisted they stay right there in the hallway until the red splotches had disappeared completely.

But of course, time would never be on their side when danger lingered so close by.

Flames ate through the rotted door. Fuel poured into the hallway, igniting higher flames along with it. They all had to run just to escape the growing fire.

Each step brought them closer to the door to the kitchen, but with how fast the flames moved, they might get cut off from the door soon.

Screams shook the castle walls, followed by the roar of a dragon. The walls had been shaking since they entered, but the shaking had increased to a precarious level. For the first time, Chloe feared the walls themselves might collapse.

"You will never make it to the door." Mishti's hardened voice filled the entire hallway when she stepped into it. Flames burned all around her, yet she gave no reaction to being in pain. She clasped her hands behind her back.

Was she not in pain?

The slightest flicker of a smile lifted one corner of Mishti's mouth. Through the flames, she looked down at her clothes with her hands still behind her back. "One of the mortals made this clothing. It can resist flames so effectively that I can walk straight through a wall of flames with no consequences."

Her boots trailed through flames as she spoke, proving her words. The flicker of the smile returned. "Just look at what we mortals can accomplish when we work together instead of being selfish like the fae."

Just then, she pulled both hands out from behind her back. One held a small bowl of fuel, which she threw down one side of the hallway until the fuel splashed just in front of the door to the kitchen.

Her other hand threw out a collection of small metal items that most certainly had iron in them. The metal objects clattered to the ground.

Gripping Quintus tighter, Chloe put all her concentration back into the enchantment. It kept them safe for now, but the fire still closed in around them. Thanks to Mishti's bowl of fuel, flames now cut them off from the entrance to the kitchen.

Ludo's gaze darted down the hallway to each of the doors nearby. He likely just wanted a quick escape. The way Quintus stared at the kitchen door through the flames worried her more though. He'd probably charge straight through the flames soon.

But if he charged through, both he and Chloe would be burned by the fire and then she might not be able to maintain the enchantment. And once the kitchen door opened, the fae inside it would be injured by the iron flames as well.

They didn't need brute force right now, they needed strategy.

Suddenly, part of the stone wall crumbled, dropping large boulders to the ground. Without another thought, Chloe grabbed Quintus tight and ducked behind the boulders. Maybe someone braver would have balked at hiding in the midst of the fight, but the boulders had blocked off some of the flames.

Best of all, part of the wall nearer to Mishti had crumbled as well. Her attention was stolen by it. When she looked up again, she wouldn't know if Chloe and the others had gone through one of the doors or behind the boulders.

Once she, Quintus, and Ludo were all hidden, Chloe closed her eyes. Blood throbbed through her veins. Shaking bursts filled her fingers. Yes, she was afraid, but she still had her mind. Maybe she couldn't fight, but she would do her best to think her way out of this.

While her thoughts whirled with ideas, sparkly sapphire-blue dragon claws broke through the wall above them. Stone crumbled, but the small bits of the wall that had broken away wouldn't injure them. Golden horns smashed through the stone next.

Her fingers dug into Quintus's arm while the dragon's entire head crashed through the wall. It roared loud enough to shake every surface around them. Bits of rock broke away to crumble onto the ground.

The dragon disappeared as it pulled its head back. Chloe's racing heart felt ready to explode. Ludo, on the other hand, jumped to his feet. He scrambled up the broken wall and disappeared through the hole the dragon had just made.

Of course he decided to run away the first chance he got. Once he got hold of the harp string reins, he'd be able to get that dragon to go anywhere he wanted. Since he had already done his part to find the fae, it didn't matter that he left.

What did matter, however, was how he had just revealed their position. Mishti's feet crushed over the bits of stone covering the ground as she charged toward them.

They only had a few seconds before she'd reach them.

Quintus stared at the door to the kitchen again. But opening it now would just cause more problems. Chloe tightened her arm around Quintus's. "Look at me."

He didn't. He kept staring at the door to the kitchen.

This time, she jammed her elbow into his side. That stole his gaze for a moment. She wouldn't waste it. "Most kitchens have more than one entrance, don't they? Isn't there another door to the kitchen somewhere?"

Before he could answer, Mishti's sword came clashing down toward them.

Quintus grabbed Chloe by the waist again and ran past Mishti in a blur. At least one of his arms was pressed against Chloe's so she could still maintain the enchantment that protected him from the iron. His free hand whirled out in front of them and suddenly, they both disappeared from view.

The glamour he had created turned them invisible, which kept Mishti from seeing where they went, but it was highly disconcerting to be carried by an invisible fae while also being invisible.

Chloe's stomach flipped each time Quintus's feet hit the stone floor. But soon they entered a much smaller hallway with only a few doors. Even better, this hallway didn't have any flames inside it.

Considering the speed Quintus had used to get there, it would take Mishti at least a little while before she caught up, *if* she even found out where they had gone.

Removing the glamour hiding them, Quintus then gestured toward a door at the end of the hallway. "The kitchen is just through there."

She would have voiced a response, except they both stepped past a room whose door stood wide open. Quintus pushed her behind himself before she could get a good look into the room. It didn't stop her from feeling how his muscles tensed beneath her fingertips.

She'd felt his muscles harden before, but this was different. The tension didn't just stretch tight, it stretched *too* tight. His fingers curled into fists too. From behind, she couldn't see his face, but she imagined a snarl burning across it.

Heat even seemed to radiate off his skin. This wasn't frustration. It wasn't even anger. It was rage like she had never seen him wear before.

He pushed her farther back and untangled his arm from hers. Now she had to slip her hand under his ombre cape just so she could maintain skin contact. Her hand pressed against the bare skin of his back. It felt even hotter and harder than his arms had.

Only then did she attempt to peek around him and into the room.

Portia lounged on a cushy chair, plucking small chocolate truffles off a plate and into her mouth. She wore the midnight blue pearl-encrusted dress that Mishti had been wearing the night before. Her stockinged feet were propped up on a small stool.

Quintus reached into his pocket. The wooden end of his spear just began to appear when he gestured toward a desk at the edge of the room.

"Get behind that thing."

He used that special fae whisper that came out inhumanly soft. Portia didn't hear it, but Chloe did. She wanted to dig her fingernails into his back and shout at him. If she hid behind the desk, she couldn't touch him anymore. And if she didn't touch him, she couldn't maintain the enchantment that kept him safe from iron.

But she didn't have the special fae whisper Quintus had, so she couldn't say anything without being heard by their enemy. Instead, she just pressed her hand a little harder against his back to remind him they had to maintain skin contact.

Portia glanced up just then. Her mouth flew open wide and the last truffle tumbled right out of her mouth. "Mishti."

She had clearly meant to shout the name, but it came out too tight and too shaky.

In a flash, Quintus shoved Chloe behind the desk and out of Portia's sight. He had moved so fast, she couldn't have possibly noticed Chloe's presence. Now he charged straight at her.

Chloe tried peeking around the desk to see what he did, but his fae speed was too much for her to follow. One thing she did feel was how the entire room seemed to shudder with his fury.

He must have been mad at her for capturing the fae. He hadn't been furious like this when they saw Portia at the party, but maybe he had finally snapped.

The blur of Quintus's body eventually stopped. His spear had left gashes on both her cheeks from the corners of her mouth all the way back to her ears. Deep gashes also wrapped around both of her wrists. The gashes covered her cheeks and her wrists.

Oh.

The realization hit Chloe right in the chest where it then burrowed deep inside. Aches tugged at her heart, her throat, even her chest. Those gashes hadn't been made just anywhere. They hadn't been meant to cause the most amount of pain.

Those had been made in retaliation.

Quintus had cut Portia in all the same places where the needled ropes had cut Chloe. Was Quintus angry because of that? Because of how Chloe had been hurt?

"Mishti." Portia's voice shook as she called the name out again. Her chocolate-stained fingers disappeared into the folds of her dress.

Quintus lifted his spear for a killing strike. Red splotches covered his neck and cheeks as he leaned in closer to the woman. His teeth gritted together so tight he had to speak through them. "You never should have hurt her."

Chloe's stomach flopped over on itself. Her heart pounded while sweat broke out across her palms. He *was* mad about the wounds she had endured at Portia's hand then.

But before he could use his spear again, Portia produced a sharp metal stake from the folds of her skirt. Faerie had many metals that didn't contain iron, but the chances of that metal stake being one of them were basically nothing.

It only took a single strike and Quintus collapsed to the ground in a heap. The metal stake drove into the soft skin between his collar bone and armpit. A few inches lower and it might have found his heart. Portia had likely been aiming for the heart.

But if the stake had iron, it might not need to pierce the heart to be fatal, especially with all the iron floating around.

Chloe swallowed her scream. Another one tried to burst through her lips, but she swallowed that one too. If she ran to

Quintus now, Portia would kill her. Quintus would die not long after.

Instead, she waited a little longer. Just as she predicted, Portia stumbled away almost as soon as Quintus hit the floor. Blood streamed from the gashes in her cheeks and wrists now.

Once the woman left the room, Chloe counted to twenty-five before she rushed to Quintus's side. She had meant to count to sixty, but how could she wait that long while an iron stake stabbed him?

Her fingers reached out for his arm, grabbing it even before she knelt down at his side. An enchantment protecting him from the iron in the air circled around him again, but it would do nothing for the stake in his chest. She had to remove it, but she'd have to do it carefully. She'd have to use her magic.

A gray tinge mottled his skin just under his hairline. With all the iron in the castle, it was no surprise a single stake of iron had already made him collapse and succumb to scurpus.

She took it back now. All the anger at him for forcing her to give up the harp string. Maybe she hated him for it, but she didn't want him to die either. And maybe she didn't actually hate him at all.

A sob tore from her mouth as she cradled his head in her hands. Blood oozed from the wound in his chest. She had to bite her lip just to keep from screaming.

Leaning closer to him, she attempted a smile. "You can't die."

He lifted one hand, stroking his knuckles across her cheek. The gentle gesture would have been nice if it hadn't been paired with the defeated look in his eye.

"No." She squeezed his arm tight, making her enchantment even stronger than before. "You vowed you would tell me what happened to your home, remember? You said you would tell me once we took back the castle, so you can't die. You vowed it."

"Did you not know?" His voice came out low and husky as he stroked her cheek again. "Vows were made to be broken."

258

Tears welled in her eyes too fast to hold back. Her lip trembled while she tried to suck in a breath. *No.*

This couldn't be happening. Quintus was fae. Fae were supposed to be able to heal from anything. He would not die.

But then his eyes rolled back in his head, and he let out a tortured groan.

Could things get any worse than this?

Of course, as soon as that thought entered her head, it got worse. Much worse.

She should have been quieter. She should have waited longer before she rushed to Quintus's side. Because now, she wasn't alone.

Portia stood in the doorway with eyes flashing wildly. She held an axe with enough precision to show she knew how to wield it. When she stepped before Chloe, one thing was clear.

That axe would soon meet flesh.

34

AN AXE SWUNG TOWARD CHLOE, and like the coward she was, she closed her eyes. It always happened that way. She'd flinch or slam her eyes shut or cry or faint. Yet all those times she expected death, it still hadn't come.

For just a moment, in that haze before pain took over, she wondered if her fear had actually saved her. Was it harder to kill a person who flinched or fainted when faced with death? Was it harder to kill someone who cowered?

If weapons or tenacity couldn't save her in a fight, maybe her body had still found a way to protect her. Maybe fear had protected her when her fists couldn't.

Even if it had saved her life, it hadn't saved her from pain. The first shards of it crept in just as her brain started to process what had happened.

She hadn't been killed, but she'd still been struck with the axe. Struck hard. It didn't just leave a gash either. It cut straight through flesh and bone, severing one of her limbs completely.

Her right foot was gone.

Warm blood spilled from the jagged cut just above her ankle. But the warm turned cold as more blood poured from the wound.

Her eyes flew open. She reached for her severed limb, using both hands to stop the blood.

She tried to avoid it, but her gaze kept catching on the foot with her boot still on it. Her foot that no longer attached to her body. A weight rammed into her chest at the sight of it, which crushed her just as much as the pain.

The bloody axe hung at Portia's side now. Her eyes flashed as she clenched her jaw. "You have a choice now." Using the axe, she pointed toward the blood pouring from Chloe's leg. "You can be selfish like the fae and save yourself."

Now she stepped backward, going closer to the door. Her arm waved to the side, gesturing toward the door that led to the kitchen where the fae were captured. Her eyebrow raised. "Or you can save the fae without stopping your own blood first, sacrificing yourself in the process."

Pain clawed at Chloe's eyes so much she almost didn't feel the tears prickling there. Her chest heaved, struggling just to breathe. She gripped her leg tighter, but her hands couldn't stop the blood like she needed them to.

Portia was right. The truth of it ate at Chloe's heart. It gnawed on the bits of it that had managed to keep a little hope. Now it shriveled and blackened until soon her heart would be no different from a jagged chunk of ice.

Whatever expression passed over Chloe's face, it caused Portia to grin. A horrible, wicked grin that only froze Chloe's heart a little faster.

But then a tiny spark lit in her chest. The tiniest spark that flickered like a candle flame in a horrible wind.

She and Quintus had left the castle when Julian attacked with that explosion. They had left to save their own lives, but that hadn't meant everyone else would die.

A slow and steady inhale worked through the kinks in Chloe's chest until she looked up into the woman's eyes. Chloe gripped her leg tighter, hardly feeling the shooting pain now. Her own teeth clenched tight.

"Just watch me." Her resolve hardened, giving her the power to sit up a little higher. "I'll save myself and then I'll save everyone else too."

It was not lost on Chloe that the last time she had said something similar, it was about the Nashes, and she had horribly failed at saving them. But this time, she had a strength she didn't have back then. Now she finally understood that taking care of herself was just as important as caring for others.

The flash in Portia's eyes dimmed. She even took a step back from Chloe, almost as if afraid of her.

Before she could say anything though, Mishti appeared in the doorway.

Portia immediately dropped the axe and glared at the young woman before her. "Finally. I called you twice. Where were you?"

"Fighting." Mishti's stoic expression flickered with a single moment of widened eyes when she noticed Chloe's severed foot on the ground.

Her gaze jumped up to Chloe's then, but she quickly pulled it away to look at Portia. "We have control of the dragon. Whoever touches its reins can control it. Ivanna says we can use it to escape."

Portia lifted her skirts, sneering at the puddle of blood that nearly soaked into the hem. "Everyone can escape on it?"

"Everyone who is still alive." Mishti glanced back at Chloe's foot again, then immediately flinched and turned away. "We also captured a fae who tried to escape on the dragon."

Sheer delight brightened Portia's eyes. She nearly dropped the skirts she'd been so careful to lift only a few moments earlier. "How poisoned is he from the iron?"

"Not much." Mishti's voice came out tighter than before. "He's not sick like the others in the castle."

Portia let out a cruel chuckle as she started toward the door. "Good. We can finally enact the next step in my master plan." She looked back at Chloe and wrinkled her nose. "Let's go."

Blood poured over Chloe's hands. Cold snaked up her leg with each breath. Her head was already getting woozy from the loss of blood. It wouldn't stop her from speaking though. "You can still escape her, Mishti. Just stay with me and leave her."

Portia whirled around and flashed her teeth. Then she grabbed Mishti and pulled her toward the door. "Do not let her infect you with her selfishness. I won't let her trick you again."

After only one step out the door, Portia dashed back inside just long enough to snatch Chloe's severed foot off the ground. If that weren't bad enough, she even stole the other boot off the foot still attached to Chloe's body.

The woman wore no shoes, but it still seemed impossibly rude to take the boots off a dying person.

But what could Chloe do when her foot had just been severed? Nothing. She knew it. Arguing or threatening Portia would accomplish nothing.

Instead, she wiped her bloody hands off on her dress then retrieved the magical book from her bag. Tears sliced down her cheeks like knives.

Using one hand to hold her severed leg, she then used her other to flip through the pages of her book. She chose to ignore how many bloody fingerprints she splattered all over the pages. This wasn't the time to get sentimental over a book.

But no matter how she turned the pages, she couldn't find what she needed. Pain wriggled into her mind, crushing and twisting thoughts just as they began to form. She'd never needed her mind more, yet it had become almost completely inaccessible.

Tears poured onto the book, leaving behind their own stains along with her fingerprints. The stone beneath her shook. Somewhere in the castle, a wall had definitely fallen.

She turned another page, which only had information on treating burns.

"Help me!" she screamed at the book. Her fingers flipped through the pages even faster now. She sniffed. "How do I grow my foot back?"

Before she could touch the paper again, the pages started flipping on their own. She held her bleeding leg with both hands as a golden glow appeared between the pages. It flipped one last time, turning to a blank page. Her body leaned closer when words appeared on the page.

Mortals cannot regrow limbs.

Her heart clenched. She shook her head, throwing bloodstained hair in haphazard waves around her face. "But I have magic. Fae can heal missing limbs, can't they? If I have magic, can't I do the same?"

When the book did nothing, she turned a page on her own. But the next page said exactly the same as the previous.

Mortals cannot regrow limbs.

She turned to another page, which just said the same thing.

Slapping her hand across the book, she screamed.

But clarity hit her again, cutting through the pain that had nearly claimed her. "What if I had my foot? Could I reattach it?"

When she turned another page, it had only a single word on it.

Yes.

Did she have time to go out into the hall and check if Portia had left her severed foot behind? Black spots filled her vision, indicating dangerous levels of blood loss.

She had already pulled her hand away from Quintus to try and stop the blood from her leg, which had left him susceptible to iron. No. She didn't have time.

She *would* save herself and then save everyone else too, but she couldn't be stupid either. Closing her eyes tight, she accepted that her foot was gone.

But maybe it didn't have to be permanent. If she got her foot back, she could reattach it with magic. A thought tugged at the back of her mind, feeling much more true than she wanted it to. Maybe she'd never get her foot back. Maybe this was just a part of her now. But how could she continue while dwelling on that?

Shoving the thought far from her mind, she pressed her hand against Quintus's chest. Her eyes fluttered closed as she reached for the magic inside her. It sparked at her fingertips then spread down to her leg.

The golden magic tingled over the wound. She slowly thought through the process of healing a leg after losing a foot. Tears kept flooding her eyes whenever the finality of this healing caught up to her. But she would just shove her fears away and think back to the wound scabbing and then on to new skin growing over the spot where her foot had once attached.

When she finished, she didn't even bother looking at the leg to make sure it had healed properly. If she thought about it too much, she'd just get stuck on how she'd once had two feet, and now she only had one.

Blood caked over her fingers as she turned her attention to Quintus. His heart still beat, but each beat felt fluttering and weak under her fingertips. She grabbed the stake in his heart and slowly began removing it.

In her mind, she went through the healing process of each layer of his chest as she removed the stake. Only once one layer was healed did she pull the stake out a little more. By the time she finished, only a tiny drop of fresh blood escaped the wound where the stake had been since all the rest of it had been healed as she went.

She threw the stake across the room now and then ensured that the enchantment keeping out iron was in place.

With a gasp, Quintus sat up straight and grabbed Chloe by the wrist. The initial movement happened so fast, he likely hadn't been in control. But thought clearly led his actions when he brought her hand closer to his face.

He stared at the blood covering her hands and then looked into her eyes.

Using the only foot she had left, she tugged her dress hem down until it hid her severed leg. He probably would have asked all kinds of questions if a horrible rumbling noise hadn't shaken the castle walls at that moment.

The dragon had probably just left the castle. Judging by the shaking and rumbling, the creature had probably destroyed a few walls on his way out as well.

Checking again that the enchantment still shimmered in place. She tried to push Quintus to his feet. "Come on. We need to get the fae out of here before this entire castle collapses."

He got up. Holding onto him, she put all her weight on one foot and forced herself up as well. Another wall crumbed somewhere nearby. Danger loomed, but it wouldn't win.

Not this time.

She wouldn't fail this time. She'd taken care of herself. Now it was time to save everyone else.

35

SINCE CHLOE HAD TO TOUCH Quintus to keep the protective enchantment up, she hoped he wouldn't notice how much more she leaned on him every other step. Yet of course, he noticed almost immediately.

"Why are you limping?" His voice had a note of accusation in it, but he also hugged her arm a little closer to his body. "You are not putting any weight at all on your right foot."

Her nose pointed into the air. "I just need a little extra help to walk right now. Quit complaining."

She hadn't anticipated how tired her arm would get. Even putting all the weight on Quintus that she would have put on her right foot, her arm still ached. It would probably tire out soon, which she didn't want to think about because she couldn't bring herself to admit what had happened. Not yet.

"I was not complaining." He pulled her closer and even reached his other arm across her stomach to brace her even more. "What happened to your foot?"

"Nothing." The word snapped from her mouth, mostly because the aches in her arm already hurt, and speaking seemed like a chore.

He glared at her just as they reached the door to the kitchen. He opened his mouth but had to wait until a nearby wall finished crumbling so she'd be able to hear his voice. "There is no need for such a blatant lie. If you are injured, just heal yourself."

"Not now, Quintus." She spoke in a breathless rush. "Forget about my foot and just open the door."

After a sidelong glance, he did as she asked. Inside, at least a hundred fae stood and sat in various positions. Every face in front of her had turned entirely gray. Most of the Crystal Thorn fae had dark skin like Quintus, yet the rich browns and bright copper undertones had been leeched from the skin, leaving behind a sickly gray.

Two narrow troughs sat on the ground near the door. Iron flames burned above them, trapping the fae inside. Similar troughs sat in front of every door in the room.

It only took a swift kick for Quintus to knock the troughs over. With the trough upside down, it smothered the iron flames until they had gone out completely.

Chloe had to suck in a gasp before the initial shock wore off, but then she got to work. Holding tight to Quintus's arm, she sent an extra blast of strength into her enchantment. To make it easier to see, she even turned the invisible enchantment to a golden one.

The bubble of magic grew larger and larger until it enveloped all the fae. Their faces brightened once her enchantment encircled them. Many had closed eyes or bent heads before, but now they glanced up. A few of them even noticed her and Quintus at the door.

Scurpus had infected every single fae in the room, but she didn't need Swiftsea salt to help them anymore. Now, she just needed magic.

She focused in on the nearest fae, a woman with short black hair and a suede dress that looked as wilted as the fennel Chloe had gathered from under the snow in her town. Closing her eyes, she quickly imagined the process of making a poultice and then administering it.

Imagining the process in her head took more time than she would have liked. When she moved on to repeat the healing process on the next fae, Quintus had already started walking into the room.

Several fae came up to him and asked all sorts of questions. Since he mostly explained everything that had just happened with the mortals, she didn't bother paying much attention.

By the time they got to the middle of the room, she had only healed a dozen of the fae, but there were at least a hundred more to go. They didn't have time for this.

Even worse, her bubble of enchantment started to flicker.

Quintus turned to her, concern in his eyes. Before he could say anything, a crack formed in the ceiling above them. Stone scraped against stone while another larger crack formed right through the first.

"Everybody out!" Quintus shouted the words and gestured toward the open door. "Go somewhere safe until your body can heal itself from the iron."

If they'd had any more time, Chloe would have put out the iron flames blocking the other doors, and she would have healed the rest of the fae.

But once again, she had to choose who would receive care. Her eyes zeroed in on the fae who were curled into balls or who had despondent eyes. The other fae would be able to heal themselves once they got far enough away from the castle and all its iron. Right now, she only needed to heal the fae who couldn't escape otherwise.

Another crack tore through the ceiling. Her arms shook as she leaned harder on Quintus. Even her eyelids started to ache from how often she closed them to concentrate on healing the fae. At least she had gotten faster.

Once they reached the door with the chains on it, only three fae still remained in the room. The others had already escaped.

Her left foot throbbed from having so much weight on it. If she hadn't been busy healing and hopping around, it may have taken longer to tire. But with so many other things going on, preserving the energy in her left foot had not been her highest priority.

Chloe still had two fae left to heal when Quintus reached for the chains on the door. Her mind was so focused on a fae with green and gold eyes that she barely noticed when Quintus's hand shot back from the chains. A sizzle of steam erupted from his fingertips.

"Let me do that." Her eyes slammed shut to finish healing the last two fae. The poultices she imagined in her mind were sloppily made, but hopefully they would work well enough.

Once her eyes flew open again, she reached for the chains. Quintus stepped to the side to give her more room to work. He continued to hold her arm, but the movement had been so unexpected, she lost her balance anyway.

With only one foot left, she hadn't even realized how much she'd been leaning on Quintus.

He glanced toward her. All thought of the chains before them seemed to have been forgotten. He only seemed to care about her as he squeezed her forearm slightly. "You cannot put any weight at all on your foot?"

Instead of answering, she just hopped forward and wrenched the chains off the door. He continued to touch her arm, but all the healing must have tired her out more than she realized. The bubble of enchantment around the room flickered again. When it did, Quintus let out a grunt.

It took a deep breath, but she managed to strengthen the enchantment again. Still, they needed to get out of there soon, and not just because the walls might collapse at any moment. Her ability to use magic waned with every second she stood.

Two hard wrenches later, the last of the chains finally fell away from the door. How ironic that the chains didn't even need a lock to hold the fae in. By simply having iron inside them, the hundred fae in the room had been completely unable to move the chains and free the more powerful fae inside the cellar.

But Chloe could.

Even with only one foot, she threw the doors open.

Light spilled into the room that had clearly been dark only a moment earlier. About a dozen fae blinked back at her. With mortal eyes, it took her a moment to adjust to the darkness. The fae inside didn't need that much time though.

"Chloe!" Elora called out from the back of the cellar. Scratchy tightness filled her voice, but it still had the unquestionable determination it always did.

In only a breath, Elora dashed across the small cellar, her long brown hair flying behind her. In another breath, she pulled her sister into her arms. "You came." Elora's voice broke as she squeezed tighter. "You saved us."

When she pulled away, the sickly gray of her skin matched her raspy voice. But she still smiled. A brilliant smile full of the pride that only an older sister could display.

Her arms looked ready to drag Chloe into another hug, but then her gray face tilted to the side. Elora reached out and touched the skin just under Chloe's right eye. "What is this?"

Chloe had already started to imagine the makings of another poultice in her mind, but the single touch stopped it at once. She had forgotten about the tattoo.

Before she could answer, a crack sounded from above. Tiny pebbles dropped from the ceiling, crumbling at their feet.

From the shadows of the cellar, a tall fae with shoulder length black hair came to Elora's side. His eyes narrowed at the ceiling. Brannick always looked a bit frightening, though for someone with Elora's tenacity, that only made them all the more perfect for each other. Since a black wolf walked right at his side at all times, it only added to his terrifying appearance.

"We need to get out of here," he said. "The castle will crush us if we do not."

Elora nodded at her beloved and beckoned the other fae out of the cellar. A short fae with a long beard and black bug-like eyes edged out of the room. His snarl matched Brannick's.

"Can you all still run?" The enchantment around them flickered as Chloe spoke. Her left knee shook, ready to buckle under the weight of her entire body.

Letting out a chuckle, Elora drew her sword. "Of course we can still run. Why do you think they had to lock us up separate from the others? They got tired of recapturing us after all our escapes."

When another crack snapped through the stone above them, all the fae in the cellar darted toward the open door leading to the hallway. Chloe reached for Quintus's arm, but he just raised an eyebrow at her.

Without another word, he lifted her into his arms and began running. When a noise of protest left her mouth, he just set his jaw. "You cannot run. Do not try to pretend you can."

Her mouth scrunched into a knot when she failed to find a response. At least without having to support her weight anymore, it would be easier to maintain the enchantment that kept the fae protected from the iron.

Quintus ran after the others, catching up by the time they reached the end of the hallway. Stone walls collapsed, often just missing them as they ran.

Despite the danger, Elora glanced back at Chloe with a smile. "Mother would have fainted if she ever saw you with a tattoo. And on your face too." Elora chuckled now, just as they entered a long hallway. "I do like the stars though. You used to love stars."

The words twisted Chloe's gut only slightly less than the sight of walls crumbling all around them. Of course, the danger didn't faze Elora in the slightest. None of the other fae seemed bothered either.

In fact, Brannick even glanced back, eyeing the spot under Chloe's right eye. But then, his gaze trailed over to Quintus.

Even while he ran with gray tinged skin and limp clothes, he spoke as evenly as if he'd been sitting on a throne. "Quintus has a tattoo as well. A moon."

The declaration made Elora shrug, but it didn't stop her from running. After a few more steps though, her head suddenly whipped around. For the first time, her feet faltered as she stared at Quintus.

With eyes even wider than before, she turned back to Brannick. They stared at each other while running, sharing some communication that no one else around them could possibly understand.

Fire flashed in her eyes when she glanced back again, her gaze locking onto Quintus. Her teeth clenched tight. "What did you do to her?"

Chloe squirmed at how her sister directed the question at Quintus, especially since it had been Chloe's fault the tattoos existed at all.

She might have found the courage to admit the truth, except flames suddenly appeared in front of them. At the same time, a jagged boulder crashed through the ceiling, heading straight for their heads.

36

STRONG ARMS TIGHTENED AROUND CHLOE as the boulder came toppling down, straight toward her head. Quintus held her as his body curled into a tight ball. He ducked toward the ground, rolling forward just in time to miss the stone boulder.

Flames flickered around them, but his body smothered them before they could burn.

Her eyes slammed shut as soon as Quintus rolled onto the ground. Both of their bodies whipped around as he rolled a few more times. The sensation tightened her belly, and yet, a part of her knew she'd be safe.

Danger had always frozen her in place, but no one had ever protected her as well as Quintus either. Now she simply focused on keeping the enchantment in place so she could protect him as well.

After another moment, he jumped back onto his feet and kept running toward the other fae. His grip on her had never faltered the entire time.

And now, Chloe could see the castle doors that led to the forest. They were almost free.

"Hurry." Elora glanced back, her gaze finding Chloe right away. "We are almost there."

As soon as the words left her lips, the walls around them shook and crumbled. Even the stone beneath their feet shook and cracked until it resembled gravel more than a solid stone floor.

Quintus's feet stumbled for the first time. The other fae stumbled as well.

And more flames had snaked into the space around them. Quintus ducked and darted to avoid the flames, but they were closing in fast.

"Get that tapestry." Chloe gestured toward the wall.

Quintus snatched the tapestry from the wall with a single tug. Once it was free, Chloe took it from him and shook it out straight. Then she let it float to the ground to smother the flames.

The castle walls continued to collapse. Pebbles, rocks, and boulders crashed down all around them. Quintus narrowly avoided each one as he sprinted toward the castle doors. Just a few more steps.

A rock struck Chloe on the knee and then one hit her on the shoulder. An even larger rock struck Quintus in the head. She gasped when his feet faltered.

Only two more steps.

He took one and the remaining walls shook with more ferocity than ever. The other fae had escaped now.

Wrapping her arms around his neck, she held him as tight as she could.

Instead of stepping forward, he lunged.

Just as his foot left the castle entrance, every bit of stone crumbled into nothing more than a heap of rubble. His body curled into a tight ball around her again, rolling when he met the mossy forest floor.

They had made it.

Chloe could barely breathe, Quintus was probably the same, but they had made it.

Her heart leapt in her chest while the realization hit her with more force than the collapsing castle they had just escaped. They had made it.

Quintus's body slowly uncurled. He had landed in a sitting position, still holding Chloe tight. Now she sat on his lap with her face entirely too close to his.

"We did it," she said breathlessly.

Her face turned toward his, which was most certainly a mistake because now she was acutely aware of how only a tiny shift forward would put her mouth against his.

It became all the more obvious when his gaze latched onto her lips, as if eager to close that same tiny distance she had just noticed.

A flash of logic triggered in her mind, giving her just enough reason to scramble off his lap. She'd meant to get to her feet and take a few steps away, but of course, she'd already forgotten that doing something like that required *two* feet.

Her heart clenched when her scramble turned into her dragging herself onto the mossy soil of the forest. Using both hands, she arranged her skirts to make sure they didn't reveal her missing foot.

She wanted to glance toward Quintus to be sure he hadn't seen her severed leg, but that idea got swallowed up when a tall fae with a wolf walking at his side appeared before both of them.

Brannick's eyes flashed and swirled in a galaxy of colors as he stared down at the two of them. "Are the mortals dead?"

"No." Quintus lowered his head as soon as he answered. Then he rubbed one hand across the back of his neck. "Not all of them."

The lights in Brannick's eyes brightened. "Where are they?"

"We don't know," Chloe answered.

That made Brannick's nose wrinkle, but hopefully only because he was disappointed in the answer and not disappointed in them.

Quintus hurried to his feet, addressing the fae before him. "I will find them. They will not survive much longer."

After a long sideways glance at Quintus, Brannick turned his attention to Chloe. He reached a hand out to help her up.

With the throbbing pain in her only remaining foot, it probably wasn't a good idea to try and stand right now, even with help.

"Let her rest." Respect lined Quintus's voice, but it was still firm.

Brannick eyed him again and then glanced at Chloe. After another moment, he nodded and pulled his hand away. "What else do you know?"

Letting out a sigh, Chloe curled her legs crisscross underneath her. "The mortals escaped on a dragon. The dragon has magical reins so the mortals can control it. They also captured a fae, Ludo, and they have some sort of plans for him, but I don't know anything about that."

Brannick's eyes narrowed at these words. "Ludo?"

Quintus nodded, a dark expression filling his eyes. "It will be much more difficult to find them now. I know."

Sitting up higher, Chloe almost asked where Elora was. But then she saw her sister's sparkly purple wings above the castle. She flew over it, diving down close every once in a while, probably to get a better look at things.

Once finished flying over the castle, Elora joined the rest of them. She looked straight at her beloved, Brannick. "I could not find any more flames. I believe they have all gone out now. That will make things much easier for us."

The slightest smile twitched on Brannick's lips while he listened to Elora. Once she finished speaking, he stepped out in front of the other fae who had been captured inside the castle with him.

"Crystal Thorn Castle has been destroyed." His nostrils flared. "Again." After a single head shake, he continued. "This destruction is obviously worse than any other the castle has ever known."

Still standing tall, he looked over to Elora now.

She came to his side and then addressed the fae herself. "We will rebuild the castle, but this area is not safe for fae right now. All of you must leave to other areas of Crystal Thorn until it has been rebuilt again."

Brannick nodded. "The mortals are still in Faerie. Beware of them. But know that my beloved and I will do everything in our power to keep you and Faerie itself safe from their wretched iron and flames."

At the end of the speech, Chloe drew her gaze away from Elora and Brannick and down to her skirts. As her gaze shifted, it stopped for just a moment on Quintus.

He was staring at her.

Once he caught her eye, he looked pointedly at her legs, which were still curled crisscross beneath her. She knew what he wanted to know. What had happened to her foot? Why hadn't she healed it yet when her magic could heal?

Even if she wanted to explain, now certainly wasn't the time.

That truth became even more evident when Elora stomped up to the two of them. The other fae had mostly all left now. The few that remained were all preparing to leave.

Elora's eyes had turned frosty as she wagged an accusatory finger at Quintus. "What did you do to my sister? Why do you have matching tattoos?"

"It's my fault." The words tumbled from Chloe's lips.

Elora answered by slamming her hands onto her hips. "Explain."

Thick aches spread through Chloe's throat when she tried to swallow. Brannick joined them now, which only made swallowing harder.

Chloe's gaze flicked over to Quintus before she found the courage to speak again. "Did you notice the enchantment around you that kept you safe from the iron?"

"I noticed." Brannick turned to Quintus. "How did you create such an enchantment? Even I could not create anything so powerful with iron nearby."

Quintus just let out a chuckle. "I did not create it." He gestured toward Chloe. "She did."

Both Elora's and Brannick's eyes opened wide, staring at her expectantly.

"Um." Chloe bit her lip. "Apparently, when I touched that creation magic last time I was here, it gave me access to Faerie magic. But I had to do a ritual, and the magic only works if..." Her voice trailed off. When she spoke again, it came out much softer than before. "If I touch Quintus."

Elora's jaw dropped lower and lower with each word her sister uttered. At the end, she touched the skin just under her eye, right in the same spot Chloe's tattoo sat. Elora stared at Chloe's face and then her gaze turned toward Quintus's.

Brannick folded his arms over his chest. "You two are bonded together now?"

"Yes." Quintus lifted his chin as he said it. He didn't even mention how much he hated the mortal mark of a moon being on his face.

Chloe had to turn her gaze to her lap. "We're hoping we can still undo it. Maybe after the mortals have been defeated for good."

"Good idea." Elora spoke in a biting tone. She threw a glare toward Quintus. "My sister will not need magic once she is back in the mortal realm." Her eyes narrowed. "She will not need you either."

Energy pulsed in the air. It drifted between them, making everyone's fingers twitchy. But while Elora's jaw kept clenching tighter the longer she stared at Quintus, his face only grew more relaxed. Something like resolve melted the worry off his face until, somehow, he looked the more sure one of the two of them.

"Elora." Brannick spoke in a low voice, tilting his head back toward the rubble. "The castle needs us."

A heavy sigh left her mouth. "I know. I can feel it too." Her eyes narrowed again. "I just don't want to leave these two alone together."

Chloe rolled her eyes. "We have been together the entire time since I came back to Faerie, which has been several days now."

Instead of helping, that comment just turned Elora's face into a snarl.

Quintus stood taller, showing off every inch of his impressive height. "I will keep your sister safe, just as I have done the entire time she has been in Faerie."

However the castle called to Elora, it must have been insistent because nothing less would have pulled her away in that moment. Throwing one last glare at Quintus, she stalked off with Brannick toward the castle.

The moment she and Brannick stepped out of earshot, Quintus crouched down and stared Chloe straight in the eye. "What happened to your foot?"

Her shoulders squirmed as she turned away. "I don't want to talk about it."

"Let me see then." He reached for the hem of her skirt.

"No." She used both hands to hold the hem against the ground. "Not here. Not where..." Biting her lip, she glanced up to where her sister and Brannick stood among the rubble of the once great castle.

No matter how the castle held their attention, Chloe couldn't bear to lift her skirts when the others might see.

Leaning closer to her, Quintus reached one hand out. "Then I will take you away from here."

Chloe raised an eyebrow at him. "Elora will be angry if you do."

He shrugged. "I can handle her wrath if it is for you."

A skip fluttered through Chloe's heart as she nodded.

Without another word, Quintus whirled his hand in a circle, and a swirling tunnel of black and golden stars appeared before them. Only tiny hints of forest greens and browns still remained within his door.

Tucking one arm under her legs, he lifted her and stepped into the door. He hadn't mentioned where they would go, but she wished it would be to the crystal caves.

37

GLOWING GOLDEN LIGHTS TWINKLED FROM the ceiling of the black cave Chloe and Quintus had just stepped inside. Instead of landing on the island like they had before, they now stood at the edge of the cave on a little spot of ground right next to the stream. Except the stream was bigger than just a stream. Now it had grown almost big enough to be a small river.

Hopping over to the wall, Chloe set her back against it then slid down to the ground. The tears that had stayed back through all the running welled up now.

Quintus positioned himself directly in front of her. The golden yellow flecks in his dark eyes seemed to glow as he repeated the words he'd said so many times already. "What happened to your foot?"

A shivered breath shook through her. "What about your home? You said you'd tell me about your home."

He tilted his head to the side. "I will, but not while you are supposed to be talking about something else." He pinched his eyebrows together to show that he meant it.

Sniffing, she looked down at her hands, which she was wringing in her lap. "I already know what happened anyway. I figured it out."

That declaration caused him to shrink back in surprise.

When he said nothing, she shrugged. "You gave your home to Ludo. It was part of your bargain with him, right?"

"My bargain?" Quintus shook his head.

She nodded. "When I mentioned your home, he stopped and looked at me. But then you said you have no home, which satisfied him and then he left to get the dragon."

"No." Quintus touched a hand to his forehead. "He tried to bargain for my home, but I told him I could not offer it. When you mentioned it, he thought I had deceived him somehow. But I have no home. Not anymore. I could not offer it to him, exactly as I said."

"But you did have a home. What happened—"

"What happened to your foot?" His tone didn't sting her, but it was firm. He even reached for the hem of her skirt.

After a sharp sniff, she slammed her eyes shut and jutted her leg out for him to see. Why did she always have to close her eyes at times like this?

Quintus had gone still; that much she knew even with her eyes closed because she could no longer hear his breathing. Holding her own breath, she peeked through one eyelid to gauge his reaction.

He stared at the healed part of her leg where her foot had been chopped off. His lip curled the longer he stared at it. "Portia?"

Chloe could only nod in response.

But then his stare changed. He no longer looked at her leg like he wanted to snap someone's neck. Suddenly, his stare turned calculating. After another moment, he plucked his sketchbook and pencil from his pocket and scribbled something on the page.

The sketchbook got tucked away a moment later. Now he reached into his magical pocket and pulled out a solid block of wood and a hammer and chisel. He carved away at the corners of the wood, dropping wood shavings onto the black soil of the cave.

He'd carved away nearly half of the wood before he finally looked up again. The gold in his eyes sparkled. "This wood is…" His throat bobbed as he swallowed hard. "This wood is irreplaceable."

Saying nothing more, he continued his work.

With him completely distracted, Chloe finally had a chance to inspect the severed part of her leg. Her fingers trailed over the smooth skin that had grown over what had once been her ankle. Most of it felt completely numb, but part of it prickled under her touch.

She wanted to be determined that she'd get her foot back from Portia and eventually reattach it, but a portion of her, something deep in her gut, knew this missing limb was a part of her now. Maybe she'd never get the foot back at all. Maybe she'd just have to learn to live without it.

Shuddering at the thought, she immediately pressed her back against the cave wall. Almost as soon as she did, Quintus dropped his tools and used both hands to poke and prod at the only foot she had left.

"What are you doing?" The words came out of her mouth in a hiss.

Ignoring her, Quintus continued to press and squeeze her foot with both hands. Then he picked up his tools again and went back to carving his wood block.

With her back against the wall, she stared at the spot where her foot should have been. "No one in the mortal realm will want me now." Her voice betrayed her by quavering over the words.

"Hmmm?" Quintus only flicked his gaze toward her for a split second before he went back to carving.

Cold tears slipped off her chin. "My tattoo is enough to scare anyone off, but now this?" She lifted her leg from the ground. And now her voice lowered to a whisper. "No young man will want me if I need just as much help as I can give."

"Ah, yes." Quintus raised an eyebrow as he worked. "I recall what Dunstan said to you. That selflessness is the most admirable quality a woman can have."

The words shredded through her like a knife to the gut. It hurt to hear them again, especially now that she had finally realized the importance of taking care of herself. But what young man in the mortal realm would understand when all they cared about was how cared for their future wife might make them feel?

At the time, she hadn't even realized Quintus had heard Dunstan's statement. Then again, he had fae hearing, so he had probably heard a lot of things she didn't expect. Ice closed in around her heart, curling inside it until it left behind a frosty coating.

How much had she really learned from this trip to Faerie? If it only destroyed her chance at winning a mortal young man's affection, then maybe it hadn't helped her at all.

But then she noticed what she had purposefully ignored that entire time. Quintus's fingers moved deftly as he carefully carved and shaped the wood in his hands. It had started as a wooden block, but now it had a clear shape. A foot.

He was crafting her a *foot* from the wood. Her body leaned forward, almost unable to breathe.

Finding a way to attach it to her leg without falling off might take some extra materials, but since his greatest magic was in crafting, he'd surely find a way.

The wooden foot wouldn't bend or twist or move the way her left foot did, but at least she'd be able to put her weight on it. At least she might be able to walk again. He smoothed the arch of the wooden foot, carefully eyeing her other foot as he did.

"Quintus." She sucked in a breath, not even really sure why she had said his name. But then a question escaped that tightened her throat on its way out. "Do you admire my selflessness above all else?"

"Admire it?" He scoffed. "I barely even tolerate it. Your selflessness made you sleep deprived. Shaky. You almost drowned because of it."

His nose wrinkled more and more. But then he stopped and set his tools and the wooden foot onto the ground. Slowly, his head shifted until he met her eye.

The moment his gaze locked onto hers, her heart thumped twice as hard as before. He inhaled, which expanded his chest.

Leaning just a little closer, he raised an eyebrow. "Your cleverness, on the other hand..."

A playful light danced in his eyes as he lifted himself to his knees and leaned even closer to her. "Your tongue that can spit more fire than a flame..."

He dropped one hand on the ground right next to her hip. The rest of him moved even closer still. When his chest expanded with another inhale, she could practically feel it inside herself.

Now his knee dropped to the ground next to her. His hand had landed just far enough away to prevent touch, but his knee did not. It brushed up against her thigh, sending a tingle through her leg that warmed it on all sides.

His lips curled into a grin. "Your determination even in the face of defeat..."

His palm rested against her cheek. Heat seared into her skin. But when his hand slipped back behind her neck and into her hair, her breath stopped entirely. He stared at her, his gaze jumping between her two eyes. "I admire those qualities greatly."

He leaned in until the tip of his nose touched hers. His intentions were abundantly clear, but he still held back the tiniest bit, waiting for her to accept them before he acted further.

But how could she think clearly when they breathed the same air? When his knee brushed against her thigh?

She shouldn't kiss him. She *knew* she shouldn't. It was already hard enough to settle for plain-looking mortal men after knowing the perfection that was Quintus's face.

Her hand rose of its own accord until it found the skin under his cape. She trailed a finger over his lean muscles while every part of her seemed to shiver. Not just his face. The rest of him was more perfect than any mortal.

If she kissed him too, no mortal kiss would ever be enough to satisfy her.

She knew it.

And she kissed him anyway. Taking in a breath, she lifted her lips up to his. He leaned in closer at once, slipping his hand around her waist and digging his other hand deeper into her hair.

Heat rose in her cheeks, burning with a light that seemed to spread through her limbs. When his hand caressed her back, her entire body melted deeper into his arms.

This was why she shouldn't have kissed him. Because now she couldn't stop.

Her arms pulled him closer, begging for him to take everything he wanted. His lips felt like magic.

But of course it had to end much too soon.

The sound of metal clashed against the stone of the cave.

Quintus pulled away and immediately positioned himself between Chloe and the noise. She had to lift herself with her arms just to see past Quintus's shoulder.

Mishti stood at the entrance to their cave. She held an iron stake much like the one Portia had used on Quintus not long ago. If the enchantments Quintus had put up at the entrance of the caves had still been there, Mishti had clearly found a way to break through them.

She brandished the iron stake in one hand and her sword in the other. With eyes narrowed to tiny slits, she spoke. "I've been sent here to kill you."

Maybe Chloe and Quintus had managed to take back Crystal Thorn Castle from the mortals, but that clearly meant nothing now.

How could they escape this without dying?

THE STORY CONTINUES

Find out what happens to Chloe and Quintus in Book 2,
Shadow & Crystal Thorns.

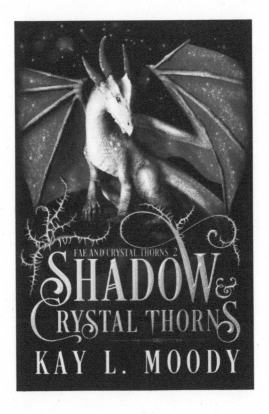

*War would be easier if she could tell who was right
and who was wrong.*

Shadow & Crystal Thorns is available now!

ACKNOWLEDGMENTS

Thank you, reader, for reading my book! Crafting stories is always so much more fun when other people, like you, can experience them too. I'm so grateful you read this book of my heart. If you enjoyed it, I hope you'll consider leaving a review.

To Angel Leya, my cover designer extraordinaire, thank you for sticking with me through the monster that was this book cover. After all the many iterations, I am so grateful you stuck with me and believed in my vision. The incredible cover this book has now is all thanks to your dedication and talent.

Deborah Spencer, thank you for your big picture edits that made this story stronger and clearer.

A huge thanks goes to my other editor, Justin Greer, for helping clean up all those confusing sentences and repetitive words, and for making my writing the best it could be.

I'm endlessly grateful for my bookstagram team, my street team, and my ARC team. All of you are the best cheerleaders ever! You always get excited about my new covers and illustrations. I am so incredibly thankful for all the work you do to share my books!

For those of you who helped me spot those last-minute typos, and who read the book early to provide editorial reviews, you are phenomenal. I am so lucky and glad to have people like you on my team.

Thank you so much to my long-time author friends, the Queens of the Quill. Having you at my side makes this publishing thing a lot less lonely and a lot more fun.

And of course, the final and biggest thanks go to my incredible husband, who believes in me probably more than I deserve. Thank you for everything.

MORE FROM KAY L. MOODY

Want Elora and Brannick's story? Don't miss this related series!

Betray a prince. Conspire with a king. What could possibly go wrong?

THE FAE OF BITTER THORN

Start with the prequel novella, which you can download and read for free! Visit **kaylmoody.com/bitter** to get your copy.

You also might like Kay's previous series.

THE ELEMENTS OF KAMDARIA

Chloe and Quintus Illustration (next page)
Artist: @artbyartemis

BONUS CHAPTER

QUINTUS

BEFORE

QUINTUS HAD NOTHING LEFT.

His knees dug into the soft soil beneath them. The pleasant chirps and scritches of the demorogs above brought him no pleasure. He'd grown fond of the sound, especially recently. Waking up to it felt like a fresh new day full of possibilities.

But now?

Now he had nothing. He couldn't wake up to the sound of demorogs outside his window when he no longer had any windows. Now he had no home at all.

Tree roots splintered above the ground in broken piles. The tree trunks that had once formed the walls of his home now lay scattered across the mossy forest floor in chips of rotted wood.

Shriveled and faded leaves dropped over the decayed wood pieces. A rug made of mossy fibers bunched up against a large pile of decomposed timber and leaves.

Stretching out his fingers, he pulled the rug away. Maybe part of it had survived the destruction. Maybe he could keep the rug and use it again. It wouldn't be the same as the magical trees that once formed his home, but it would be something.

But as he tugged the rug off the ground, he realized only a short square of it remained. It had only appeared bunched up because of the item underneath.

His eyes flew open. His heart skipped an entire beat.

A chunk of *wood* had survived. A small piece of his home now lay before him.

Trembling worked through his fingers as he ran them over the wood block. The small piece of rug must have protected it from the annihilation that claimed the rest of his trees.

The shaking in his fingers multiplied when he took the wood block into his hands. The chunk was mostly square and about as long and as thick as his forearm. It wouldn't be big enough to craft several items from, but he would be able to craft at least one item from it. One item as special as the wood block itself.

No one else would understand how important it was, but then, he knew something about his home that no one else did. He had always called his home his first creation, the first thing he ever crafted.

In truth, he hadn't crafted it at all. His hands had moved, his ideas had helped to mold it, but the *magic* hadn't come from him.

The magic had come from Faerie itself. At first, he assumed that was just how it felt to use magic. But in talking to other fae, he quickly realized that while he could *use* magic, he didn't *have* magic. Not like the other fae did anyway.

And even though fae couldn't lie, he had always managed to phrase things in just the right way that no one ever learned how different he really was.

Faerie itself had given him the magic to build his home. Faerie itself had always been there for him when he had no one else.

It gave him shelter. It found him food. It gave him a way to hide his lack of magic. It even made him appear older than he should have.

According to Faerie rules, a fae did not become an adult until he discovered his magic. Quintus had lived longer than most of the fae he knew, and yet, he had been without magic for nearly all his life.

He had gotten so good at crafting that everyone assumed he used magic to do it. Whenever he did need magic, Faerie itself provided. His skill became so well known that he never had to *say* his greatest magic was in crafting. Other fae always said it for him. Faerie itself helped him open doors and craft magnificent items, lending him just enough magic whenever he needed it.

But then one day, his magic had come.

It filled him like a hot fire and a blast of sharp wind. Abilities coursed through him that he had only ever dreamed of before that. He could finally *experience* magic. It finally belonged to him and not to Faerie itself. The magic only came once he learned to do something he had long since forgotten or maybe had never known how to do at all.

To *feel*.

The ability to feel hadn't come on its own. Just like the magic Faerie itself had given him when he needed it, his first feelings had sparked only after getting a little help. Help from a person.

A mortal girl with long blonde hair, pretty blue eyes, and a face that could stop his heart with a single smile.

The moment he first saw Chloe, his entire world changed. She barged into his life, forcing him to change and grow more than he was ready for. And even though the change had been frightening and unsettling, he always wanted more. More of it. More of her. For the first time ever, he finally felt *alive*.

And then she left.

She had said she never wanted to see him again.

His magic had stayed, but it wasn't as good. It wasn't as strong.

He gripped the wood block to his chest, breathing in its mossy, almost papery scent. Crackling energy still buzzed inside the wood that had once formed his home. Faerie had always given him help when he needed it. Somewhere deep in his gut, he knew this wood block had survived for a reason.

He would find something special to do with it. The wood chunk represented more than just a piece of his old home. It represented survival, of living even when he should have died.

After carefully tucking the wood block into his magical pocket, he took out his sketchbook and pencil. Even amidst the rubble of his broken home, the objects brought comfort.

The soft cover of the sketchbook fit perfectly in his hands. Its familiar scent of parchment and leather grounded him when nothing else could. The sound of his pencil gliding across the smooth paper surface put his mind into a focused sort of trance. Like many of his crafted projects, his fingers started drawing even before he fully formed a specific idea in his mind.

Maybe he couldn't control what had happened, but he could do what he had always done when circumstances knocked him down. He could craft.

His fingers gripped the pencil at different angles depending on how light or dark he wanted the lines. It helped that he had already sketched and crafted an object like this before. Now his fingers already innately knew the correct proportions.

The end sketch had the potential to become a stunning and magical end product. He ran a finger over the drawing while wearing a slight frown. The block of wood he had found wouldn't be big enough. He'd have to supplement it with lumber from another tree, but he could still do it.

He could make the harp that now graced the page of his sketchbook. He'd put carvings of ink pots and feather quills into its pillar. Hopefully, it could work as a peace offering.

The design was perfect for a certain mortal girl who loved to read, one who could make music like he had never heard before. Her music may have started on harp strings, but it always ended somewhere deep in his heart long after the last note had been played.

Yes, Chloe liked harps. She could play even better than her older sister. If he presented her with a harp with a pillar made from the most magical of all Faerie trees, would she perhaps forgive him?

Quintus had nothing left, except that small block of wood. Could it be that the small chunk was all he needed?

Maybe, just maybe, he'd get to see her again someday. He'd make it right between them. He'd fix the mistake that drove them apart.

Then maybe he'd be able to admit to the parts of his past he'd always buried. Maybe then he could tell her *who* had destroyed his home.

And why.

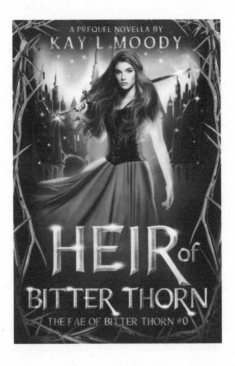

Visit kaylmoody.com/bitter for the complete prequel

Heir of Bitter Thorn is a prequel to The Fae of Bitter Thorn. Discover how Elora got the mysterious scar on her hand, how Prince Brannick escaped Fairfrost, and why the two of them don't remember their first meeting.

ELORA NEVER felt more alive than when a sword swung toward her body.

This one aimed for her heart, but she parried the blow. As always, her sword acted as a shield as much as a weapon. The two blades clashed midair. It took her a moment to regain a ready stance.

In the precious second she lost, her opponent managed to sneak in another strike. The lethal point of his sword kissed her bare arm on its way to her heart. It was too bad for him that she knew the move well.

Her steady footing gave just the right angle to slide her blade against his until the tops of their hilts clanged. With a great shove, she pushed the sword away from herself.

Her opponent stumbled backward for three steps and then landed on the dry, cracked dirt of the clearing where they fought. Faced with his defeat, Elora's father let out a chuckle as he smoothed wispy brown strands back over his balding spots. His silver eyes shined as he reached for the leather-wrapped hilt of his sword.

"I don't know how much more I can teach you, Elora." Hearing his gentle voice always jarred a bit with the ferocity of his sword fighting. He let out another soft chuckle and shielded his eyes from the sun, looking toward his forge.

The little clearing in the woods had always been the perfect spot for sparring. It sat close enough to his forge for her father to see when a customer approached. And even though their little cottage stood nearby, the clearing was far enough away that Elora's mother wouldn't see her fighting—in a dress and corset, yes, but *without* the long-sleeved under slip she was *supposed* to wear at all times.

The tight corset only barely limited her movements now that she was used to fighting with it. But the under slip that covered her arms always got in the way when she had to move fast. Fighting without it always went smoother.

Her father had sheathed his sword. He stroked her cheek with his knuckle, wearing a smile that always made her feel proud. "I think you're better than me now."

The words came with a biting reminder. Her blade sang as she slammed it into its sheath. "I'll never get to fight in the tournaments as long as I'm a woman, though. How do I know how good I really am if I'm not even allowed to fight?"

Her father managed to stop himself from wincing at her words. Maybe he'd been practicing. Apparently, he didn't want to start a fight. He leaned up against a tree filled with leaves fluttering in the gentle wind. "You don't need to fight. I won hundreds of tournaments in my day, and you can beat me. That should tell you exactly how good you are."

That was all her sword fighting was allowed to be. A hobby. Something to pass the time, like needlework or poem writing. A woman could have a talent for others to applaud and admire, but it could never be something she earned money from.

Besides that, beating her father now didn't mean as much as it used to. As a child, she loved sitting on her mother's lap and ogling as her father easily defeated every sword fighter he went up against. But he was an old man now, with three daughters to provide for and only a forge in an out-of-the-way village to do it with.

He hadn't even ordered a new shipment of ore for several weeks.

From the corner of her eye, she noticed a flash of movement. Her head jerked toward it but only found the same tree that had always been there. After narrowing her eyes for a moment, she turned back to her father.

With a handkerchief embroidered by her mother, he dabbed at the sweat on his forehead. "I have something for you."

Visit kaylmoody.com/bitter for the complete prequel

ND - #0173 - 110324 - C3 - 216/140/17 [19] - CB - 9781954335097 - Matt Lamination